The Essence

The Essence

THE DARKNESS WITHIN

IAN

authorHOUSE®

AuthorHouse™
1663 Liberty Drive
Bloomington, IN 47403
www.authorhouse.com
Phone: 1-800-839-8640

First published by AuthorHouse   04/16/2011

ISBN: 978-1-4567-6653-5 (sc)
ISBN: 978-1-4567-6652-8 (dj)
ISBN: 978-1-4567-6651-1 (ebk)

Library of Congress Control Number: 2011906598

Printed in the United States of America

The Essence: Their Past

1200 A.D.

Prologue

His name is Lynn Thrax of the house of Thrax. He is six years of age and lives with his mother, father and twin sister, Dania. Seven of his forefathers live with them also in the enormous home they have built on this vast land. Their home is in the wide open hills in the Lohar Kingdom. Their home is big enough to house his current family and a few more.

From the outside, as soon as you set eyes upon the house you can see that they lived like rich nobles. The exterior is an off white while the interior floor is lined with white marble all throughout the house. The clean black bricks on the outer wall are set in by the best masons of the land. No creases or cracks. The interior walls are made of pieces of thick oak to catch the permeating heat. The walls are adorned with various hunting trophies from their conquest of this or that animal.

His forefathers are well known nobles throughout this kingdom. All his progenitors lived to be well over one hundred years of age. They would tell him that soon he would be just like them when he got older, until . . .

It happened.

The clouds rolled so dark over the House of Thrax that it looked as if the gods were angry with them. His father commanded him to stay in the safety of the house but his curiosity always got the best of him. Even after Dania begged him to stay inside, he stalked around the house and out to a field where there was tall grass and where his father and other elders were gathered.

He snuck a peek at what was causing the sudden change in the weather. He caught sight of his eldest forefather being challenged by a dark man in a black cloak with a unique pin holding it clasped. The man's features were obscured by his cowl but Lynn took in every bit of what he could. Black cloak with red interior and smooth black boots almost completely free of dirt. The hilt of his sword showed through the bulge in his cloak.

The stranger and Lynn's eldest grandfather battled and even though he was so much older than his adversary his gift allowed him to keep his youth. They went back and forth like a pendulum swaying in a grandfather clock. His eldest grandfather eventually became overcome by his challenger. With his death, all his forefathers began die and wither away in months, weeks and days after the eldest fell with his last breath of life.

Now all that is life is Lynn, his birth father, mother and twin sister. He will never forget the name of their now arch enemy or that day and the gift that was stolen from his heritage. His name, Ruffio St. Cloud. The gift . . .

IMMORTALITY!

Chapter: 1

1220 A.D.

It has been twenty years since that terrible day that death has marked his bloodline. His father and mother are now dead, his father lived to be ninety and his mother lived to be seventy. His sister is now the last of his family left with him since their parents no longer walk on this earth to hear the birds sing or the lions roar, when the last leaf in autumn falls from the tree to when the first speck of snow flutters at their noses.

No more will they see the changes of the seasons. For him and his sister are now twenty-six years old and Lynn is on the hunt for the one man who has taken his fathers' gift. They strive by moving from country-side to country-side helping with the farms of peasants and nobles. Every where they go people ask them about the birth marks on their hands.

They tell those people that those birth marks were the same marks their ascendants had before them yet as their elders began to fade theirs stayed defined and potent as ever on their tanned skins.

Lynn and his sister are an ideal average height at five-eleven. Lynn has the athletic build of a small warrior. If seen from a distance he would look like an average man but in some of the finest clothing.

His sister is the same as himself except with full breast that can just fit in the palm of her hand. Their hair is that of the same color as the tar pits as black as Ruffio's soul. The irises of their eyes, for no reason explainable, are different colors.

Dania's left and Lynn's right is hazel while her right and his left are white as the clouds that roll above their heads. When folks see them, at times, are frightened of them because they say according to myths and tales there will be the twin siblings born to rule over the people to march them into a new millennium and beyond.

1222 A.D.

The time has come that Lynn and his sister felt *his* presence. At that very moment they awoke to look out of the hut they were sleeping in to see a dark figure spreading his wrath amongst this village. Lynn grabbed his sword and told Dania to stay there while he go and defend the village from Ruffio.

For Lynn knew why Ruffio was here. As Lynn and his sister, Dania, sensed Ruffio's presence, he sensed them also. "He's destroying the village and every one in it just for our heads," thought Lynn.

As Lynn saw Ruffio kill the host of the hut he and Dania were staying in, in cold blood, Lynn stepped out from the hut and his voice rumbled like the roars of many beasts while saying, "Enough! Your quarrel is with my blood, no one else's!"

At that moment Ruffio whirled around and that was when Lynn remembered that look Ruffio gave Lynn's' eldest forefather. The look that has been seen by the ones that perished by this monster, the last look they'll ever see.

Ruffio said with a voice that has years of wisdom but the immortality that allows him to be youthful, "You are the one that I've been waiting for," he paused. "You were taking so long that I decided to come after you myself."

Lynn then spoke, "How did you find us?" That's when he realized his mistake by Ruffio's answer.

"So there are two of you," he said through a sinister smile. "Where is your precious sister so she can see your death and her own?"

"She is none of your concern, now on your guard, I challenge you to the death," said Lynn with a shaky voice for he knew that this could easily be his defeat.

At that moment when Ruffio turned the sword to reflect off the light of the fires, Lynn realized that the sword he was holding was his eldest ascendants katana.

"My grandfathers sword, return it or perish!" he commanded.

Ruffio smiled and said, "So a duel it is, though I assure you that you, like your fathers before you, will not see past this day. Ha ha ha!"

After he finished speaking Lynn rushed him with his blade held high above his head coming down in an arch. Ruffio parried and laughed, "Is that all you got Lynn Thrax? The house of Thrax will finally fall when I'm through with you."

Lynn swung again for Ruffio's weapon hand, but this time around Ruffio parried so fast that Lynn didn't catch his next movement until it connected. Ruffio threw the hilt of his sword into Lynn's nose, then a knee to his stomach, and then followed with an elbow to the back of Lynn's head. Lynn hit the ground hard and knew that his life would end before he could avenge his ancestors of this maniacal man if he didn't think fast.

Lynn watched as Ruffio raised his sword above his head preparing to strike and spoke, "Now isn't that a surprise, you put up a better fight than your forefather, yet, you still have that same look that he had and it was the look of a man pleading for his life."

Lynn said through gritted teeth and the pain of the blows Ruffio dealt, "If I die it is with honor and knowing that my death will be avenged so that you will never take another walk nor breathe another breath."

Ruffio smiled that sinister smile again and said, "Ha, I'm too powerful for anyone to stop me . . . know my name, for it is the last name you will ever hear. I am Ruffio St. Cloud, destroyer of clans, I AM GOD!"

His blade began to fall towards Lynn's neck when with blinding speed Lynn saw his sister strike Ruffio in the back with her dagger.

He fell away with a deep cut as Dania went to her brothers' side and asked, "Brother, are you mortally wounded?"

"No," he answered back trying to stand. Then an unseen force picked Dania up and began carrying her to Ruffio whose hand was held out. The cut was already healed which was too fast for a regular man.

Once Ruffio had her in his arms he said, "So this is the lovely Dania. I'd rather keep her as my foot stool wench than kill her." Ruffio stabbed her in the womb, and as she fell to the ground he laughed the laughter of a man gone mad.

Lynn ran to his sisters' side and asked, "What were you thinking? Why didn't you stay hidden like I asked?"

"I saw you about to be beheaded and I used what I knew from watching your training. Remember when father asked you to stay in the house," she smiled, "I guess it wasn't enough to stop him."

Lynn reached with his right hand to interlock in her left. He felt a power surge throughout himself and his sister. Lynn and Dania heard a familiar but vague voice say, "It has happened, use your secrets to bend reality to your will. Use your power to defeat him."

Lynn stood up to his full height, turned around and gave Ruffio a gaze as if to look into his soul. For those few seconds, Lynn saw the death of thousands caused by Ruffio and the fear in his eyes.

"What h-h-happened to you? Your eyes have the fire of kingdoms behind them," Ruffio stuttered while stumbling back just a little.

"Your reign as a tyrant comes to an end today!" bellowed Lynn to Ruffio. Ruffio letting his anger get the best of him rushed Lynn yet time seemed to have slowed down for everything around Lynn except himself.

Lynn dodged Ruffio's attack then parried, dodged again, and then again. As Lynn ducked low he noticed an opening and struck with his fist into Ruffio's belly then with the hilt of his sword into Ruffio's chin. Ruffio flew back with the strength Lynn never knew he had.

Ruffio jumped into the air higher than a two-story house and to Lynn's surprise, he jumped up there right along with Ruffio. When they met in the air, it seems like they floated there as Ruffio began to strike.

Lynn parried, parried again, dodged, parried and then Lynn struck Ruffio for the third time since the battle began. Lynn connected with an elbow to the face of Ruffio causing him to fall back to the ground. When Ruffio hit the ground, Lynn's grandfathers' katana flew free of his hands.

Lynn landed on the ground and charged at Ruffio while holding his hand out using his mind to call the katana to him. Ruffio began to rise up and as soon as he stood straight up, Lynn, still charging, lunged at Ruffio thrusting the katana into Ruffio's abdomen.

Ruffio shook as he fell to his knees and said, "My blood will flow today but my bloodline will hunt you and take back what I sto—, 'er won." Then Lynn brought his katana down through Ruffio's neck severing his head.

As Ruffio's head rolled apart from his body, a small orb of light came to Lynn and he touched it causing a force he never felt to shake his body. Taking Ruffio's Essence, Lynn saw the deaths of people killed by Ruffio, even his eldest grandfather.

As Ruffio's Essence began to subside, Lynn felt a presence beside him. He turned to see his sister standing there fully healed and their eyes were back to normal.

Chapter: 2

1301 A.D. AUTUMN

Lynn, as far as his sister is concerned, is now alone. Dania begged and pleaded with him to let her take the true death into her embrace. After so many times of hearing her make the request he finally obliged by taking her head and having her Essence strengthen him. Although Dania went to join their father and mothers' spirit, she left Lynn a gift.

Lynn looked at his left hand to see his sisters' birthmark embedded on the backside. The only immediate family Lynn has are his children, their children, and their children who live with him on his fathers' old land. After the death of Ruffio, Lynn decided it was time to come back home and rebuild the home the way he remembered it. He tended to the land and brought it back to its former glory all in honor of his family that has passed.

One evening as he was walking around the rolling hills of his land, he encountered three men wearing black cloaks and hoods hiding their faces with a red interior to their cloaks that made it look like an ocean of blood were in the cloaks. Their cloaks adorned with the same pin Ruffio was wearing when he killed Lynn's grandfather in battle.

The pin was a golden dot with membranous wings flaring out to the sides like a demon. Their tunics were hip length and were the color of flowing blood. Their tights were black and made of fine silk for mobility. Lynn didn't recognize the type of material on their boots except that they looked like scales in the twilight of a setting sun. Seeing the bulge in their cloaks from the hilt of their swords, Lynn thought, "I can best them in battle if it came to that but they are mortal men, so why are they here."

"May I ask why you are here?" Lynn asked while trying to read any type of sign their bodies might give off.

The man in the middle stepped forward and spoke in a raspy voice, "We've been sent to deliver a message from our master to Lynn Thrax of the House of Thrax."

"Speak your message and be on your way," said Lynn while reaching down to his left hip with his left hand to grab his scabbard.

The man on Lynn's right stepped up some showing that he was the taller of the three and said, "How are we sure you are the Lynn Thrax? Our master said that Lynn Thrax is believed to be some sort of master swordsman, so if you best us then the message is truly for you."

All three pulled their hoods free from their heads to show their faces obviously meaning to kill Lynn since he set eyes on their faces. Lynn knew all too well how an assassin works from the many years of experience and living.

The man to Lynn's' right stood tall at six-foot-four with a thick beard and mustache. His face from what Lynn could tell looked around forty years of age with the crow's-feet forming by his blue eyes. His build was a muscular one that made it look like he weighed close to two hundred and thirty pounds. His hair was brown and cut short but long enough to fall down to his neck and be pulled behind his ears.

The middle mans' face had a pencil mustache and trimmed goatee with sideburns extending to his goatee. He stood about six-foot-one with cut black hair parted on the left but combed to the right. His eyes were brown and set back by a protruding nose.

The man to Lynn's left was a lot different than the other two. His head and face was bald of any hair except for his eyebrows and lashes. He had a nose piercing, three above his left eye and five in each ear. His eyes were green but were barely noticeable since his eyes were naturally squinted. This one was the shortest at five-eight but made up for it in his build by being the bulkiest.

The three men began to flank Lynn from all sides except behind him. Then he felt it. "They are immortals, but how could I not tell until they got so close," thought Lynn. "You are not mortal then?" asked Lynn still looking at the middle man in front of him.

"Our lord has blessed us and granted us not immortality but a longer life than any ordinary man with these pendants, also with the ability to hide from detection by true immortals until it is too late," answered the middle man while groping the pin holding the cloak together.

What those three messengers were about to witness, was that Lynn was no ordinary immortal. The three men moved swift for the eyes of an average man as they began their assault, yet not fast enough for Lynn's eyes.

The middle man charged Lynn and jumped to his side a good distance not attacking. The shortest to the left charged and barely brushed against Lynn's robe. The tallest man on Lynn's right charged and Lynn thought, "This must be how they overwhelm their targets."

The last man to charge brought his sword up to attack Lynn. Lynn dodged, with his hand still holding his scabbard, asked, "Are you sure you would like me to teach you the art of swordplay?"

The man who was in the middle replied, "We are more than enough for you and your kin!"

"So be it," said Lynn calmly unsheathing his katana and holding it down to his side.

This time all three attacked Lynn but he dodged them jumping over their heads. The shortest of the three attacked Lynn by himself. Lynn parried, then parried again, then dodged. After dodging that last attack the tallest man tried to surprise Lynn.

Lynn dodged, dodged again, parried, and then struck at his knee. The challenger fell to the ground holding his right knee where Lynn sliced through flesh. The middle man lunged at Lynn but he dodged by spinning around him to throw his balance off.

The short man attacked so Lynn cut his arm then swooped low and sliced through his Achilles tendon. He fell to one knee leaving himself open for Lynn's finishing blow. Lynn took his head and embraced his Essence as the other two hit the ground so as not to be harmed by the spectacle. The Essence felt so genuine that Lynn could feel the others taken by this assassin and feel the assassin himself.

The taller of the two that were left was already healed at the knee when Lynn turned and asked, "Would you like to carry on or deliver the message?"

By the sound of Lynn's voice, he sounded like an angry king passing judgment for a heinous crime.

"Our master sends this," started the shorter of the two, "Know this Lynn Thrax of the House of Thrax, I will have your dead body for my own pleasure. Your head will be mounted on my wall in the name of my grandfather, Ruffio St. Cloud."

Lynn took in the message and delivered his own, "Tell your master. After so long, he shows his cowardous tail. Well, I will be waiting, but, not for long."

Lynn turned away when the two defeated combatants took off. He looked one more time in their direction and noticed three horses. Two had the messengers and the other one was a beautiful black stallion with a grey mane and tail running free in an opposite direction.

When Lynn made it to his home, he told his children that he must leave for their safety. They begged him to stay but he knew he had to hunt Ruffio's heir before he stretched his evil to this land. He left the land without looking back because he knew if he did it would surely brake him.

Chapter: 3

1319 A.D. SUMMER

Time has passed greatly since Lynn last seen his family. Lynn feels as if time has shifted around him, but for an immortal, time stands still. Lynn is now one hundred and twenty-five years old and has seen kings come and go, battles won and lost, and still he breathes.

He has been counsel in the castle Maru, in the city of Fawn, in the Lohar Kingdom where he has lived most of his life. He answers second to only King Ganon and resides in the castle with the royal family.

When you first enter into the castle, you step into the throne room. There the throne room is decorated with purple velvet draping on one wall, blue on another, and white on another. The throne was made of pure gold and cerulean colored back and sitting cushions and the armrest also.

About four corners were the towers, one door leads to a dungeon where there are three cells and chains along the walls to hold a few extra unruly criminals. If thrown into one of these cells then it has been done under great reflection over the evidence brought up against a defendant. King Ganon goes through a very detailed investigation during his trials so as to not convict an innocent man or woman.

Another door that leads to the second floor is the dining room. There you have three tables parallel to each other. Those three tables seat sixteen each table. There are two crescent tables on the outsides of the former three. Those tables seat only eight each table with all seats facing inward. The last table is the royal table where it stands perpendicular to the others.

The king sits in the middle with the queen to his immediate right and the duke beyond her. To the left of the king sits the prince and beyond him would sit the princess but there is none at the moment even though the king has been hoping for one.

Back on the throne room floor another door leads to the third floor. There it houses fifteen servants, four along three of the walls and three in each of the other towers. Along one wall housed two rooms for guests. In the middle there are eight more rooms for more guests.

From the throne room there's one more door leading to the royal chambers. The stairs that lead to the royal chambers branch out right under the tower of one of the servants. Then leads up along the wall to a door where you will find the room. This is the only passage leading up to the royal quarters and its the only passage that's found outside. It may not seem safe from first glance but King Ganon has made sure to incorporate a handrail and a cloth-like covering to protect against implement weather.

When you step into the room the kings' bed is in the right corner and a fruit table in the far left corner. The princes' bed is in the near left corner since he's the only child. His bed is small but there isn't any in the whole city or maybe even kingdom who's bed is worth more than this young prince.

In the near right corner is a rack holding different swords. There were kriss style blades to snake blades that loosen into a razor like whip. There were small to medium and large katanas. The king even had a sword that only the strongest of men could pick it up. Even then that person might need some help. That sword was one sword that was owned by a person that was deemed a god by most men and has not been seen for many of centuries.

The castle may seem small but there has been little need for renovations. Since there have been no destruction done on the castle or city itself, King Ganon never felt the need to. He was waiting till his next child was brought into the world. Hopefully a daughter. He and the queen wanted a daughter just as much as they had wanted little prince Aurelius.

Every now and then Lynn would send a messenger to his family to keep them from worrying. They would send him back within a few days saying that the family has grown a little and still ages with youth. Deep down Lynn longs to go back but he can't lead Ruffio's heir to his home. Lynn knows that he must leave soon or bring the wrath down upon the castle Maru and the city of Fawn.

Chapter: 4

1323 A.D. SUMMER

Lynn felt that his time as counsel in this kingdom was drawing near its ending. Lynn has served under King Ganon for about seven years and knows that the king will help him in any way. Lynn asked King Ganon, "My king, I wish to embark on a journey of . . . discovery. I would like to have your blessing as I partake of this task before me."

King Ganon does with no argument as he thanks Lynn for his friendship, counsel, and help in winning many battles.

"Of course you have my blessing my dear friend. Why would I not do that for the most trusted man in my life. You have stood by my side in many battles and at many occasions. You have been counsel to me in my time of need whether it was during courts or just to help me chose my attire for the parties we hold."

Lynn bowed to the king, took his hand, kissed it and said, "Thank you. You have truly been great to me and a gracious host. You were like a brother and a father and you will be missed."

Lynn left the city of Fawn peacefully and quietly seeing that he wanted no recognition by the people. As Lynn makes it outside the city gates, he feels a presence.

"A mortal, but where," he thought to himself while looking around. Still unable to find the person he senses, he makes his way towards the bordering forest, Forest of New Life.

Before he could enter, a woman leaps from the limbs of the trees to land about twelve feet in front of him. He immediately spots her clothing and remembers the three messengers that wore the same clothing who attacked him on his land.

She wore the same cloak and pin as the others and she stood about five-foot-seven with a curvy figure that only accented her garments even more. "The tunic and tights look better on her," thought Lynn as she walked forward. Her eyes are a light blue like the sky on a clear summer day.

She had tiny freckles upon her cheeks right under her eyes. Her hair was a curly reddish blonde that extends to just below her shoulder blades. From her appearance and her movements, any body else would have suspected her for a strega but Lynn knew better.

"Are you Lynn Thrax of The House of Thrax?" she asked Lynn stopping about five feet in front of him.

"Who's asking?" asked Lynn while checking her out and noticing her sword on her well rounded hip.

"I am Maria Maccio," she said.

Lynn shrugged his shoulders and walked past her but was halted when she said, "I am on the run from my master, Niccolo St. Cloud."

"Well keep running."

"You don't understand," she pleaded, "I will die if I am left alone. I'm lucky I made it this far."

"I understand well enough. I understand that you were with the man who is out to take my head and now you want my help."

"I have betrayed him. I left his side when I was the only one he would allow there. Please allow me to accompany you and I will tell you my story."

Lynn took Maria into his company after much pleading on Maria's part and listened as she told him about Niccolo's hatred for him. She told Lynn about how Niccolo wanted his head and didn't accept failure or betrayal from any one, even women sharing his bed.

She told Lynn that before she ran, she saw the craziness that he so talked about his grandfather used to have. She said that he is no more than ninety-five years old, yet, he likes to act as if he's older and younger at the same time.

First thing that went through Lynn's mind was, "How could he still be alive and active after so many years."

When Maria finished telling Lynn about Niccolo, Lynn said, "Let's rest for the night and we'll be on our way when day breaks. You're welcome to come if you like."

She agreed with the rest and laid amongst some leaves like an unworthy servant. Lynn caught her attention and offered her some space in his tent. "Come now, that's no place for a comrade and friend."

She more than accepted and slept under Lynn the whole night, warm like a bird being protected from the weather by its forbearer. Lynn watched her fall asleep and saw that the stress from her escape and search only wore off when she was sleep. When Lynn finally felt that the forest was quieted down he dozed off himself.

They awake to the birds chirping and singing their songs that will live on for as long as Lynn breathes on this earth. Lynn looked at Maria and thought, "If only I had a stallion, she wouldn't have to walk."

As they exited the forest, they came upon a valley that seemed to barely curve left and right but still going straight through. The only problem is that going around each turn; you can't see the next one.

Before they made it far they came upon men in sandy baggy pants appeared. Their shirts hung open showing off their tone and tanned skins.

"This valley is run by our leader Verne. Pay our toll and you may pass. If you don't, we will take what we want," said one of the men loud enough to echo through the valley for Lynn and Maria to hear.

There were at least ten of them and Lynn thought while holding his scabbard readying to unsheathe his katana, "I can easily take them down if they cause any trouble."

Lynn began to walk forward but Maria stopped him with a hand on his shoulder. Lynn looked back at her with a questioning look on his face. The group of bandits began to edge forward to take the payment by force if necessary.

"Let me be of some service?" Maria said while unsheathing her sword.

Lynn looked to tell her 'no' but the gaze she gave him showed him that she has a warrior's heart and a survivor's story. The men attacked and Maria showed off her prowess that belied her small frame and her dainty looks. She handled her own pretty well and even impressed Lynn how well she could handle a blade and multiple foes.

Maria made short work of the men but didn't kill any so they could tell the others of Lynn and Maria's coming. Lynn will soon figure out that letting them go was probably a bad idea.

They walked through the valley slowly anticipating an ambush from those same men. The valley was no easy feat so they rested for the night on the valley floor by one of the massive stone walls. Lynn watched as Maria rested. The moon and the clouds made the shadows dance along the rock wall. Here and there he would think that some one was approaching but it was just his anticipation for an attack. He went on through the night letting Maria sleep and not needing the rest himself.

The next morning Maria was gracious that there was no attack or anything stolen during the night. That day, they finally made it to the other side of the valley. When they approached the end, three men walked out from the left of the opening.

Two giants among men at about seven feet and one that was shorter than the two giants at about six feet. The two giants held a single bladed crescent axe. They wore their leather chest straps in an "X" across their chest with shorts as not to be affected by the heat.

The shortest of the three wore those same pants as the men Lynn and Maria encountered when they first set foot in the valley. His sleeveless shirt hung open to show his tanned and toned body. His wrists were adorned with thick gold bracelets as well as a thin one on his upper left arm.

His gold chains flashed in the sun against his athletic build. He had a thin black mustache that extended well past his lips with a thin straight goatee stretching to just above his collarbone. His hair fell to his shoulders behind his ears with bangs down each side of his face, no where near as long as Lynn's.

"So you are the two trespassers in my valley refusing to pay the toll and beating on my men. You will pay the toll or you will pay with your life." said the smaller man.

"We want no quarrel with you or your men. We are just trying to reach the land of Mooray," said Lynn while pulling Maria behind him a little bit.

"You shall not pass without my leave," said the leader then signaling for five more men to come out from hiding and attack Lynn and Maria.

They ran blindly into the fight against Lynn and Maria and were easily defeated with no casualties. When they finished Maria asked, "Why let them live?"

Lynn answered still keeping his eyes on the leader, "They are not immortal so it would be almost like cold blooded murder taking their lives."

The leader then snapped his fingers and sent the two giants forward. Each attacked one on one against Lynn and Maria.

The one that attacked Lynn swung his axe from side to side trying to hit Lynn. Lynn leaped over each swing until the giant tried to aim higher forcing Lynn to duck low. Lynn quickly stepped forward about to strike but the giant kicked a large boot up into Lynn's face.

Lynn caught the boot above his head and slashed at the back of the thigh. The giant fell to the ground holding his thigh not wanting to do battle anymore.

Maria was being chased by her attacker. He chased her behind a small boulder and tried reaching around it going from one side to the other. When the giant dedicated to one side, Maria jumped atop the boulder and then jumped onto his neck.

He began spinning and thrashing his arms around wildly. Maria started pummeling him in his head. The giant swung the side of his axe up at Maria. Maria quickly jumped off making him hit himself and knocking himself out cold. Lynn and Maria came back together to face the leader.

He stepped forward a few steps and said, "Battle me one on one. Just me and you." He pointed at Lynn upon finishing his statement.

Lynn accepted the challenge and they circled each other in a face-off then stood still as the wind picked up. Once it settled, they charged each other attacking and parrying each others moves.

The leader backed Lynn up to the valley wall and thought he had him trapped. He swung at Lynn's' mid-section but Lynn jumped and kicked off the wall to fly over his challengers head. Lynn turned quickly and connected with the hilt of his katana to the back of the neck.

He dropped to his knees, looked up at Lynn and said, "You have bested me and I lay down my life. Make it swift and remember who fought valiantly against you."

Instead of taking his life, Lynn raised him to his feet and told him, "I wish not to harm you or your followers any more than what has already taken place. You should learn not to try not to bully people who come through this valley and act like thieves."

The leader replied while shaking his head, "Oh no, me and my men are far from thieves. We are like rangers or of that sort that help unfortunate people and make the rich suffer. If we perceived to be thieves, then I sincerely apologize."

"No harm done, just be a bit more careful," said Lynn as he began to walk off with Maria by his side.

The leader ran to cut Lynn off and said, "I owe you my life. Let me follow you on your journey and protect you and your lady friend."

Lynn stopped and asked, "You expect to protect us? What is your name?"

"Verne Wingo of the Wingo clan." Verne answered Lynn's question.

Lynn spoke loud enough for the valley to echo, "You are now Verne Wingo of the Wingo clan, protector for the House of Thrax." Lynn then spoke in a hushed tone to Verne, "Before long you will be asked to receive a gift. If you wish to protect me then it would be wise to accept."

"Of course, anything to learn from you and travel with some one as versed in the language of swordplay as you are. Shall we go to my camp?"

Lynn accepted the offer and was taken to a mighty camp alongside Maria and Verne that he didn't expect these men to have. The camp sat North West of the valley and coming upon it there are four guards, two archers hidden in the trees and two swordsmen on the ground.

The camp had a number of fifteen tents from what Verne told Lynn. Four tents stood like castles compared to the other tents. One is where Verne resides, another for his guards, another for the injured which Verne sent men to pick up the injured men in the valley and the last is the dining hall.

Verne has more than two hundred men to accompany him and more than enough women to go around. Eight tents just a bit smaller than Verne's is where the men and women live. One of the smaller tents is a blacksmiths' workshop. As the company walked past they could see inside that it was darker than the other tents from the soot and ash. The heat rose from that place almost as if the sun itself was in there.

Another small tent is for collecting goods that might be needed on the road. The last tent was a pretty large tent that was their own bordello where for enough gold; you will receive a very good show. Verne offered to pay for Lynn and Maria, if she wanted, to have a good time. Of course they declined without disrespect to Verne or the women of the bordello.

Verne threw a gracious celebration for Lynn and Maria that went into the night. Close to the end of the celebration there was a loud raucous and screaming outside the dining hall.

Lynn, Verne, Maria and others went to inspect what the commotion was about and noticed those black cloaks with their red interior and the pins holding the cloaks fast around their necks. Their black silk tights reflected the fire and barely swayed in the wind from their chaos.

Lynn pulled Verne back into the tent and told him, "Now is the time you fulfill your oath and receive my gift."

Verne nodded and knelt down with his head bowed. Lynn placed his hands to the sides of Verne's head and directed Verne's gaze to meet his. When they locked eyes, Verne began to jerk as Lynn sucked his life force and sent it back empowered with the gift of immortality passed down by Lynn's ancestors.

The markings on Lynn's hands began to glow and burn, a sensation he has never felt before. When they finished, Verne looked at least twenty years younger as the lines by his eyes began to fade.

Lynn stepped out of the tent into the camp with Verne and Maria at his side. They went from tent to tent helping to put the fire out. Every now and then they would encounter those black cloaked men and make quick work of them.

When the fires were nearly extinguished, a raspy voice came from around the three friends that Lynn knew all too well . . .

"Lynn Thrax, I hope you remember me from our last bout for now I am much stronger than before," said the mystery person before showing himself and . . .

He wasn't alone.

He was flanked by four men to each side. He began to speak again, "Our first battle, we weren't properly introduced. I am Lionel D'arjuan. Now its time you feel the wrath of Niccolo St. Cloud."

When the last words left his mouth, the men with Lionel began to descend upon Lynn, Verne and Maria. Two attacked Verne, three on Maria and three on Lynn. Verne dodged his attackers by using his speed and new found youth.

He ran to one of the tents with his attackers close behind. Verne grabbed one of the ropes holding the tent steady, cut it and flew to the topside of the tent and back flipped off the top. The men stopped and watched Verne fly over their heads and pull the tent down over them.

Both men stood up under the downed tent but one quickly fell again never to rise again as Verne took his head. His Essence erupted into Verne and shot the other challenger out of the tent and onto the ground out cold.

Maria, steady on her prowl, kept dodging and parrying their attacks but never attempting to show the side of her that she showed in the valley.

While Lynn was dodging his attackers Verne surprised one and cut his weapon arm and when he faced Verne, his head separated from his body. Another Essence erupted through Verne exhausting him down to one knee.

Clutching his head Verne shouted to Lynn, "What is happening to me?"

Lynn still battling the other two answered, "You're immortal and so are they. You must be careful of how many of their Essence you endure when you first become an immortal. Too many can destroy you!"

Lynn saw his opening as his attackers came from both sides lunging at him. Lynn placed his hands together to bring about his ancient power. He molded reality with his mind by freezing time, reaching down to grab a handful of dirt and throwing it in their eyes.

He then moved and let them impale each other in their chests. Lynn then took both their heads and tried to steady himself as both men's Essence hit him, one in the chest and on in the back. It brought him to his knees while the energy just erupted around him.

Lionel began to approach Lynn until Verne jumped in his path. Lionel stopped but Lynn spoke, "No Verne, he's mine."

When Verne turned to look at Lynn, he was standing straight up as if nothing happened. Verne moved out of the way then Lionel spoke, "You and me, now!"

Lynn accepted his challenge for a take all duel. Lynn thought, "He doesn't realize that in this game, everything is for keeps."

Lynn and Lionel placed their blades directly in front of each others' almost touching tips. Neither moved an inch once the blades came into contact. Lionel kept his eyes on Lynn. Lynn let his eyes veer just barely and that was enough for Lionel to make his move.

Lionel struck first but was stopped short by Lynn's parry. Lionel tried again, again and again to no avail because each time Lynn parried his swings. Lionel did an all out assault but Lynn dodged to the side. Lionel pivoted on his right foot and did a roundhouse with his left. Lynn did a sweeping kick at Lionel's pivoted foot to knock him down.

When Lynn came up, a dagger was thrown into the small of his back bringing him back down to his knees. Lionel jumped up and tried to seize his moment.

He stood over Lynn about to raise his sword but Lynn placed his palms together to bring about his ancient power passed down from his ancestors. Lynn pulled the dagger from his back dropped it and delivered a side slash to Lionel's stomach. He then leapt up and whirled around behind Lionel to bring his katana down in an arch over his back.

As Lionel fell to his knees in pain Lynn said, "You have been bested twice. You should have stayed away when you had your chance. Now, your Essence will help me defeat your master."

Lionel breathed heavily through clinched teeth with nothing to say. Lynn took his head and embraced his Essence as it surged through his body. With Lionel's death, his followers began to withdraw from the camp. Lynn allowed them to run because he had more important business to attend to.

Lynn found Verne and told him, "You must choose your successor so that we may be on our way."

Verne answered with, "Yes, I have chosen Sir Peter Macdowl. I know he will guide my people righteously and protect them with his soul."

"I hope you are right. Anyone can be a spy for Niccolo," Lynn told Verne with the eyes of the survivors from the battle on them.

Lynn, Maria and their new companion Verne began to set out as the crowd part like the Red Sea when the prophets used to command the air, sea and land. As the three new friends exited the boundaries of the camp, the people began to roar in applause and praise their names.

Lynn, Maria and Verne walked east because Mooray lay north but the Grand Straight blocked any crossing. By going east, there lies the city of Kamma and the ports of Iggarius. From there they will set sail in the Grand Straight and make way for Mooray.

Before making it to Kamma they must cross through a pretty large wooded area with a large ravine, then through a meadow. Lynn told the others to stay on guard since there is a possible danger when and where ever they travel. They have been traveling for days and still no sign of the woods.

Every night Lynn would ask Maria if she could remember anything about Niccolo's stronghold, layouts, and weaknesses before she fled but it was no good because she claimed to not have much of any helpful memory of the inside.

When they came to the woods, they paused for a minute while Verne asked, "Are you sure these are the woods and not a forest?"

"They're woods alright, and not to be taken lightly." Just as they began to set foot in the woods an arrow struck the ground in front of Lynn's foot. From the way the arrow was cut of fine wood and left no mark in the ground to show it didn't even move the dirt a little is how Lynn knew who shot the arrow.

"Who goes there?!" commanded a voice that sounded like the voice of hymns, yet so masculine.

Lynn answered respectfully, "I am Lynn Thrax of the House of Thrax. My fellow companions are Verne Wingo of the Wingo Clan and the lovely but deadly Maria Maccio."

Lynn paused to take a closer look into the trees then said, "Show yourself, elven archer, protector of these woods."

When Lynn finished speaking a being showed himself by moving from limb to limb with such swiftness that even Lynn could barely keep an eye on his movements. He made one last gracious leap into the air to land directly in front of the three friends.

He stood to his full height at six-foot-one. His hair was long to his waist, braided back behind his ears, and to their surprise, a clean blonde. His facial features were so perfect it seems as if he has never aged and to where they almost seemed feminine behind his dark green eyes.

Verne thought, "No wonder we couldn't see him through the trees, his clothes are the colors of the leaves and they seem to be getting lighter in the open sunlight."

His boots were made of fine cow hide rolling up to his knees. His quiver was one of the most beautiful ones they have ever set sight on. His long bow was made of the same wood as his arrows but there was some type of design on it on both sides of the bundle.

His two daggers stuck out from behind his lower back. They also looked as if they were made of the finest steel forged in the depths of a volcano.

"I'm sorry if I frightened you in any way," He said to the group.

"Why be so hostile for an elf?" asked Verne.

He answered while putting his bow around his back, "We must be careful because the dao-tug threatens these woods."

"The dao-tug?" asked Maria curiously.

He started to describe them, "They are evil elves. They resemble us wood elves except for their gray skins. Their hair is as white as your eye."

He said that while acknowledging Lynn's left eye then finishing, "Their eyes are as red as the blood they so lust for and their clothes are a little too gothic for our taste."

Verne asked in his best manner, "So, basically you're at war with them!"

"No, but they would love nothing but war. They see themselves as the true masters of every living being. They wouldn't hesitate to make humans as yourselves into toys, slaves or just a torture subject just for their sick sadistic infatuation," said the elf while looking around to see if anything was out of order.

"We thank you and ask for your pardon to pass through these woods and in return, you don't have to worry about us doing anything to defile the woods," said Lynn while getting an agreement from Maria and Verne.

"It is not for me to grant, yet if you'll follow me to see my king, he might grant you your request," He said while motioning for the three travelers to follow him.

"So be it, we will attend you to see your king," said Lynn not knowing what he was getting them into, but trusting his intuition anyway.

When the elf turned away from Lynn, he caught sight of a pendant hanging from a silver chain around his neck. The symbol that it perceived to be made Lynn ask, "Excuse me for asking, but what might that be around your neck?"

He said while looking over his shoulder, "It is the symbol of the chosen ones that will one day come to right the wrong and rid us of this unknown evil that plagues us now."

He added after a brief pause, "It also grants us to live for centuries like the chosen ones and to await them when they come and need us."

Eventually they came to the well known ravine after traveling through the woods and trying to avoid wild animals and feral dogs such as mastiffs and the like. Verne wasn't as gracious as the others walking through the woods so he was nicked by branches and thorns that would catch on to his clothing and various articles.

He turned to face the others and said, "No human may see this. If you'll please face the other way?"

When he finished asking politely, Lynn, Maria and Verne did as he asked. There was a bright light and a sucking wind from behind them. They turned quickly to see a thriving city in the once empty ravine.

"W-w-where are we?" Lynn said with a stutter about the breathless sight.

"We are at my home, the city in the woods, Nospherat," he said with a warrior's pride but holding his composure. The elf then reached up and grabbed a tree limb and teleported the party right up to the front of the city gates.

"Speak your names and your business or prepare to be taken!" yelled a voice from behind the gate.

"It is I, Lilander, prince of Nospherat!" screamed the elf back through to the other side.

Lynn was in total awe and shocked that he wasn't told that their host is a prince. Lynn didn't even have to look, he knew Maria and Verne were in the same form of shock.

Lynn had a little clue why he didn't tell but couldn't get it out before Maria asked, "Why didn't you tell us you were a prince?"

"If you were dao-tug informants, you would have wasted no time at taking me had I mentioned it," Lilander said just as the gates flew open and there stood obviously, the king.

He stood at a colossal six-foot-five with a crown upon his head. His clothing was a long white garb with a silver sash around his waist. His facial features looked almost like he could be an older Lilander. His hair was the same color and braided in the same fashion as Lilander's.

He wore many rings with different stones and gems embedded within them except one that had the same markings as Lilander's bow. Briefly looking around, Lynn noticed that all the elves that he could see, with the exception of the children, wore that same pendant as Lilander.

"Lilander, where have you been my son? You know as well as anyone that the dao-tug wouldn't hesitate to seize you and do the inevitable to you . . . to us," said the king with authority but also a tone of a worrying parent.

Lilander said while pointing towards the gates with an open hand, "I'm sorry father, but I would like to adventure outside of these walls."

The king accepted the answer without much complaint and turned his attention to the newcomers. "Who might this be, if I may ask?" asked the king directing to his son about his new friends.

Lynn bowed at the waist but kept eye contact with the king and said, "I am Lynn Thrax of the House of Thrax. This is Verne Wingo from the Wingo Clan and the lady Maria Maccio."

Verne and Maria bowed and curtsied when their names were mentioned. The elf king put out his hand to take Lynn's. Lynn did while still bowed not knowing what to expect. Maria and Verne watched as the elf king turned Lynn's hand over and said, "Rise, royalty does not need to bow to royalty in my domain."

"This man," he began again, "is one of the chosen ones we've been waiting for. Where is your other half?"

The crowd gasped and chatter began amongst them sending the message that one of the chosen ones are amongst them. The news traveled before the fleetest bird could fly. News of one of the chosen ones being in their city caught like wild fire with no one to tend to it.

"How did you know I was one?" asked Lynn.

"Of course elves eyes are practically the best. When I first set eyes upon you, I noticed the markings but had to be sure. Now we know," said the elf king over the chatter of the crowd. The elf king motioned for Lynn and Lilander to walk on each of his sides with Verne and Maria close behind. The citizens walked close behind as the king and his guest walked through the streets of the city.

Elves began throwing rice into the air along with banners that had Lynn's birthmark on them followed with the cheers of thousands. They finally made it to the palace, then the elf king turned and said to the following crowd, "Me, my son, and our guest now depart from your company for the evening. I now see a brighter future for us more clearly." He turned back towards his guest and said, "Shall we?"

They entered into the palace to set eyes upon one of the most beautiful palaces in existence. Lynn knew that this one stood out from any other castle he has seen, and he's seen many of them. None he has been in has ever looked this extravagant or wide open. Even the walls were partly made from the nature of the bush around them.

Before entering, Lynn noticed three large towers that he now saw stairs and doors leading to each and other unseen places. There are two sets of stairs along the left and right side of the hall that came around to connect the balcony. The elf king pointed to the stairs on the right and said, "The first door is where the guest stay."

To the left was a portrait of Lilander above to a door so Verne asked, "What lies beyond that door?"

"That leads to my dwelling," said Lilander showing Lynn and the others up the right side stairs to the balcony. A narrow walkway lead to two large doors with, to Lynn's surprise, his birthmark imprinted on the doors and the doorknobs were little silver handles forged in the shape of his birthmark also.

The elf king saw Lynn look towards the doors and said, "That is the kings' court if you're the least bit curious."

The king paused in front of everybody at the top of the stairwell and said, "The doors below the kings' court on the first floor leads to our dining hall. The doors to the left of those leads to an enchanted training ground for our archers and our knights. The doors directly below us lead into a sauna that has miraculous healing qualities. Also there are some very exquisite robes around down there if you would like to wear any."

They all walked towards the middle of the balcony after the elf king pointed to the door next to the guest rooms and said, "That leads up to my dwelling. Above that is where I keep the gifts that different races and species has awarded us with."

Verne's mouth stayed gaped open as they were being shown around since he has never seen anyone live so richly. Maria stayed with a neutral expression while Lynn, even though he has lived amongst royal families, never has he seen the beauty of the elves palace until now.

"How about that one? What lies behind that door?" asked Verne while pointing to the locked door beside Lilander's tower door.

The elf king answered, "That is where my soul-less son is being kept."

Maria quickly advanced on him angrily and said, "Your son!"

"Wait, please listen," said Lilander while stepping in front of Maria to stop her.

She looked Lilander in the eye and then peered over his shoulder to wait for the elf king to explain. The look she had on her face was not one to be tampered with, Lilander knew that for sure. Lilander almost felt a tinge of nervousness.

"As I said, he is soul-less. The dao-tug have done this to him and will not release him until they are defeated or have my body. And I, King Ravenholme, will not tolerate this assault on any one under my rule," He said with pain behind his eyes that began to shed tears.

"Is there anything that we can do?" asked Verne.

"No one has been able to speak to Lilandro, for he rambles on and rages about being released." Lilander intervened with, "I'm the only person that has been able to get his attention, but, he refuses to answer any questions or talk back."

"Well there has to be something we can do to help!" said Maria with a mixture of anger and anxiousness.

"No. I'm sor—" started King Ravenholme but was interrupted by Lilander.

"Wait there is. You must travel to the caverns of the dao-tug, Cinlae, and take their accursed Staff of Locked Souls," finished Lilander.

"Is this possible? Can it be reversed?" Lynn asked Ravenholme.

With confusion on his face he answered, "I'm not sure. We never had this happen before."

"We will venture out tomorrow to this cavern of the dao-tug," said Lynn.

"I shall join you to save my brothers soul," Lilander said unexpectedly.

"No. I will not have Ravenholme's only other child in danger," Lynn said to Lilander almost sounding like a father figure.

"I have been training for decades waiting for you to come and I will not let this pass me by. I will not sit back and place my brothers' soul in someone else's hands. Plus, whose going to show you how to reach the cavern?" said Lilander defiantly but also having a point.

Lynn responded, "I can't let you come."

Maria grabbed Lynn's forearm and said, "Let him come. What harm could it be to have another good hand to come along and show us, plus battle alongside us?"

Lynn took a deep breath, let it out slowly and said, "Alright, but know this, we are a team, don't get us all killed. Even though that will be hard to do."

"I understand," said Lilander in acknowledgement.

That night, King Ravenholme threw a feast in the four companions favor afterwards they slept the night away resting for their long day ahead. As Lynn slept, he dreamt that he was surrounded by Lilander, Maria, Verne and two other unknown figures only to have them snatched away except Maria.

She just stood there glaring at him as if he has failed them all. Lynn awoke suddenly in a cold sweat with Maria staring at him with frightened eyes as Verne began to stir and awaken also. Verne sat up and looked through drowsy eyes over at his two friends as they spoke.

"What were you dreaming about?" asked Maria.

Lynn looked at her then turned his eyes away and thought, "What if it was a vision. I need more time to sort this out."

Lynn contemplated for a few seconds then said, "I dreamt that I failed all of you."

"That isn't possible if you're the chosen one," said Maria while taking Lynn's hand in hers.

"If you say. Lets rest and not worry about the dream anymore tonight," Lynn said while pulling the covers back up to his chin.

Maria obliged and didn't say anything else about it. She went and got in her bed and looked over at Verne. They gave each other a shrug and rolled themselves up in their covers.

Maria and Verne fell back into a deep sleep as Lynn laid there thinking, "What could it mean? Was it a vision or just another nightmare? All I know is only time will tell."

Lynn rose the next morning to the smell of a great breakfast. The aroma of freshly roasted venison wafted through the whole of the castle. The smell of grounded coffee beans made Lynn sit up with a refreshing smile on his face. He wiped the sleep from his face as his eyes began to gain their focus.

"Will you get up already and wash up so that we can feast and be on our way!?" Maria said frantically moving about the room at top speed trying to gather all their items together.

"Alright, just a moment till I get a hold of myself." Lynn responded back a little rudder than intended. He stretched and got to his feet. He proceeded to get dressed and then made his way to the sauna where Maria was waiting for him.

Maria sat in the water relaxing and said, "Come on get in, its very relaxing and relieves many ailments."

"What about the water getting dirty?" asked Lynn.

"Don't worry about it. The elves have this magical stream that keeps the water pure and clean," she responded behind closed eyes.

After washing up, Lynn went to Ravenholme's court. "Could you please gather your party and have them meet me in the dining hall," asked King Ravenholme.

Lynn went to the lower magical training grounds and found Verne taking advice from one of the warrior elves. Lynn stood at the entrance and said, "Verne, it is time to eat. King Ravenholme is in the dining hall waiting for us."

Verne bid his goodbye to the warrior elf and made his way off the training grounds to follow Lynn. They searched for Maria and found her where Lynn last saw her. She was still in the sauna taking in some of the beautiful sunlight.

"Maria, my lady, Ravenholme requests our presence for the feast," Lynn said behind her.

She leaped up in surprise and rounded on Lynn then kissed him before he could react. Lynn stood there with a look of shock jumping from one side of his face to the other to form one whole picture of awe.

"Let's eat. I'm very hungry," she said as she walked towards the door.

Lynn and Verne looked at each other in confusion and just followed Maria out the door. Verne tapped Lynn on his arm trying to gain a reason for her illicit kiss. Lynn just shrugged his shoulders and mouthed, "I don't know."

They then went up the tower to Lilander's room to retrieve him but he wasn't there. His room was humongous compared to the guest room with his bed big enough for at least five grown men. The comforter was kept so plush that just a brush of it with the back of the hand would make any body instantly relaxed and ready for a tranquil sleep.

There were three portraits adorning the walls. Two of him and one family portrait but one look at the family portrait and they saw the other two were not two portraits of Lilander but some one that closely resembled Lilander.

Lilander burst into the room with the look of astonishment on the faces of everybody in his room. It took a minute before any one could think to utter a word to Lilander for being in his room. Lynn said while gesturing to the portraits, "Lilander, you never told us you were a twin."

"Yes, that is why I must save his soul," Lilander said while getting his bow, quiver and daggers and placing them on his body in their respective places.

"Where were you when we were looking for you?" Verne asked as they left the monstrous room.

Lilander kept walking for a moment then said, "I was seeing to my brother in his room."

"What!?" asked Verne and Maria in unison while trying to keep up with Lilander after slowing their pace a little.

"Let him be. They have a bond that no spell or curse can break," Lynn said to the two interrogators.

They did as Lynn asked and followed into the dining hall to feast. As the four companions entered into the dining hall the king rose and then his subjects. Lynn and Lilander took Ravenholme's right while Maria and Verne took to his left.

Ravenholme motioned for everyone to sit while he stayed standing. He began with a clearing of his throat that also meant for the chatter to cease. "My fellow counsel and friends," he began, "we are here to celebrate the coming of the chosen one, Lynn Thrax. Also, we are here to grant my son leave to go with them on their quest to rescue Lilandro's soul from the dao-tug. Yay if he may travel with them. Or nay that he remains in the safety of the city."

He paused to let them agree or disagree. Some voiced that he should be able to explore the world for what its worth even if the peril is great the outcome may bring back Lilandro. Others who disagreed were voicing that he was the only person who could take the king's throne without a civil war erupting if something were to happen to the king.

Once they were through and the majority agreed, he said, "Let us eat of this fruit and meat and drink of this wine and be merry."

After that everyone began to eat and talk casually. There was laughter all over the dining hall as the nobles reminisced with each other. As it got late in the afternoon, people began to leave. Lynn, looking around, couldn't see Maria anywhere.

He began asking about her from what was left of the crowd. "Have you seen which way Maria went to?" he finally asked Lilander.

Lilander was the only person to give him a probable clue as to where she was by spotting her leave the dining hall earlier. Lynn went out into the main foyer and went up the left stairwell from his position to head for the guest rooms.

He stopped as the once locked tower door now stood partially open and struck his curiosity. He approached the door slowly and cautiously, peaked in and saw the stairs circle to the top. Lynn went in and felt a cold atmosphere but he kept going. There were torches in the walls to provide light as he worked his way up the flight of stairs.

When he made it to the top, he stood there and saw, to is surprise, Maria standing in front of the door. Lynn heard the hissing voice of Lilandro behind the thick oak door, "No! I will get free and I will destroy you and your-!"

"Maria, what is going on?" Lynn asked cutting off Lilandro's last few words. She spun and ran towards Lynn and hugged his waist tight. Before they knew it, Lilander, Verne and Ravenholme were standing behind them.

"What are you doing up here? Don't you know it's dangerous just to be in his presence?" said Ravenholme while checking Lilandro's door to make sure it was securely locked.

"I just wanted to see what the dao-tug did to him," answered Maria like a young child being disciplined.

King Ravenholme showed everyone the way back down like the gentle elf he is. Lilander locked the tower door as the group exited and motioned for some elves to stand guard. They did as they were told without uttering a word of displeasure.

"Shall we begin our journey?" asked Lilander making his way for the front doors trying not to show his frustration with the situation that just happened.

Lynn answered as they followed Lilander out the palace, "Let's be on our way at once."

As they left the city, more citizens were celebrating and bidding them a safe return. When they exited the outer gates, they slammed behind them. Lilander pressed a button on a podium and teleported everyone to a small shrub.

Verne looked around in confusion and asked, "Where are we? Where is the tree?"

Lilander answered with a hint of a wry smile that doesn't usually come from elves, "We are on the other side of Nospherat."

Lilander pointed and Verne's gaze followed and fell upon the odd shaped tree on the opposite side of the ravine. Lilander held his hands out to his sides at shoulder height and began to bring them together and focusing his will. Doing this, an invisible veil fell back over the city to show just an empty ravine.

The four adventurers turned with no words to say and began their search for the dao-tug home, Cinlae, to recover the Staff of Locked Souls. Instead of heading east to Kamma, they journeyed south through the Malchor Desert. They traveled leagues through the desert only able to rest safely at an oasis surrounded by eight boulders in the shape of a horseshoe.

Every now and then Verne would complain to Lilander saying, "Is going through the desert really necessary? They just had to live out in a desert. They couldn't pick a beautiful beach or lush forest but a desert." Lilander just smiled every time Verne would rant.

Yet, Maria kept on insisting that they should hurry and get back on track. Why she was in a hurry, no one knew why. Maybe she had seen something in Lilandro. Even Lilander with his keen elven senses couldn't see what was driving Maria so hard to get back to her old master, Niccolo.

After traveling a great distance, Lilander stopped the group and pointed to a rock face. Behind it were more giant rocks, that when seen from above, looks like fingers sticking up out of the ocean of sand. "That is the entrance," said Lilander, "It means to suck you under and never release you . . . ever."

"We shall return. I am as sure as I have lived this long to see so many generations come and go," said Lynn while keeping his eyes on the landmark studying it.

Lilander led the way into what seemed to be the palm of the rock hand. He held one hand, palm down towards the ground, and the other hand, palm up towards the sky.

"What is he doing?" asked Verne in a hushed tone.

"I can't say," answered Lynn in the same hushed tone.

Lilander overhearing the two answered, "I'm acting as the key to their caverns. Their world."

After a second or so, the sand around them began to whirl up in a cyclone. The rocks then closed on them like a fist and began to vibrate madly. When it opened, apparently they were below the surface, and into the dao-tug territory. The caverns would've been pitch black had it not been for the lit torches.

"How are the flames able to stay alight down here this deep in the ground?" asked Lynn.

"It's part of their magic that they developed," answered Lilander.

Every one except Lilander began looking up at the cavern and were caught in what seemed like a trance as the cavern shifted and moved.

"Don't worry about that, it's just nature," Lilander said when he saw what had caught everybody's attention.

"Nature?" asked Verne, "Like how is that possible?"

"It happens all the time. We call them tremors. We just don't always feel them topside. They're what cause the ground to shake. This world is more alive than most nations or races can comprehend."

They started walking down a maze of corridors, taking time to pause as Lilander remembered the right paths to take. When finally coming to the end of the maze, they were taken aback by a large tremor. Lilander looked concerned.

"What's wrong?" asked Lynn when he saw the look on Lilander's face.

"That was no regular tremor we felt," The elf answered.

From just beyond the exit of the maze a towering rock golem dropped from above in a reverberating crash. Its eyes burned a fiery orange-yellow when it stared upon the four trespassers.

It attacked them but they moved just out of reach of its attack. It swung its massive fist around to hit Verne with full force. Verne flew back into a wall with little harm done now that he was immortal. Verne got to his feet dizzily knowing if it wasn't for Lynn's gift, he would be dead flat against the rock wall.

Thinking that Verne was no longer a threat, the golem began attacking Lilander. Lilander used his swiftness to dodge the assaults. Lynn approached the golem with blade out ready to strike until Lilander stopped him saying, "Man made weapons have no effect on this thing."

"How do we stop it?" asked Lynn watching anxiously wanting to do something.

"Well, you are one of the chosen ones. Use your gift that radiates from you body like the sun beating down on the earth. I know its in you I can feel it," said Lilander.

Lynn drove his katana back home into its scabbard, and then focused while placing his palms together. His powers rose to the surface making both his irises in his eyes white as untouched snow. As the golem cornered Lilander, Maria stood back attending to Verne, Lynn sent out his mind to the creature.

The golem turned to face him, held in his gaze. Still frozen, Lynn released a mental bolt to send the golem flying into the rock wall. The golem slowly rose to its feet. It looked at Lynn with a confused look from the power in such an insect compared to itself. Its face quickly turned into a mask of horror and dread as it charged Lynn. Lynn focused his will even harder and stopped the golem in its tracks. Slowly the golem began to float in the air. Pain began to register on the golems face as Lynn fed more power into it until it exploded into a million little pieces of rocks and pebbles.

Lynn and Lilander joined Maria and Verne back near the exit of the maze. Lilander caught sight of a fairy that flew in front of him as if to tease him. "Follow me, but let's try to make as little noise as possible. We probably already alerted the dao-tug," said Lilander.

They followed Lilander, which in turn followed the fairy to a hidden spring just to the left and around the bend from the exit of the maze. Lynn,

Verne and Maria were following Lilander and the fairy in confusion. If you didn't know what to look for you would surely miss it.

Lilander reached up and struck his hand inside a circular crevice that made the large boulder in front of them slide down. They stepped through where a clear blue spring revealed itself to them. They took in the underground water spring and could see their injuries heal even faster than before.

"We must be off. Thank you little fairy," Lynn said to everyone then the little fairy.

"Tweet tweet tweet tweet," responded the fairy.

"She said she knew a chosen one would come one day," translated Lilander for everyone.

They bowed to the fairy and were on their way. They went back to the exit of the maze with no difficulties. Maria asked Lilander while inspecting the lone corridor before the maze, "What now?"

"We go confront the dao-tug and take back those locked souls," Lilander said cautiously stepping into the corridor.

Walking through the corridor it was as if the spiders and webs they spun became greater as they went in such a dangerous environment. They made it through the jagged corridor to an opening that opened into a gigantic cavern. The group all walked the edge of the subterranean cliff to look down into the open cavern and saw Cinlae, the dao-tug city.

From where they stood, the city looked like a giant web with the insects crawling amongst the silk spun lines. There were torches lit in the streets and the homes but their main source light came from an emerald green flame hanging from the ceiling of the cavern.

Lynn's eyes were stuck to the unnatural flame. Anger and rage began to swell up in Lynn's loins until Lilander spoke. "There's a set of stairs to descend into the city over here."

Lilander caught the glimpse of rage in Lynn's eyes but was unable to comment since Maria stepped in his face and asked, "Are there no guards or gates to the city?"

"'Yes. The gates can't be seen from here, but they are massive with towers surrounding the city. The gates are patrolled by male and female warrior's alike waiting for anyone to be careless enough to stumble into their web," Lilander answered and began walking with Lynn ahead of the group down the stairs.

Lilander said to Lynn very low, "I know what you felt. That's what first lured Lilandro. The staff finished the rest."

Lynn looked at the elve's unchanging face and thought, "What could be in store for us down here."

The stairs led from the right of the maze and circled around the stone wall to the bottom. They walked over a bridge made by nature over thousands of years ago to the entrance gates. The towers and gates loomed overhead like dark clouds covering the sky.

They made it halfway through the gate just to have a merchant's cart being pulled by a Nightmare shove ahead through them. The pitch black horse with the blazing fire tail and mane snorted and bit at the passers only to come up short. Lilander informed them, "Don't let the people of Cinlae upset you. It's like that around this whole city. It's just the way they are."

Upon entering the city, Lynn, Verne and Maria gasped at how gothic the buildings appeared to be with spiders and their webs everywhere. The citizens walked around as if they didn't even notice the arachnids. The children played in the streets like they didn't have a care in the world and that their underground world was a normal one.

Just about everyone they would try to ask for directions would get suddenly upset and challenge them. Before any of the challengers would get an attack off, they would see Lynn's markings and say the same thing over in the elfish tongue and retreat. Lilander would translate the first couple of dao-tug until the sounds and their words were embedded in Lynn's mind.

They called him 'a chosen one of their myths come true.' Lilander eventually told the rest of the group that to the dao-tug a chosen one is a curse upon anybody in their presence.

"How far does this city stretch Lilander?" asked Verne while trying to dodge the young dao-tug children.

"It stretches almost a mile and a half," Lilander answered while at the same time, seeming to be looking for something.

A what?" demanded Maria.

Lilander explained, "It is a term we elvenfolk are using instead of yards and leagues."

Maria accepted the answer allowing Lilander to talk about the city. "The city is made up of eight sections. Starting from clockwise of our current position is Foreigners Section, where we will most likely be staying."

"Beyond that is the Scholars Section where a majority of humans visit. There you will hear languages you never knew existed. North of that section is the Artisans section. Rarely any humans or outsiders for that matter go there. Let's just say if you're not known, you're not welcome."

"North of Foreigners section is the Performers section. That is where shows for your theatrical, music or almost any other entertainment can be found. You would do good to avoid the mimes there. They are all deadly."

"To our right is the Chattels section. This is where people come to find slaves and livestock pens. They purchase living, dead or undead as slaves."

"The Verdict is like their courthouse where outsiders are taken when arrested. Don't get caught because the verdict is always guilty. The punishment is either slavery or death."

"East of that is the Outcasts section. That is the undesirables of Cinlae dwell. Among them are beggars tainted with diseases; the half-breeds mixed blood by either human, elven or outside; and lost foreigners. They all live in poverty."

"Thieves dwell here also but there's one name known everywhere down here in Cinlae. He's a half dao-tug named Chakran."

"North of the Outcasts section is the Dead section. This is commonly called the Tombs. Vampires of the city dwell here as well as ghouls craving flesh and necromancers. The necromancers can practice their arts here unrestricted. A massacre is held here once a year."

"Lets hope it isn't that time of year," said Maria with a little shiver.

Lilander shook his head while saying, "It isn't, and we are a little late. Suraala Keep is where the vampire warlord Keogh resides. He was once a mighty warrior now plagued with vampiric blood where he has lived for the last three centuries."

"Finally north of the Chattels is the Savage section. That is where non-dao-tug soldiers reside. The Ceremonial Bowl is where battles and other rituals are performed for entertainment . . ."

By his sudden silence Lynn figured he was through so he asked, "How do we know where to go and what do we look for?"

Lilander waved for everyone to follow and said, "There are four groups of male patrols and six groups of female patrols. The female dao-tug are ruthless ones and lead the race."

After a few minutes of pondering, Maria finally speaks up, "So we have ten patrol groups to watch out for and this race is run by the dao-tug women?"

"Yes," answered Lilander but steadily walking the streets and alleys looking for something.

"Where are we going? What are you looking for, Lilander?" asked Verne.

Lilander answered almost robotically, "I have a plan. We need to attract the attention of the leaders and there's only one way to accomplish that. But first we need to go to the Foreigners section."

"How the hell do you intend to attract attention?" demanded Maria trying to keep up with Lilander's long strides.

Without answering her Lilander stops in front of a sign that read—The Dark Night-. "Here he is," said Lilander.

"He who?" demanded Maria.

He ignored her question again and entered into the building. Lilander explained, "This is where surface dwellers can have a drink and convene and be protected. We would do good to use this establishments services."

Lilander spotted someone talking pretty loud telling a story to his fellow drinkers about his exploits. Lilander approached him and grabbed his arm, pulled him away from the other drunken men and said, "Chakran, I need your help."

"I don't know who you're talking about but-"

Lilander didn't let him finish. Lilander dragged the drunk with him to a booth Lynn and the others found open. "I need one of your radars!" Lilander got straight to the point.

"Lilander, you can't just barge in here and demand things from me. Where is a heartfelt greeting to your friend, Chakran," said the drunken Chakran.

Lilander and Chakran grasp each others wrist and presented broad smiles to one another.

"It's good to see you again, Chakran. These are my friends Verne Wingo, Maria Maccio and Lynn Thrax, one of the chosen ones," said Lilander bringing the attention to the others for a split second.

Chakran's eyes stopped on Lynn for a moment. "What do you need, Lilander?" asked Chakran with a smile on his face as he turned back to him.

Chakran stood about six-foot-one with white hair falling just to his ears like a short mullet. He wore a long brown trench coat with three straps adorning the wrists and two on the upper arms.

At the shoulders was small pads and the coat was being held closed by three of the seven straps that lined the middle of the coat. Three of the straps at the top of the coat hung loose to show off his toned chest.

His pants were two-tone with the inside seams a darker brown and the outer part yellow. His boots were black and extended to his knees with steel toe tips on the outsides. He kept on his brown leather gloves showing that he would be ready at a moments notice.

His skin was like any other dao-tug at a pale gray with red irises in his eyes. His body deceives people to think he is an easy push over at one hundred and seventy five pounds but no one lives to tell any body about their push. He keeps his hand on his single edge sword in his lap being on the defensive.

"I need a radar to locate the patrol groups," said Lilander.

"What are you planning?" asked Chakran.

Lilander shook his head and said, "Please, leave this to us. We are here on business not pleasure."

"Alright, but if you need help, don't be frightened to call," Chakran said while passing Lilander a small compass like radar and small recorder instrument.

Lilander thanked him and made his way out of the tavern with Lynn, Maria and Verne in tow.

"What is the instrument for?" asked Verne once again his inquiring mind always open for information.

"It's to call Chakran. It is magically bonded to him so that when any one plays it, he will come. It only makes music though if he plays it," said Lilander as he began to walk off.

Lynn asked, "How are you and Chakran such good friends?"

"He's a half dao-tug rogue-," said Lilander but was interrupted when Maria snapped.

"A thief!?"

"No," said Lilander clearing it up, "He's like an avenger to overthrow the dao-tug nobles. We met when he came through my woods. He wanted blood but I was able to reason with him and allow him to stay in the palace until he rested. Since then he holds me in debt for not killing me and I hold him for allowing him a place to rest."

Lilander pauses when he steps in front of another eerie looking building and looks up. "Here we are. The Pit. We can rest here safely without any problems anytime we wish."

They went inside of the small five story inn to speak with the proprietor. Inside was crawling with spiders and shabby walls adorned with webs. An old dirty torn red carpet lay on the floor.

Upon closer inspection of the carpet, there wasn't just dirt built up over time, but blood also.

The check-in desk stood to the left of the entrance door. The desk looked better than the floor. Dust, stains and spiders lay there as if they were priceless trophies. The proprietor was an older looking dao-tug with an attitude that suites their race and the living conditions.

After settling in, Lilander explained to the others some of the attractions here. The most popular gambling house is Dead Mans Hand Casino, a five story building that looks as if only the wealthiest beings would go there. There's a place called Widows Sting which is a bordello, casino and an inn.

The prostitutes there are pretty expensive for the average citizen. More gambling houses are Dragon Breath, Rolette of Death, and Gangis Khans Wrath. The other bordellos are called The Green Flame, Serpents Kiss, and Dark Orb.

After resting, they began their tract through Cinlae to find the patrol groups. Lilander activated the little magical radar to begin tracking their movements. The whole radar fits in the palm of the hand but without knowing the proper words to invoke the magic, it would just be a regular compass.

"It's good you found Chakran when you did, Lilander, or it would be harder to find the patrols without his help," said Maria to Lilander's back as he kept walking.

"Hmm," said Lilander, "Yeah. He is of great help to our cause as are we to his."

"Why would he have a magic radar anyway?" asked Verne.

"He's a rogue. He has to watch where his potential threats are whenever he's on a mission," answered Lilander without taking his eyes from the little blue and purple arrows on the radar.

They took care of the male groups with little ease. After finishing the last female patrollers, and accomplished what was trying to be done, they were being sought for by the officials. The group ran but just about everywhere they turned, the dao-tug Enforcers were there.

Dao-tug Enforcers are the grittiest and deadliest of the dao-tug's law enforcement. The Enforcers only consisted of the female sex and they had to be full blooded, not even the least bit doubt of being half dao-tug.

Finally after being apprehended, a large female dao-tug at about six-foot-two stepped in front of Lynn. Lynn smiled and was about to speak until the dao-tug threw a punch into Lynn's stomach doubling him over then struck the back of his neck with the hilt of her sword. Lynn hit the ground and the last scene he saw was of his friends hitting the ground beside him before darkness took him.

Chapter: 5

After being kept in a blindfold for a while, he was finally aloud to take it off. Upon taking it off his eyes set sight on an arena full of people staring at him in silence. The arena was mixed with adults and kids. Dao-tug, humans, trolls, orcs and even ogres. Just about any race that traversed these underground caverns could be seen in the audience.

A voice erupted from high up, "Here we have this insolent outsider breaking our laws!"

The crowd showed its disapproval with boos. With the arena settling down a bit the voice rang again, "He will battle for his life and for our entertainment of course. Bring on his challenge."

The arena erupted in cheers as the same female dao-tug that knocked Lynn out before, entered the area. "His first battle will be our preliminary battle. Sheera place his weapon down. He must start out without it. Begin!" came the voice over the crowd.

Sheera placed Lynn's katana on the ground behind her. Lynn's bonds magically loosened from his wrist and fell to the ground. She unsheathed a long sword and a crooked dagger with its tip dipped in some green substance.

She attacked with a swing at Lynn's head with her long sword. He ducked. She then swung a backhand with her long sword at his torso. He jumped back out the way from her attack. Just as fast as he backed up, she lunged with the tip of her dagger.

Lynn rolled under her attack and ran for his katana. The crowd disagreed with a sigh. Lynn turned around just as she was attacking him. She kicked him in the diaphragm, then an elbow to the side of his face. She did a spinning kick to his chest to throw him back a few paces.

Lynn's head was spinning from her powerful blows. When Lynn looked up, the dagger was being pushed deep into his chest. The crowd erupted into a monstrous cheer as Lynn fell to his face and felt his body go cold. She circled Lynn taking in the applause and stalking him like a tiger does its prey.

Feeling that his time was slipping, Lynn put the marks of his hands together and felt the ancient power rise in him. The energy from it threw Sheera on her back. Lynn could feel the effects of the poison slowly wearing off giving him enough time to rise and get his footing.

Sheera arose quicker than she hit the ground. Lynn was surprise, but it wasn't the look on her face that shocked him, it was the crowd's silence. Blinded by her anger, she rushed Lynn but didn't notice his speed. She attacked his head with a lunge then brought it down to cut through his body.

He dodged both attacks and stepped on her sword when it hit the ground. The blade snapped in two as she tried to pry it from under her targets foot. She still fought with the broken sword and crooked dagger in hand.

She swung out of rage with her sword and dagger. Lynn sent his power surging through his katana as he swung his blade and deflected hers out of her hands. No sooner as she lost her weapons she dived for Lynn like an angry cat. He squatted under her attack and plunged his katana into her stomach.

She stopped short taking short sharp breaths. Lynn withdrew his katana, spun around and took her head. The crowd erupted, whether it was approval or disapproval, he didn't have a chance to find out. Guards chained and blindfolded him then took him back to his cell.

Lynn sat there awaiting thinking, "What's next," when a familiar voice came from outside his cell. There was a tiny slit in his cell door that was only opened for feeding and when ever being addressed. The feeding didn't come regularly. In fact it was very rare.

"You, you, what is your title?"

Lynn just looked at the little slit for a window in the door with a scold on his face. The only light came from the slit when it was open and he really didn't want it closed but he didn't want to seem needy.

"Answer me damn it!" said the man behind the voice.

Lynn gave a smirk and said, "I'm Lynn Thrax of the House of Thrax."

"Lynn Thrax. Lynn Thrax you say?" He let the name roll off his tongue before speaking again.

"So you're the one my master seeks to destroy. Wait until he hears this. James Stratton caught the evasive and elusive Lynn Thrax. I know he shall reward me handsomely for this," said Stratton with a hint of anxious excitement in his voice.

Lynn needing to see just how far up the chain Stratton was he wittily responded, "You think that an underling like you can hold me? You are nothing but a pawn in this game. If you wish to live, stay out of the way."

Lynn accomplished what he was trying to find out with Stratton's next statement. He said with rage that you only see in an ambitious scout, "I am stronger than you think! Until I can get word to my master, you will do for entertainment."

The little slit shut and footsteps faded in the distance as he left. Lynn now knew that Stratton was actually basically at the bottom of the totem pole in Niccolo's regime. After what seemed like a day or two, Lynn was brought back into the arena. He went through the same ritual as before with the blindfold and chains except he had his katana this time.

"We are ready for our next bout!" Stratton bellowed from high up in the stands.

The crowd erupted in cheers as a ninja with a short dark blue tunic and tights with a mask that covered only his mouth stepped into the arena. His hair is white like that of a dao-tug and pulled up into a ponytail. His katana rested on the back of his hip with his right hand groping the hilt.

He stood in a stiff straight posture with his legs together until he went into a battle stance. He stood about five-foot-ten but when he crouched, it seemed like he was more than a foot and half shorter. Lynn and the ninja circled each other like two lions fighting for leadership of the pride.

Lynn caught sight of his odd gauntlets with open slits on the underside of his forearms. What caught Lynn off guard were the ninja's eyes. Lynn's marks encircled the ninja's eyes like tattoos. The two combatants rushed their targets and parried each others blows.

"Who are you and why are you fighting me?" Lynn asked him.

"No need for names on this stage just blood."

The two warriors were engaged in a deadlock neither wanting to give way to the other. Both warriors strained against the others might but knew that there was even more strength lying behind the others visage.

"I ask you again, who are you and why are you fighting me?"

"I'm Uri Tanko, and I'm fighting what you're fighting for . . . life." Uri answered then pushed off Lynn's blade then they both stalled for a moment staring each other down. Uri inched his right foot forward just a bit to bring about his combat stance. Lynn slowly raised his blade on guard.

Lynn attacked but Uri dodged his every attempt, yet Lynn matched Uri's speed by dodging his attacks also. During a brief pause, Lynn spoke, "We can escape. I just need your help."

Uri responded, "There is no escape from the dao-tug! Death is the only release and even that's not guaranteed."

Uri began his assault again and Lynn thought, "I could try a counter attack and use that to my advantage." Uri brought his katana down in a slashing arch. Lynn spun to the left out of harms way but also slashed at Uri's arm in doing so. Uri spun through the air and landed on his side. He quickly jumped back to his feet and stole a glance at his flowing blood.

His eyes suddenly changed and reminded Lynn of a feral animal readying to attack. He pulled his mask down free of his face to show elongated fangs beginning to form. His arms grew to twice their original length and sprouted leathery wings on them. His ears grew out very large to extend over his head. The brown fur rose to the surface just as his feet turned into giant talons.

Lynn sat in shock as the hybrid form of a werebat flapped its enormous wings to take flight. Uri swooped in fast and cut Lynn's arm with one of his talons. And just as fast as he attacked the first time, he turned and attacked again, again and again. Uri stopped in the air and bore his chest to suck in air for his sonic wave.

Before he was able to complete his next attack, Lynn placed his markings together once again to bring forth his ancient power. Lynn slowed time just as Uri released his sonic wave. Lynn circled Uri and saw the high frequency sonic waves from Uri's attack as Lynn made his way behind Uri. Lynn jumped on Uri's neck and held on with all his might as Uri flapped wildly.

While trying to hold on, Lynn put his hands over Uri's beady eyes and felt their marks unite as one. Lynn felt Uri's body relax under his thighs as his power coursed through Uri and back to him. Lynn knew a connection was made when he was able to see into Uri's mind and see not only the ninja bound by chains but the werebat running rampant throughout his mind. Uri broke free of his bondages and gained control of the raging beast within. Lynn jumped off Uri's neck seeing that he calmed down a bit.

Still on guard, Lynn asked Uri, "Uri can you hear me? Are you alright?"

Uri answered with a low growl while trying to shake his dizziness off, "Yes. I have control over my lycanthrope now, but how?"

Lynn explained, "I really don't know, but, I think we were destined meet."

Lynn showed Uri his hands, "You have my birthmarks around your eyes."

Uri and Lynn both looked around the arena from the corners of their eyes. The crowd silenced to a barely audible whisper. The crowd began to boo as they noticed the fighting had stopped and it didn't seem to be starting up any time soon.

"What are you doing?! You're supposed to be killing each other and we're supposed to cheer. You are stealing from my patrons who have paid to see one or both of you die now finish this bout," demanded Stratton from high up.

Lynn said in the direction of Stratton's voice, "Your games are over. You will soon find my katana slicing through your neck."

Before Lynn could finish, eight guards surrounded him and the werebat Uri. Uri took flight and drew a few of the guards his way. Lynn took up his defensive stance just as some of the guards lurked forward and the crowd went crazy in fright of the two prisoners rebelling.

Uri shot his sonic wave blast at the guards that were chasing him to knock them off their feet. While they were scrambling to get back to their feet, Uri dove in and lifted one of the thralls by his neck in his talons. With one effortless twist, Uri pulled the head free from the body and let both fall to the ground.

Three guards attacked Lynn back to back. In the heat of battle, Lynn let his intuition guide him.

'Duck to the right. Side slash your blade back to the left. Kick out behind you. Twist katana around in hand and thrust to the right.'

Lynn's katana entered into the chest of one of the guards. Lynn turned to see Uri diving at the four other guards over and over again like a lure just out of reach. Lynn swiftly made his way to the unexpected guards and quickly ended two of their lives.

The other two turned their attention to Lynn. No sooner had they done that, Uri dove onto one and bit his heart out of his body. The last guard didn't know what to do so he attacked Lynn. Lynn avoided his attacks and let Uri dive on him to pin him to the ground. Uri bared his fangs for the kill but was halted when Lynn put his hand in between the two.

"Wait. We need to find my friends. Where are they being held?" Lynn asked the dao-tug guard.

The guard spit at Lynn's feet and said, "I embrace death. You will get nothing from me." Uri readied himself to take a bite out of the guard's chest but Lynn stopped him again.

Lynn got down by the guards head and said, "Wait, I have an idea. It's a long shot but it's our only chance."

Uri nodded his furry head and moved back just a fraction. Lynn put his hands on the sides of the guards head and concentrated on the task. The guard's eyes took on a far off look then he let out a gruesome scream as he took his last breath.

Uri transformed back to his human form and asked, "What did you do to him?"

Lynn rose to his feet and started off as spectators were exiting the arena as if it was due to fall at any moment. Lynn answered Uri, "I guess I did a mind drain."

Uri shocked said, "A what?"

"A mind drain. I took information from him and it killed him. I think I am fatal to the dao-tug if I try to enter their mind. I only was able to gather very limited information but not much. We must move . . . now."

They ran out into the streets as if nothing unusual happened and made their way to where Lilander, Verne and Maria were being held.

Lynn and Uri made it to the building called 'The Verdict' in the Chattels section without much interruption. There were two guards which Lynn and Uri took care of quickly. Lynn looted one of the bodies for some keys to gain access to one of the floors. When they entered the building a sign on the wall shown that they were on the second floor.

This floor was one long hall with ten steel doors, four to the right and left sides and two at the end of the hall. Uri and Lynn split the eight doors to the cells amongst themselves to search. Peering in each cell, they saw nothing but a few spiders crawling around the rectangular cells. Coming to the end of the floor, they shook their heads to each other showing no positive result of the search.

Lynn tried the keys to the steel door with 'To Third Fl.' above it but to no avail. He then tried them on the door that had 'To First Fl.' The keys turned easily in the locking mechanism to grant them access.

They slowly went down the stairs to the first floor. The first floor was only visible by four well placed torches. In the ground were six pits with walkways leading halfway over each one and rounded off at the end. They walked on to the walkway of the first pit to their right.

Inside was an orc, to the left of that pit was a zombie. Diagonal from there on the other side of the first pit was a skinny frail looking human, and to the left of that pit was a very pale humanoid of great beauty except for the fangs protruding from his upper lip.

Diagonal from there was a troll and to the left of that pit was Lilander. Lilander lay there in the dirt and grime barely recognizable but Lynn could tell who his follower was. Lilander lay there not bothering to give attention to what the other prisoners were getting riled up about. His eyes stayed shut tight not wanting bring his mind back to the hell hole he was in.

"Lilander! Wake up. We've come to release you and the others!" Lynn screamed down at Lilander stirring the other prisoners even more in doing so.

Lilander looked up and squinted, "Lynn? I knew you would come. Who is that with you . . . a . . . a werebat?"

Uri then said, "My name is Uri Tanko. My clan is called the Flying Stalkers dojo."

Lynn asked Lilander, "How did you know that Uri is a lycanthrope?"

"I'm an elf, Lynn. He knows I can see deeper to his true power. I can see his beast rumbling behind his eyes yearning to be released, yet, he now has control of it."

Lynn then asked, "How do we get you out? Do you know?"

Lilander stood up, "There should be a switch box close to the door. It's locked in place but there's a code box on the wall by my pit. I'm sorry, I don't know the code."

Uri looked back the way they came then to the box on the wall by Lilander's pit. Uri tapped Lynn on the shoulder and directed his attention to the code box. Lynn went to the box with Uri close behind. A piece of parchment over the box read, "These numbers in order are very close, yet, in the right order, can be so far apart."

Neither Lynn nor Uri could figure it out so Lynn reached for the numbers but a very heavy raspy breathing came from behind him.

"Uri, could you please calm down and back up some?" Lynn said swatting at his shoulder trying to get Uri to back up just a pace.

Uri then said, "That's not me, Lynn."

They rounded on their heels slowly to see a female dao-tug with a spider mask on resembling a brown recluse. She stood there twirling two sai in her hands. Her skin rolled as something moved beneath the surface.

Every few seconds her skin would burst open in a spot and tiny spiders would make their way to freedom before her wound could heal over. Her boots extended all the way to her knees and had a symbol resembling a spiders head on the knee.

She wore some type of warrior garb that resembled underwear but with that same spider head symbol on the front. The top of her outfit completed what looked like an armored brassiere. Adorning the front like the other two pieces to her outfit is a spiders head on each breast.

She spoke, "You will not progress any further."

Uri unsheathed his katana and said, "Who will stop us then? Surely not just you."

Two male guards came to her side. They brandished their weapons and said not a word. The mask wearer looked back at the two guards and smiled through her full mouth of fangs. A brown recluse crawled out of her mouth and slid down its web from her teeth.

"I think these two will do well to help capture the likes of you two," she hissed through her teeth.

The two guards and the mask wearer attacked Lynn and Uri. Uri drew the attention of the guards while Lynn fought the masked female. Lynn struck at the masked dao-tug's arm to disable her. She winced back at the blow but showed Lynn her arm that was quickly healing over.

She lunged both sai at Lynn's head. He leaned back away from the attack then dodged right a few paces to avoid the next attack and to get some breathing room. Uri jumped around the two guards causing them to miss on their attempts.

The guards anticipated Uri's next spot but never his next move. Uri let fly two shurikens which caught the two guards straight in their throats. Before Uri touched the ground, the two guards fell face first to the floor. Lynn attacked the masked female with an onslaught of slashes. Lynn had the dao-tug teetering on the lip to the pit where the frail human was waiting with an eagerness that belied his nature.

Right then, Lynn felt a power awaken from behind him. Before he had a chance to see what was happening, Uri flew past him and knocked the masked dao-tug into the pit. Lynn peered into the pit just as he felt another power awaken from within the pit.

The human turned into a white furred werewolf and ravaged its prey. The dao-tug stood no chance as the loping werewolf was on her before she could regain her footing. He bit into her chest and tore her heart out. Lynn went to the code box and began putting numbers into the correct order. He looked across the room and signaled to Uri to try the switches. He threw all six switches not knowing which one was the one to Lilander's pit. The walkways extending halfway over each pit began to lower and break off in small pieces to form steps.

If not for Lynn and Uri releasing them there would have probably been a massacre. Instead the man in the werewolf spoke, "We know what you came for and we all thank you for releasing us. We are in your debt and will hinder you from your objective no longer."

"Thank you," Lynn said while helping Lilander get his balance as he was coming up out of his pit.

The prisoners went upstairs and made their escape. Lynn, Uri and Lilander followed them upstairs but could not make their own escape until they freed Verne and Maria. They tried to go through the third floor door but it remained locked and Lynn didn't have or know where to find the key.

Uri stepped forward with a set of keys, "I think these could at least try to unlock the door. I picked them up after finishing the two guards."

Lynn clasped the back of Uri's neck in a relieving manner showing that his mind was a little more at ease.

Lilander asked, "Where shall we be without you?"

Uri answered in a humorous tone, "Probably stuck here on the second floor."

Lilander just smiled as Uri fit the key into the lock to allow them access to the third floor. When they came onto the third floor, Lilander said, "Lets search all the floors thoroughly before moving on. Maria and Verne can be in any one of these cells on any floor."

There were eight more cells on this floor like the previous floor, except when they peered in the first cell on their right, the walls slanted to give it a triangular look. In the first room was a decaying corpse with spiders feeding on its bones.

Everyone covered their noses as Uri spoke, "Let's hope that's not one of your friends."

They moved about the floor checking the cells, but it seemed empty until they reached the last cell on the left. His feet bound by chains in the middle of the cell, well away from the door or cell window, was Verne lying flat on his back.

Lynn thought, "I'm guessing they heard about his escape tactics. They even stripped him of his weapons and jewelry and threw them into the corner."

Lynn said, "Verne . . . Verne wake up. It's us. Lynn, Lilander and Uri."

Verne stirred awake and asked, "Where have you been and who is Uri?"

Uri answered, "I'm a friend and I'm bonded to Lynn now."

"Well, thank you, whoever you are. So Lynn converted another to his cause."

Lynn smiled as he handed Verne back his possessions. Lilander asked, "Verne, think, do you know where Maria is being held?"

Verne sat there pondering hard while putting his jewelry and scabbard back in place.

Lynn impatiently shouted out, "Come on, you have to remember something."

Verne looked at Lynn, "All I remember are the guards taking her further up. Said something about being held trial."

The four companions exited Verne's former holding cell and headed for the stairs. Four dao-tug guards stepped through the door leading to the next floor to block their ascent.

The Guard in front spoke up, "Give yourselves up and we might consider death rather than torture."

Verne unsheathed his blade and said, "Can I get that on a parchment?"

Lynn spoke before unsheathing his katana, "We came for our friend and to help another, if you wish not to perish, **you will move.**"

The guards stumbled back a bit at the refusal but regained their composure just as quickly. The guards charged but little did they know who they were up against. One attacked Uri but Uri moved so fast, it was as if he magically shifted to the side.

The guard swung his sword around at Uri's chest. Uri flipped into the air over the attack and landed two kicks of his own across the guards head. Before coming down Uri had his katana buried deep in the guards' forehead.

Another guard rushed Lilander, but an arrow caught him in the thigh. He looked down at the infliction and looked up just as Lilander was plunging both of his daggers into the dao-tug's neck. Lilander withdrew the daggers and let the guard slump and die on his injuries and his own blood.

Another guard spun a two blade sword resembling a stick. In mid spin he attacked Verne repeatedly. Verne blocked each one but got backed into the cell. As he kept blocking the attack from the dao-tug, Verne knelt down and rested a hand on something metal that bumped his heel.

The dao-tug tried to impale Verne but Verne rolled under the attack to head for the door. Verne brought his blade around and knocked the dao-tug's weapon from his hand. The guard ran to his weapon but was stopped short by what Verne had done.

The guard looked down to see his ankle chained to the wall. He reached for the keys on his belt but felt nothing on his side where his keys wee supposed to be hanging. Verne stood in the door in a casual stance tossing the keys in the air while saying, "I'll be on my way now. Enjoy your stay . . . like I did."

Verne closed the steel door and let the lock fall in place. The last guard was attacking Lynn with no efficiency. Lynn ducked and dodged the attacks until the guard tried to sweep his leg under Lynn's. Lynn buried his katana into the dao-tug's ankle as it came around. The guard screamed out in pain but was cut short when Lynn took his head.

Since the guards left the stairs leading to the fourth floor unlocked, the group of escapees made their way quickly up the stairs. They checked all the cells and there were only three cells empty. The prisoners begged for help, food, or to be released. Lynn instructed to the others, "Set them free. They shouldn't be bound to this place, not like this."

After releasing the prisoners, Lynn and company made their way to the door leading upstairs but were stopped when four female guards stepped through. The females charged without a word but fell short when four arrows hit them directly between the eyes.

Uri turned to Lilander and said, "That was almost assassin like. I need to keep an eye on you."

Lilander didn't answer just directed Uri to follow Lynn and Verne up the stairs. The next floor had one door in the middle of a semi-circular room. Four female guards stood next to the door leading into the cell. One guard stood to each side of the stairs as Lynn and the others stood there.

None of the dao-tug made a move as if the intruders were invited and expected to be there until one of the dao-tug by the cell opened the door. Verne took lead and was followed by Lynn, Uri and then Lilander. Upon entering the cell there were four prisoners chained to a section of the wall with steel mask covering their faces. Verne felt the power and knew Lynn felt it too when he walked towards one of the prisoners.

Lilander grabbed Lynn and pulled him back just as one of the prisoners leaped for his neck. Uri thought, "Of all this fresh blood on the floor and on them, how are they still alive?"

Lynn spoke, "Be calm, all of you. I'm here only in search of a friend. Do you know where I might find her?"

"Sorry," said one of the prisoners, "we thought you were the torturer returning."

Lynn checked around but couldn't think of a way to release them until his eyes fell on Uri. He then said, "Uri, I need you to transform and break those chains and mask."

Uri responded, "As long as they're not silver, I should be able to."

A few seconds later, Uri was changed into his hybrid werebat form and working at the chains. Lilander kept looking out the door to see if the dao-tug made any moves, but they didn't. After being freed, one of the other prisoners spoke, "We thank you and are truly grateful for showing us mercy. We can sense your immortality and know you could have followed your senses and taken our heads. We shall flee back to the surface and tell about your graciousness."

The prisoners quickly ran out the cell. Lynn was about to speak until the screams of the immortals erupted from outside the cell. Their Essence shot through the door and hit Lynn and Verne in the chest filling them with power while bringing them to their knees.

When Lynn and Verne came back to their feet, they walked out of the cell. The dao-tug stood in the same stance and place as when the intruders entered. Lynn walked slowly to the center of the room with an angry scold on his face.

"Lynn, don't. We did all we could," Lilander said from behind Lynn watching his body movement.

Lynn let out a long breath that he didn't know was being held, "No, we didn't."

Lynn unsheathed his katana and no sooner the guards had their weapons out and ready. Lilander and Verne followed suit and bared their weapons. Uri snarled showing his fangs and squatted a few inches readying to pounce. Lynn smiled what looked to be a slight snarl as the dao-tug guards inched closer.

The dao-tug fell on them from all sides but was halted when Uri let out his high pitched scream. The dao-tug fell to the ground holding their heads as if trying to keep them on. Lilander was riding the floor also since his elf ears could hear the noise. Verne and Lynn grabbed Lilander and pulled him into the stairwell.

Verne called out, "Uri lets go!"

Uri stopped the noise and made one giant leap to the door. Just as Uri made it through Verne had the door shut and locked. The dao-tug started pounding on the door and shouting obscenities at their escaped quarry.

Uri reverted back to his human form and waited till Lilander was a little less shaken up. "You could've warned me," said Lilander grunting while getting to his feet.

"There wasn't time," said Uri putting his hand under Lilander's elbow.

"What would it have been like if I warn my prey of my attack? They would avoid it," said Uri.

Verne asked while following Lynn up the stairs, "Why did the dao-tug recover quicker than you, Lilander?"

Lilander answered, "They dwell on pain. Pain is like a lovers embrace to them. Yet, there's some things I guess even they can't endure."

Lynn leads the way through the large steel doors to enter into a courtroom. The courtroom was the dome roof of the structure with the jury stands all around the room and one very large judge's bench parallel to the door. There was a figure sitting behind the bench with another spider mask on.

She stood and spoke with a voice like a demi-god, "You've made it thus far to find the one you search isn't here. Your lives are mine to decide!"

"What makes you think we will comply?" Lynn said relieving his scabbard of his katana.

The dao-tug answered, "We will destroy you on this plane. Once that is complete, we will reanimate you with our necromancy and you will be ours forever."

"Where is Maria?" asked Verne stepping forward a few steps.

She leaped onto the bench and bellowed, "You dare demand answers from the Phase Spider!"

Her leaping on to the bench aloud the four travelers to see her body. She wore skin tight leather pants with fin like spikes sticking out the side of her legs. Her boots extended to her knees and the same spike protruded down to mid-calf. Her top covered her ribs and breasts but left the cleavage and slim stomach exposed. Her arms were bare except for the black wristbands and those fin like spikes riding up her arm.

"Either it's me or her body sends out waves of power that are almost visible," thought Lynn.

She turned to jump on to the wall and climb around the room. They all noticed her fin like spikes sticking out of her back. She stopped just over the door and smiled a deceptive smile at her prey. The hairs on the backs of their necks tingled as if some other being was about the room.

"Uh, Lynn," Lilander said, "we have company."

The other three turned to see what Lilander was looking at. Their eyes set on a huge spider twice the size of a mere man. Before Lynn had a chance to register the monstrous arachnid, both spider and dao-tug attacked.

Chapter: 6

All at once Lynn, Lilander, Verne and Uri scattered to different parts of the room expecting the two monsters to collide into each other. Yet, to their astonishment, the dao-tug seemed to have gone transparent therefore phasing straight through the arachnid.

"What the hell is going on?!" yelled Verne.

Uri was first to answer, "I have the least knowledge to say on the subject!"

Lilander gave some insight to the others, "She or it is a Phase Spider. She is able to phase herself to the astral plane and back at will."

"Brace yourselves! Here they come!" Lynn warned the others.

Verne and Uri battled the oversized arachnid, while Lilander and Lynn battled the mask wearing dao-tug. It seemed that every attack Verne or Uri inflicted did no damage significant enough to stop the arachnid. Uri used his speed to run around and under the spider confusing it and giving Verne an opportunity.

Verne ran up into the jury stands and leapt off on to the spiders back. When the spider began reaching for the pest on its back, Verne kept its appendages at bay with his sword. Uri used his strength to kick the other legs from under the spider causing it to stay off balance.

Lynn and Lilander were having no better luck with their target. Every time they would attack, the dao-tug would phase just before the attack connected. Lynn thought, "It's like we're fighting a ghost that strikes back."

Lynn felt their time coming short and resulted to his only other weapon. He put his palms together to bring forth his ancient power and feel its warm embrace around and through him. Uri sensed Lynn's desperation and transformed to his hybrid werebat form.

"Lynn, I'm ready when you are," Uri sent telepathically to Lynn.

It surprised Lynn that his bond connected them to this extent. Lynn nodded to Uri but to his surprise, so did Verne.

"Don't forget, I'm bonded to you also," Verne sent telepathically to Lynn.

Verne jumped off the spiders back just before Lilander shot four arrows linked together by a net. The spider cringed, thinking that the arrows would impale it but instead caught it to the wall. Lynn attacked the dao-tug only to have her phase, yet, as she came back, Lynn used his powers to slow time. Uri then shot his sonic blast at the dao-tug. The blast knocked her off balance only to stumble into Verne's outstretched sword.

"Quick, before she gathers her senses and phases herself!" Lilander yelled to Lynn from across the room.

Lynn slowed time once again to gain some space. It was just enough time for Lynn to take her head as soon as she looked up. Once the body and head were separated, the mask came off and the spider disappeared. The net holding the spider fell slack as the quarry being held was no longer in its grasp.

Lynn picked up the mask and pocketed it, hoping that he could study it at a later date. "Well, no special theatrics, no Maria popping out of a secret compartment. Maria is no where in the building," Verne was going on in exhaustion.

"We can't go back. We know what's waiting on us down stairs," Uri said looking around real attentively.

Lilander then put in his own sense, "So, where do we start looking for her?"

While they were rambling, Lynn watched the dao-tug's body wither into spiders and scatter about revealing a note. Lynn picked up the note and read it.

"Hey, look what was left behind!" he called out to them.

They rushed over to Lynn to see what he was reading. Verne snatched the note out of Lynn's hands almost tearing it and read it out loud, "If your reading this, congratulations, you've obviously defeated my Phase Spider. She was a very adept dao-tug and her death will not go in vain. If you want the girl come to the arena and claim her. Know this; if you leave the city, you have sealed her fate."

Verne finished the note and Uri asked, "Well?"

"Of course, we'll go and get her out of who's ever hands she's in," Lilander said before Lynn could answer.

Suddenly, those six female guards were pounding on the door, on the verge of entering.

"Uri, the wall behind the bench, quick!" Lynn commanded.

Uri transformed into his hybrid werebat form once again and used his sonic blast where Lynn directed. When they made the jump, the guards were on their tail but stopped for fear that if they were to follow Lynn and the others, they would die or their prey would.

Uri caught a hold of Lilander and Verne's hands in his talons while Lynn used his power to slow his descent. When they hit the ground, before Uri could fully revert back to his human form, they were on their way to the arena. Running through the crowds of people the six dao-tug guards were watching their prey from high up in 'The Verdict'. They knew where their prey were going and knew it was only a matter of time.

Lynn and his entourage rushed through the underground city not daring to stop less they give the six female dao-tug guards a chance to gain some ground on them. As they came into the presence of the arena, a giant banner hung outside with writing that Lynn couldn't make out.

"Would anybody like to tell me what that says?" Lynn asked the group but Lilander knew it was for him.

Lilander answered, "It is of the elven writing."

Verne not waiting for Lilander to finish asked, "Well, what does it say?"

"It reads," Uri started before Lilander, "there's an award of whatever is desired for the capture of the four escaped hostile prisoners . . ." Uri paused before saying, "dead or alive."

"How did you know that?" Lilander asked Uri.

"Being an assassin, you must learn and blend in with the environment. I was taught to pick up on just about any language just as perfect as any elf. I've also had almost a millennium to perfect my art. Let's move. There's a friend who needs saving."

They moved into the arena after that was said and done, but Lilander felt shocked and awed by Uri and quickly hid his expressions. Lynn seeing this thought, "Lilander still needs some training. He's only a novice in a very large battlefield."

They came into the arena through the gates they escaped and seen Maria strapped to a table. All four ran towards the table but was cut short by a man in expensive looking but far from any royal robes.

"I see you made it. No problems getting here I hope," said the man blocking their passage.

Lynn and Uri knew at the sound of the voice who he was. His mellow voice was unmistakable. Even without the loud speaking device he loves to uses.

"So Stratton, you finally decided to face me without hiding behind something," said Lynn taking in the mans features.

Stratton spoke," You actually think that me, one of Niccolo's elite generals needs to hide from you?! I will soon be one of his Children once I present you to him."

Stratton smiled after revealing his hopes for the future. Standing at six-foot-two with a firm jaw and a nose that looks more like a snub with little outcropping flares where you can barely see his slits. His eyes were held partly shut as if he was squinting behind blue orbs making him look blind. His hair was pulled over his left shoulder in a ponytail.

A very handsome and mesmerizing man he would be if not for his scar coming from his left eye down his cheek to stop on the side of his neck. Lynn couldn't calculate Stratton's build beyond his hanging robes.

Stratton spoke again, "Now, do you actually think that you can defeat me?"

Verne not concerning himself with Stratton's rambling asked him, "What are you doing to Maria?"

Stratton smiled a sinister wolfish smile, "That device she is strapped to is called a desiccator."

He paused and looked in Maria's direction. Everyone followed his gaze to the table. "The desiccator," Lilander spoke to himself activating his memory before speaking to everyone directly, "The desiccator is a large iron table which is used as a torture device. There are four solid iron bands for the victims' arms and legs. The bands are flexible and can hold any creature that's the size of a half-ling to the size of a troll. The desiccator hypnotizes its victim to lull them so that it could suck out the life force and vital fluids."

Lilander pointed to a jar at the head of the device, "Her vital fluids are used as a powerful poison that is most potent on its same race. The victim must be drained to death to produce enough of the essence. The desiccator mixes torture, necromancy and alchemy all into one terrible device."

"I knew the elf would be able to determine what it does," Stratton said while pulling a staff from inside his robes.

The staff stood bout waist high with a black orb with a green core shining from within. It had an odd type skull with elongated fangs biting down on the orb as if to hold it in place. Lynn thought his eyes were playing tricks on him until on closer inspection, the length of the staff had transparent eyes blinking on it.

"Feast your eyes on my Staff of Locked Souls!" basked Stratton in the presence of the staff.

"That's the staff. Lynn we must retrieve it," said Lilander.

Stratton held up the staff in front of himself in admiration and said, "So this whole fiasco of yours has been for my staff? No worries, your souls will be of use to me just as all the others."

Stratton pointed the staff at Uri as the core of the orb rose to devour the blackness by what looked like other souls. It happened within an instant and just as fast as it began it ended with Uri falling to the ground, immobilized with no soul.

"No!" yelled Lilander rushing to Uri's side.

"Lilander, take Uri into the stands and stay by his side. Verne you try to free Maria from that thing . . . and I'll handle him," Lynn commanded the other two of his conscious friends.

"So you wish to die in front of your friends and crush their hopes?" said Stratton twisting the staff in two different directions to unsheathe a glowing green double-sided jagged edged blade.

"My blade is embedded by a talisman that allows me to slowly drain your soul with each wound inflicted," Stratton said while swinging the blade smoothly from left to right repeatedly in front of himself.

Lynn unsheathed his katana without blinking for he knew as well as Stratton did that this was a death match. Stratton approached Lynn at great speed so Lynn readied himself to parry his attack. Instead of attacking how Lynn anticipated, Stratton used the sword as a pole vault to dropkick Lynn in the chest.

Lynn slid back about fifteen feet before he caught himself. This time around, Lynn rushed Stratton just as Stratton rushed him and surprised Stratton with a forearm to the head. Stratton twisted in the air and was barely able to catch his balance.

His blood flowed from his mouth. He spit the blood on the ground like froth. Lynn thought, "He didn't like that. Now let's see what his next move could be."

Stratton pulled another item from underneath his robes. When he brought it to a halt, Lynn knew exactly what it was before Stratton spoke, "This is the Black Widow mask. The most powerful of the three mask. Remember, pawns advance in rank once they reach the other side of the board."

He placed the mask on his face and went through a slight metamorphosis as the mask molded to his face. He just smiled his sharp evil smile showing rows of elongated fangs while frothing at the mouth.

"See my power that will gain me favor in Niccolo's sight. With this he will finally allow me to become one of his Children," said Stratton with a voice that could possibly make a mountain tremble.

Stratton and Lynn locked in battle once again. With the powers of the Black Widow mask enhancing Stratton's abilities, it seemed as if Lynn couldn't even touch him.

"I got a bad feeling about this Lynn! Get out of there! He's too strong!" yelled Verne still struggling to release Maria from the desiccator.

"So the effects of the mask are already taking affect, said Stratton with that bellow of a voice.

"What effects?" asked Lynn.

"My Black Widow mask gives me the ability to climb like an arachnid, great vision, a poisonous bite, to leap like no other man and to induce fear into my victims."

Lynn tried using his powers in battle but Stratton seemed to be able to counter those. "I have activated a spell on the arena to where only talisman magic is permitted," said Stratton.

Lynn thought, "So that's why my powers are not working."

Stratton spoke again, "As you see, I have the four combinations to make me a god."

"What are those if you'll permit me to ask?" Lynn asked while trying too think of a solution to beating Stratton.

"One is my Staff of Locked Souls, two is my desiccator, three is my immortality soon to come and four is the last of the three powerful masks."

Then it dawned on Lynn.

"The Phase Spider mask from the jail," he thought.

"So only three? Well let's even the score with one of those three," Lynn said while pulling out the mask.

Stratton's mouth gaped open in surprise to see the mask in Lynn's hands. Lynn thought, "How powerful are these masks and is mine powerful enough to defeat his?"

"That mask was supposed to vanish when the wearer died. How is it possible that you have the mask?" Stratton said while doing a good job of hiding his fright and surprise.

Lynn answered while taking a proud look at the mask then at Stratton, "I guess a head without a body can't go through the same fate as the body."

"You mean you?" Stratton said in frustration.

"I decapitated her and soon you will follow!"

Stratton charged at Lynn with his sword raised high. Before he could make contact, Lynn already had the mask on and using its phase powers. Lynn opened his eyes to look through eight eyes instead of two.

He was able to see a blurry figure looking right through him but unable to see or touch him. Lynn phased back to the material plane to stand face to face with Stratton. Stratton attacked Lynn but Lynn used his new found prowess to leap far from him.

Stratton quickly followed pursuit. Once Lynn landed, Stratton was within striking distance. Stratton attacked again but Lynn phased behind him. The momentum from his attack sent Stratton on to the ground. Lynn flipped over Stratton to land in front of him and delivered an uppercut with the hilt of his katana. Stratton rose quickly but stood still in exhaustion.

"So, are those the four combinations that will make you a god?" asked Lynn with a hint of humor in his voice.

Lynn heard his voice for the first time since putting on the mask and noticed it sounded as evil and deafening as Stratton's.

Stratton yelled, "I will not let you succeed Lynn Thrax!"

Stratton rushed Lynn to have his attack miss but Lynn's attack hit right on target. Lynn's target was the talisman that Stratton used to augment the staff. The skull on the Staff of Locked Souls shattered under Lynn's attack. The power from the sword struck out at Stratton causing him to release the sword.

"My talisman! You will pay with your life!" Stratton yelled in a fury.

His body began a slight metamorphosis as his fingers turned into deadly claws. Stratton attacked in a blind rage missing Lynn by mere inches. Lynn kept dodging and taking little slices at Stratton but every cut that would open, little black widows would emerge and weave some new skin out of their web.

Stratton charged Lynn but Lynn had a surprise waiting for him. Stratton lunged out at Lynn. Lynn phased into the astral plane but not his katana and allowed Stratton to impale himself. Lynn phased back to the material plane and just as fast withdrew his katana then quickly spun and took Stratton's head at the jaw line. Stratton's soul was snatched from his body and sealed into the Staff of Locked Souls, its purpose going into effect even if the master isn't controlling it.

Chapter: 7

With Stratton's death, the Staff of Locked Souls lay on the ground as well as the Black Widow mask. The desiccator disappeared and Maria was slowly coming to. Lilander and Verne stood staring at Lynn.

Lynn thought, "It seems like they're scared of something or some one. Me?"

"What is it? What's wrong?" Lynn asked with that evil sounding voice gnawing in his ear and mind.

Lynn set eyes on the Black Widow mask and immediately knew what must be done. He picked up the mask and was about to phase until Maria asked, "What are you going to do with that?"

"I'm taking this to the astral plane and abandon it there. Afterwards, I'll try to remove this mask," Lynn said looking the mask over slowly and capturing a glimpse of the evil within the mask.

He phased to the astral plane and took one more look at the mask before launching it into the void around him. He phased back to the material plane and began taking off his mask. As he grabbed the mask around the nape portion and tried to pull it off, the mask seemed to have gained a mind of its own and held on to Lynn's head.

After much tugging on the mask, Lynn was finally able to get a slight hold on his own power to help him remove the mask from his face. Everyone approached Lynn just as the mask was coming free. Lynn's power radiated out like a bright light shining from the spot where he stood that froze everyone in there tracks.

When the light died down, Lynn stood there with the mask in his hands. Lynn could still feel the power that the mask boast inside itself, slowly receding and yearning to be set free, tempting him to put it back on. His hands began pulling the mask back toward his face. The mask was calling out to him. Yearning to be back on. Crying out to Lynn to embrace the power that it can give him. Power beyond his wildest imaginations.

"No," Lynn said to himself shaking his head, "I must be stronger than you."

Lynn finally resisting the urge to put the mask back on put it in his pouch and went to the Staff of Locked Souls. He bent down to pick it up but stopped when he remembered what happened to Stratton when his talisman was destroyed. Lynn closed his eyes and braced himself for the unexpected as he wrapped his fingers around the hilt.

Nothing happened so he placed the sword back in its long scabbard so that it can take on its staff look. Lynn went to the now conscious Maria and Verne to make sure they were alright. He went by Lilander and the soul less Uri.

"Do you know how the staff works?" Lynn asked Lilander.

Lilander shook his head, "I saw no special rituals used against Uri except will alone."

Lynn looked deep into the orb to see the core rise with his will. For a moment the core seemed to fade back into itself so Lynn focused even more of his will deep into the orb. He sought out Uri's soul then aimed the staffs orb at the ninja's husk of a body once it was found. A green celestial strip reached out from the orb into Uri's body. It drifted through the air like a snake as it made contact with the ninja. It gripped Uri's lifeless body as he convulsed with reinforced life. The small light show took only a matter of seconds.

Uri didn't seem to show any signs of life until his body began to transform into his werebat form. Then without warning, he let out an ungodly roar or scream of terror.

Lilander quickly held him down and said, "Uri. Uri. Calm down, we're here for you. You're ok."

His heart was speeding rapidly from his soul and body being reunited so quickly. Uri calmed down a bit. Everyone seemed to be back to normal and ready to make their way to the surface until Lilander and Uri paused.

"What is it?" asked Maria stepping closer to Lynn.

Lilander looked around intently and said, "I think . . . Lynn quick give me Chakran's recorder."

As soon as Lynn had the instrument free from his pack, the six female dao-tug guards from 'The Verdict' were coming from all directions towards the group. Lilander quickly played the instrument but no sound or spectacular feat erupted from it. The guards halted their advance as Chakran appeared quickly from the stands to leap with a supernatural ability to land by Lilander.

Lilander handed the instrument back to Chakran and said, "We need to get back to the surface."

Chakran smiled and twisted the recorder then placed it on the ground. A white transparent barrier surrounded Chakran and the five adventurers blocking off the guards. The guards then sat with their legs folded in a meditative position on the ground just waiting.

"This is the best I can do for you until we can think of a way out," Chakran said.

Lynn thought for a few minutes then snapped to an idea. He pulled the Phase Spider mask out and took a nervous look at it before putting it on his face. Everyone stood frozen, staring at Lynn like he was the legendary hideous Medusa.

"Come on. I will teleport us to surface," Lynn told them but nobody moved.

They hesitated until Maria ran to Lynn's side and faced the others. Then Verne and Lilander followed suit but Uri stood stiff as if his legs were made of stone.

Maria shouted out at him, "Uri, come on its safe."

Then Verne added, "We're running out of time. Those guards could have some sort of magic to counter the barrier."

Uri broke what fear was stopping him and stepped closer to the group. "Let's get out of here," he said.

"Stay close and remember, I'm new at this," said Lynn with that sinister voice. Lynn paused for a second and said, "Chakran, come with us. It would do good on my conscience that you allow us to repay you."

Chakran smiled, picked up his instrument causing the barrier to dissipate and ran to the group. Lynn closed his eyes and began to concentrate. Lynn felt everyone move in closer. He also felt the guards rise quickly from their positions and charge once again. Lynn feeling the anxiety around him phased the group just in time.

Then with his will, Lynn lifted everyone through roof, rock and sand to sunlight. Lynn phased everyone back to the material plane and they all seemed to be ecstatic to be safe and whole.

"Did you guys see the Black Widow mask?" asked Verne.

"Yes, I believe all of us spotted it," answered Uri.

Lynn pulled the mask off easier than before. "I guess I'm growing in power," thought Lynn.

Chakran pulled Maria to the side and said, "I know what you did."

Maria retorted, "What are you talking about?"

"Don't play stupid because I tried to call for the mask myself."

"Please."

Chakran cut her off, "I thought I could use the mask in Cinlae but you summoned it before me. Your secret is safe with me."

"They don't know how skilled I am on the astral plane," thought Maria.

Lynn walked over to the two and said, "Chakran, you should come with us."

"No thank you. I have too much work down under."

Lynn then said, "But you're surely a wanted man for helping us."

Chakran said jovially, "I've been wanted since I was born."

Chakran turned to the rock face entrance when Uri, Lilander and Verne joined them. They watched as Chakran got enclosed in the rocks and pulled underground to make his trip back to Cinlae.

"Lets get back to Nospherat and," Lilander was cut off when Uri mentioned other plans he had.

"I have a companion that has been taken to a ruined coliseum to the east," Uri said.

Lilander lost what enthusiasm he was showing to let the familiar featureless elf face stare at everyone.

"What has Stratton done to him?" asked Verne.

Uri glanced at Verne with an oblique look, "Her actually. I over heard him saying she'll be there until the eclipse then it would be over."

Lilander thought for a moment then said, "Eclipse, eclipse. They're preparing for the massacre of the year. She will be their first to start their bloodlust and keep them from going back into Cinlae and running through the city."

"Well, let's go save her already," Maria said anxiously.

Chapter: 8

Lynn, Maria, Verne and Uri followed Lilander as they traveled southeast. Lilander mentioned that he only knew of one ruined coliseum and that was 'The Advent'. While traveling, they came across a new coliseum being built. They were immediately approached by two royal guards and what seemed to be the architect.

"If you are not permitted to be here then I'll have to ask you to leave. Instructions from King Augustus the Just," said the architect.

Lilander took the floor, "Well, I am Lilander Ravenholme, twin son of the wood elf King Ravenholme. King Augustus is our good friend and ally, and I assure you, he would tell you to let me and my companions pass if he were here. Our business is at 'The Advent', not this new massive one."

One of the guards was about to speak but held his tongue when a young woman came out of the new coliseum to intervene. She stood about five-foot-ten with green eyes. A petite brunette with beautiful dimples whenever she smiled. She wore white riding pants with black leather boots, black blouse and white cloak. Her age was barely twenty but with knowledge and wisdom well past her years.

"Lilander, is that you?" she asked.

Lilander stepped past the guards towards her and said, "Princess Le'Anne, could it be?"

She hugged Lilander with affection of a longtime friend. "Why yes, and I haven't heard from you since your brother was changed," she said.

"Yes, but me and my friends have the Staff of Locked Souls and will be off to free Lilandro as soon as we can."

How did you get it? I know, stay with us for the night and tell me about it," Le'Anne extended the invite to the travelers.

Lilander looked at everyone else for their response. They more than happily accepted making Le'Anne smile showing off her dimples and spreading the word to the rest of her company. Prince Lilander was amongst them and he brought friends, illustrious friends who's deeds proceed them only to now finally put a face to some of the legends that have transpired decades before their time.

They sat, ate and reminisced on their adventure since Lilander met the others and since he last seen Princess Le'Anne. "That's what we've been through so far," Lilander finished telling her their story.

"Wow," she said, "Lynn Thrax of the House of Thrax, Lady Maria Maccio, Verne Wingo of the Wingo clan and Uri Tanko of the Flying Stalkers dojo. I thank you for bringing Lilander home safe, but I sense that his journey is only beginning and he can't stay."

"Yes, we must go to save another captive of the dao-tug who should be at 'The Advent,'" Lynn explained to Le'Anne.

Le'Anne replied, "I will not hold you back any further. Sleep and at first light you may resume your journey."

Le'Anne departed from inside the new coliseum followed by Lilander and the others. She took them to the northern side of the coliseum where two giant tents and a gracious carriage were pitched and waiting. Verne and Uri set their tents up on the side of Le'Anne's carriage away from the coliseum.

After a lot of rambling and adjustment of the bodies, everyone dozed off except for Lynn and Maria. Maria laid there watching Lynn search through his thoughts but unaware that he wasn't the only one awake.

Lynn lay there thinking about his forefathers, parents and sister until the hairs on the back of his neck began to prickle. He rolled over slowly to see Maria just closing her eyes trying to look as if she were asleep.

"Maria?" Lynn said in a whisper without a response. "Maria, I know your not sleep so what's on your mind?" He asked.

She opened her eyes and said in the same low whisper, "I was just admiring your strength and valor but are we ready for Niccolo?"

Lynn rolled back over to look at the ceiling of the tent pondering for a few seconds. Lynn finally spoke, "I can't say except that I would battle him right now and not stop until his head and body were in two separate places."

Maria smiled a masking smile and thought, "He has no idea what he's going up against, but no matter what, whoever comes out on top, so will I."

"Niccolo is a very powerful man and has influence in many places. I just want you to be careful," she said while touching Lynn's face.

Lynn smiled at her, took her hand and kissed her palm. "We'll be alright in the end," he said while watching her doze off. Lynn soon followed into that same dream state that everyone else were embraced in.

"Father? Father? Where are you?" yelled Lynn from his six year old body and voice, "Father!"

"No, don't come this way!" he yelled back at Lynn.

Lynn knew better than to disobey his elders but curiosity overwhelmed him. He crept a little closer to see what the sudden excitement was all about. He noticed all his forefathers in a line, backs to him, just standing there.

Without warning, all fell with their heads rolling every which way with only one dark figure standing amongst their bodies. Lynn saw those feral eyes and beastly smile from his hiding place. The figure stepped forward allowing Lynn to see that it was Ruffio.

Lynn looked around and immediately thought that he couldn't have picked a worse place to hide. He jumped up and ran away from the figure in fear.

Ruffio caught sight of Lynn and screamed, "Niccolo, capture him!"

Lynn ran for his life but his legs were not fast enough. A hand gripped the back of his neck and lifted him clear of the ground. The hand slowly turned Lynn to face the owner. Lynn barely got a glimpse of the face until . . .

"Lynn. Lynn wake up. Someone is trying to capture the coliseum," Lynn heard Maria's voice in his ear as she shook him by his shoulders.

Lynn quickly jumped to his feet, grabbed his katana and exited the tent. He ran around the carriage to see Le'Anne's guards battling men in, to his astonishment, black cloaks with red tunics and red tights. One ran to Lynn, sword held high, readying to strike. Lynn unsheathed his katana and dodged the attack. He paused for a split second to see that same pin holding his cloak around his attackers' neck.

He kept coming at Lynn until Lynn struck him down and took his head. The Essence was a brief one which Lynn felt was a novice. Lynn ran inside the coliseum to see the builders running around like chickens scared in their coop by a wily fox while the guards tried to fight off all those immortals.

Lynn found Le'Anne running behind two of her guards until they were unexpectedly slain by one man. The man who struck down Le'Anne's guards was a muscular six-foot-two warrior of a man. He wore the same tunic and tights but, his cloak was red, and flowed like a river of blood, distinguishing him as the leader of the raid.

His hair was black and pulled back into a short ponytail with an angular jaw line that makes him look like a force to deal with. His eyes are light green like Lilander's tunic in the sun, yet, there was something that showed he has the wholeness of an eagle but the range of a hawk. Even though he had a muscular build, he was no more than twenty or thirty pounds heavier than Lynn.

He grabbed Le'Anne up into his arms and began looking around scanning the frenzied battle around him. Then his eyes fell on Lynn and seemed to show a hint of hatred behind them. "Come after her and lose your head," he mouthed inaudibly while gesturing for Lynn to come then raking across his neck.

Lilander saw the exchange and made a beeline through the immortals, cutting them down and taking their heads. Lynn intercepted Lilander and asked, "What are you doing?"

"I'm going to save her and end his miserable existence."

"No. It's me he wants. You'd lose your life going after that one. He's no mere novice but an adept with a blade."

Lynn made his way through the maze of battling guards and immortals. On his way to face Le'Anne's captor, Lynn assisted a few of the guards and his friends take some heads. Lynn finally made it to the steps where he last saw Le'Anne and her captor. He looked further up the steps to see the man dragging Le'Anne behind him.

The man looked over his shoulder to see Lynn right on his heels. All in one motion he threw Le'Anne, with remarkable strength, further up the steps and swung around with his sword out on his guard. He still had that smirk on his face awaiting Lynn to come closer. Lynn kept running, barely unsheathing his katana until he was within a few feet of the man's blade and lunged at him.

He dodged and parried to throw Lynn's weight causing him to stumble on the steps. "So you're Lynn Thrax, the one my master has commanded us to bring to him alive," said the man.

Lynn took a glance above him to see that Le'Anne was alright then back at the man responsible for this situation. Lynn asked, "Who are you, might I ask?"

"I'm Zane Lumley, but to my victims I am known as master."

"I asked only so I can tell **your** master who helped me."

Zane not understanding asked, "How can I help you?"

"When I take your head, your Essence will make me that much stronger to beat Niccolo."

After saying that, it seemed at first frighten then anger Zane. Zane thought, "Could he really be stronger than master Niccolo? No, he's not even stronger me!"

Lynn and Zane rushed each other valiantly. Lynn slashed from left to right at Zane. Zane leapt over the attack and Lynn. While in the air behind Lynn, he delivered a kick. Lynn blocked by bringing his katana behind his head to intercept the blow. When Zane landed, he brought his sword down in an arch over Lynn's head.

Lynn dodged the attack by sliding to his right. Zane's attack had so much strength and power behind it that his sword dug into the steps and destroyed them where Lynn was just standing. He pulled his sword free of the rubble and smiled at Lynn feeling like he was about to bring him to his master. Lynn rushed Zane but threw his katana at Zane's head. Zane ducked under allowing the katana to fly over his head with an inaudible swish through the air.

When he stood straight again, Lynn delivered a side kick to send him flying off balance. Lynn retrieved his katana before Zane was able to stand.

"You're truly a competitor, but, your days of running wild are over!" Zane said when he got to his feet.

Lynn responded with a sharp wit, "Oh yeah. Well, come tame this wild beast."

Zane rushed Lynn in a rage. Lynn parried under Zane's blade and thrust his katana into Zane's chest to the hilt. The blow cut through his sternum and one of his lungs stopping Zane in his tracks. Lynn withdrew his katana spun to gain momentum and took Zane's head. No sooner did Zane's body hit the ground, his Essence over took Lynn's body.

Lynn felt the immortals Zane had slain and the faces of innocent souls he killed out of bloodlust. For a minute, Lynn felt nothing but hatred for all good but soon gained control of himself and pushed back Zane's personality.

A figure sat in a fairly large chamber dimly lit by two torches. An ivory top table stood to one side of the room with an empty basin adorning the top. On the other side of the room was a large bed in the corner with black and red comforters and pillows. Two windows were perpendicular to each other with a chair placed in front of both. In the far corner is a ladder that can be easily overlooked but was the only route to the roof area.

Still the figure seemed comfortable in such a dreary and eerie place where evil is encouraged. "So, he's getting stronger every time he battles," said the dark figure, "His blood will run freely in my hands and his Essence and body will fuel the fire."

A younger man walks into the chamber without presenting himself but the seated figure shows no anger after seeing who it was. "Master, would you like for me to bring your enemy to your feet?" he asked.

The dark figure turned slowly from the frame on the wall to face the young man. "No, my son," he said, "you're not needed at this moment."

"Yes, Master Niccolo," he replied eyeing his fathers beauty.

Niccolo wore a black tunic that extended to his ankles with a pair of red tights underneath. His red cloak was worn over his left side, while exposing his right side. The cloak hid his sword on the left but the hilt still bulged out under it. His beauty was unnatural with his full blossom red lips and his clean cut eyebrows. He stood at about five-foot-eleven with an average frame.

His eyes are the crimson of a true vampire but hung low to hide his power. His black hair flows like the wind and extends to his shoulder blades and down the sides of his face.

"Dante, what brings you?" asked Niccolo.

Dante stepped a little closer to his father. His features were almost a mirror image except that Dante looked to be only a teen but was well past those years and his hair was a brownish blonde pulled into a tight ponytail with two or three loose strands hanging down over his face. He stood two inches shorter than his father, Niccolo.

Dante wore the same tunic and tights as Niccolo, but his cloak was a rich emerald color with ivory trimmings. He carries two knives about the length of his forearms on the outside of his thighs. They both looked at the empty picture frame that gives Niccolo eyes to the outside world through his thralls allowing him to watch Lynn Thrax.

"Father, your looking weak and haven't fed in months. Shall I bring you something to eat?" asked Dante.

Niccolo looked at Dante for a second then answered, "No, Dante, just send her in."

Dante exited the chamber and sent in a young peasant girl and shut the door behind her. Dante put his ear to the door and listened for a second. He heard nothing at first then the screams started and the door rocked for a brief moment. Dante leaves with an evil grin on his face. In the chamber, on the frame, Niccolo's eyes are running toward Lynn up the steps.

Maria, Lilander and Verne ran up the newly destroyed steps to Lynn and Le'Anne's side. Uri dropped out of the air in the last stage of his transformation back to his human form. "Is she alright?" asked Maria taking Le'Anne's hand but talking to Lynn.

"Le'Anne, you're not injured in any way are you?" Lilander asked not giving Lynn or Le'Anne a chance to answer.

"She's fine. Lynn made sure of that," said Uri.

"Yes, he is astonishing with a sword," Princess Le'Anne spoke up.

Lynn peered over at her and caught a glimpse of admiration. They walked down to the center of the arena to lend what hand and help to the guards they could. Before long, Le'Anne stopped Lynn and his friends a little after midday.

"You should be on your way to 'The Advent' to save your friend before its too late," she said while showing them 'The Advent' from the new coliseum.

Lynn was surprised to see 'The Advent' was so close. Lilander kissed Le'Anne's hand and bowed. Everyone else bowed except Maria who just stood there looking around. They were off and on their way to the corroded and worn down coliseum.

They arrived a little before twilight. Uri stopped and sniffed the air and said, "She's here, but not alone. I can't distinguish what else I smell."

Getting the warning, they crept into 'The Advent' trying to avoid touching anything lest it gives way and tumble bringing the walls down around them. Lynn felt a presence that was unnatural and couldn't tell if anyone else could feel it. No matter what he felt he didn't want to give it away that it had more company in the decrepit building.

"Do you feel something? Like something is walking beside you?" Lynn asked everyone with a whisper.

They disagreed and just as quickly the feeling was gone. They finally made it to where Uri's friend was. She sat on the ground in the center of the arena chained to the ground with her head hanging down perceiving to be asleep or meditating. They ran to her side but before they could get within arms reach of her or say anything, she lashed out at them.

Her eyes were beat red and darting around like crazy from one person to the next. Everyone backed up out of reach as she continued to show a menacing look on her face screaming obscenities, "Come on! I'll kill all of you! Don't think these chains make me any less dangerous!"

Uri stepped forward and went to her. She instantly dropped her facade as Uri took her in his arms and began crying. "Uri, we need your strength to brake these chains," Lynn said while inspecting the chains around her feet.

When Uri released her, Lynn was able to get a better look at her. Her hair was short, just below her ear lobes, with a tree bark brown to her locks. She has some kind of armor over her shoulders connected to her brassiere but was soft to the touch.

The brassiere was white with a ruby embedded in it right between her breast. She wore nothing but her underpants, which were the same color as her brassiere, with a sword on each side of her waist. Upon closer inspection the swords looked to be locked in place. She wore gauntlets and boots of the same material as her shoulder armor. On the gauntlets, there were rubies right under the palms.

She stood five-foot-seven with a light brown skin color to her finely toned build. Her face had an angelic beauty with a oval bluish-gray eyes. Her lips were probably the most voluptuous any of them has ever set eyes upon. Lynn walked up to her with his hand extended in a greeting.

Her eyes opened wide upon seeing Lynn's face. She unsheathed her swords, striking at Lynn's head while doing so. Lynn dodged by leaning back and placing his left hand on his scabbard and right hand on the pommel.

Uri Leapt in between the two and said, "Gaia! What do you think you're doing?"

Gaia answers angrily with her head full of steam, "He's the one I've come back for!"

Maria turned to Lynn, "What is she talking about?" Before Lynn could answer, Gaia answers the standing question, "I'm from the future and I came back to stop the person who's heir created the vampires in my time. My calculations said I would encounter the fiend here in this place."

Everyone looked at Lynn except Lilander who kept looking at Gaia. Lilander spoke, "Well I can assure you, he's no vampire. I would be able to see through to his essence."

Gaia looked at Lynn kind of puzzled but before she uttered another word, Uri interrupted, "They're here."

Chapter: 9

From the darkness around them, all they could see was yellow feral and red bloodlust eyes behind an unusual mist. The eyes were closing on them when Lilander and Uri said in unison, "Dao-tug and vampires."

Seeing that their presence was detected, the vampire thralls and dao-tug fell upon the awaiting group. Lynn and his entourage battled the attackers as best they could but the situation seemed fatal. Suddenly the thralls and dao-tug that were still alive stopped and backed up into a circle around their prey.

Lynn started walking forward but stopped when a dagger was thrown at his feet from the shadows. A figure emerged from the shadows. The circle opened to where—she—came through. Lynn was surprised to see such a small woman in charge of so many gruesome—beast might sound too sane—things.

She stood about five-foot-six with shapely thighs and hips. She wore a skirt with splits down the sides exposing her calves, thighs and buttocks. Over her breast she wore two straps just wide enough to cover her nipples and leave the rest of her flesh free.

Everything she wore was black, even her long hair was black and flowed with grace. If you continued to look at her you would get caught in her hypnotic glance. Lynn blinked one time and that brief moment, her beauty dissipated into a hideous hag then back again.

Lynn thought, "Did anyone else just see that."

Almost as if she read Lynn's thoughts, Gaia said, "She's using her hypnosis on us. She's a Lady Vampire. She's no ordinary thrall."

The Lady raised her hand and with that gesture sent away the dao-tug and her thralls. When they were out of sight, she spoke with a feminine godlike voice, "You're not the one I search for. But, the scent is unmistakable-"

She looked at Maria when saying this. Lynn took a couple steps forward and asked, "Who are you and who are you looking for?"

She looked at Lynn as if he wasn't worthy of asking her *any* question but she answered reluctantly, "I am Lady Ursula, the only Lady Vampire. I'm hunting the one who calls himself Dante. You," she switched her glance from Lynn to Maria, "you have his scent. Why?"

Everybody stared at Maria waiting for an answer of who the mysterious person, Dante, was. Maria spoke finally after a moment of silence, "Dante is my son."

Ursula spoke once more, "If I smell Dante's blood on any of your hands, you will be my new prey for taking away mine. I will make you suffer his fate."

When Ursula finished speaking, she moved towards the shadows becoming one with them and slowly disappearing into the darkness. "Thank you for telling me you were the mother of a vampire," Lynn said angrily to Maria.

Maria retorted back in the same manner, "I'm sorry if you didn't ask if I had any children."

Lynn was about to address Gaia until Uri added insult to injury unintentionally, "Not just a vampire, but, a Lord Vampire. That would be the only way Ursula could become a Lady and not just a thrall."

Lynn shot Uri a glance that put him slightly on guard. Lynn turned back to Gaia, "Now do I look like I can bring forth vampires?"

Gaia, still puzzled from what just happened, said, "I must have gotten it confused. The script said I would find 'the one' here in this place at this time. The script must have been incomplete."

Lilander intervened, "Is that exactly how the script read?"

"Yes!"

Lilander responded, "Well, then the script was right. You just chose the wrong person to attack."

Gaia being confused asked, "What do you mean wrong person? The two vampires that started the threat in my time are his descendants."

Gaia gestured to Lynn with her thumb. "I can't say that it isn't his descendants, but, **the one** probably was Ursula," Lilander said taking up Lynn's defense, "You're more than welcome to come with us. Since the taint seems to start with Niccolo, we will eradicate the vampires in one fell blow."

She agreed and followed them, with Uri at her side, out of The Advent. Gaia thought, "I never factored in Uri's interference."

She looked sideways at the werebat in sheep's clothing. They made it back to the new coliseum within a few hours before daylight. Upon arrival, Lilander received word that Le'Anne went back to Kamma and increased the guard force at the coliseum. Lynn and his company immediately left for Nospherat going back through Malchor.

On their way through Malchor, a young messenger ran to Lynn and fell to the ground exhausted from his journey and cried out, "Lord Lynn Thrax! King Ganon of castle Maru has sent me to find you. I've been searching for you for a little over two days and he requires your assistance."

Lynn asked, "Assistance? For what? I am no longer his counsel."

The messenger responded, "We were under attack my lord."

Lynn shocked and angered said, "Under attack! By whom?"

"They call themselves dao-tug and there are—"

Lynn cut him off, "The dao-tug, speak no more. We will go with you at once." Lynn then turned to Lilander and said, "Lilander, I am sorry but I must, it is like a second home to me."

"I know what must be done. Lilandro isn't going anywhere," Lilander said while checking his daggers and then the tightness of his bow string.

They followed the messenger and arrived at the city Fawn, where the castle Maru is, a few nights after they left the old coliseum to see the chaos that has been brought upon the city. The city was on fire with dao-tug running amok and citizens trying to save what little possessions they could. Dao-tug and human bodies alike lay dead in the streets but Lynn knows, the human body count far exceeds that of the dao-tug's.

They encountered a few dao-tug and, to their surprise, some vampire thralls near the gate entering into the city. Lynn and his companions made quick work of them then moved into the chaotic atmosphere. They cut through dao-tug and thralls that ran across their path trying to bar their way. Eventually, the group of adventurers made it to the castle Maru.

Lynn knew this wasn't the castle he once dwelled in. The castle he remembered was one full of life and celebration. This one only reeked of death and darkness. In just the small amount of time that it was attacked it was already falling to pieces. Lynn thought, "Who ever did this will pay."

Pieces of set stones began falling to shambles in certain places. As they approached the castle doors Lilander set his eyes on one of the two guard posts by the door. One was empty, the other had a guard in it with death biting down on him lurking over his shoulder waiting to wrest his life from his body. They followed Lilander to the guards side.

"Guard of the castle Maru, where is King Ganon?" Lynn asked of him.

"Lord . . . Lynn . . . is that you?" he panted out in slow sharp breaths. Maria then spoke up, "Yes, now where is the king?"

"Please . . . my lord . . . save the kingdom," he paused to cough.

"He's in there . . . with those . . . m-monsters," he said ushering his last breath.

As he went into shock, they stood watching knowing that he was too far gone for anyone to help. When the guards body was still, Uri turned to Lynn, "Let's go save your kingdom."

Upon entering the castle into the throne room they were attacked by four dao-tug women. The dao-tug emerged from the four doorways that lead to different sections of the castle. One attacked Maria and Verne, another attacked Lilander and Gaia, one on Uri, and one on Lynn.

Verne tried to be the valiant one and quickly was disposed of by the dao-tug. When Verne rose back to his feet he saw Maria standing over the dead body.

"How the hell," Verne thought.

Lilander dodged each attack from the dao-tug attacking him and Gaia. Gaia thinking the dao-tug forgot about her tried attacking from behind. The dao-tug spun quickly with a roundhouse kick. Gaia went flying across the room. When the dao-tug turned back to face Lilander, there was an arrow pointed in between her eye.

"Enough games," Lilander said and let the arrow loose at point blank range. The force threw the dao-tug back about fifteen feet. Uri was dodging the attacks from the dao-tug while taking little slashes at the dao-tug himself. Eventually she got tired out and took one final swing at Uri. Uri dodged and let her fall to the ground. A few seconds later she was dead from the loss of too much blood.

Lynn was parrying every attack and taking jabs of his own at the dao-tug. The dazed dao-tug began seeing triple from the head rocking blows Lynn was delivering. That was the last thing she saw before Maria came from behind and ran her through piercing her heart. When Lynn turned to inspect his friends he saw Lilander retrieving his arrow from the fallen dao-tug and Gaia getting to her feet. Everyone stared in awe at the interior of the castle.

"Where do we start looking?" Verne asked kind of breathless.

"Let's try the royal chambers. Ganon could have hid in there during the assault, but, if I know him, he would fight to the death," Lynn told them.

Lynn lead everyone to the first door on the right of the entrance only to have Maria shout out, "Over there! What is that behind the throne!?"

Verne ran toward the throne but the figure hiding behind the throne jumped up into the shadows of the rafters and disappeared.

"Well, what do you think it was?" Verne asked as he made his way back to everyone.

"From the way it flowed and merged into the shadows, I would say it could be a vampire thrall," said Lilander almost sounding sarcastic when really it was naivety.

"No," said Gaia and Uri together. Uri finished, "It was definitely a thrall. Only if you could have seen the scared look on its face once we seen it. I think it was scared of us."

Gaia then remarked, "Or just scared of Lynn for failing him."

Maria turned suddenly to Gaia with an angry scowl and her blade drawn, "I can tell that there is still a little bit of doubt. Let me fix it for you."

Gaia quickly came on guard but Uri jumped between the two, with his hands up to hold them back. "Now, let's not do anything that we will regret later," Uri said.

"I won't regret it!" Maria snapped back.

"Maria! That is enough! Lower your blade and let's find King Ganon," Lynn said walking toward the door leading to the royal chambers.

He entered with everyone following close by up the torch lit tower. After climbing the stairs that lead up the tower, they exited onto a stone walkway with stairs leading further up to another door. Verne looked over the edge and thought, "That is an awfully long way down."

When they entered into the royal chamber, they entered into more chaos. Portraits were torn from the walls, Ganon's bed lay turned over in the far corner. His chairs broken to splinters, and his fruit and wine table lay in pieces.

They searched the room thoroughly checking everything for any trace of King Ganon. They were about to give up the search until Verne called Lynn over to the window sill. "Lilander, I need your help on this one?" Lynn called across the room to the elf.

Lilander made his way over and asked, "What have you found?"

Lynn pointed at the sill directing Lilander's attention. Lilander stared for a second at the sill, then stuck his head out the window looking up, down, to the left then the right. "It looks as if someone climbed along the wall to the left leaving a fresh trail of blood that isn't dripping or hasn't dried up yet." Lilander said after bringing his head back inside the window.

Lynn thought for a second and remembered the servants and guest quarters are that way. "Quick everyone follow me before we're too late. Uri, I need you to climb around to the guest quarters and stake out the floor while we come around," Lynn ordered. Uri leapt out the window and began climbing across the wall with ease.

"Nice thinking," Maria said intruding on Lynn's thoughts.

They were about to exit until the door burst in. In came two vampire thralls and one male dao-tug. Everyone unsheathed their weapons but Gaia touched her rubies together before doing so.

When she touched her rubies together, an armor came about her body where her brassiere, shoulder armor, boots and gauntlets were. The belt holding her two scabbards bulged out with the same armor around it. The three intruders suddenly fell back by a powerful gust of wind and out the door and off the edge of the stairs.

Everyone looked at Gaia in surprise and seen her blades glowing white as she still held them up to where the two thralls and dao-tug were just moments before. Before anyone said anything, Gaia did, "We don't have time and I'm kind of angry."

They made their way back down to the throne room to see that it has been turned into what seemed to be a desolate battlefield. Instead of just standing around, they made their way to the next door to their right. They ran up the stairs with a quickness. Before reaching the door, it swung open allowing them access. Everyone followed Lynn's actions with weapons drawn as they stepped through the door. Uri quickly jumped back a good ten feet.

"Wait, wait. It's me," he said frantically.

Verne stepped forward and asked, "How did you know it was us?"

"Well," Uri began but was cut off by Gaia. "He's a were-animal. his nose is ten times better than ours and since he's a bat his ears are better than any other were-animal," she said.

Verne looked at her and said, "Thank you. I forgot," then turned back to Uri and said, "You still keep amazing me."

Lynn approached Uri and asked, "Did you see anything unusual?"

Uri made a little smirk and said, "I never been here so I don't know what's unusual to look for except that there are no thralls or dao-tug's around. Yet, there are still a few servants on the floor."

They started on the hall to their right getting any stray servants out until they made it to the tower room which was the Head Chefs' room. They heard muffled talk behind the door but when they opened to inspect, the room was empty. They continued on down the adjacent hall making certain that all the servants were out on this hall.

As they passed the Head Servants room, the door stood open with someone just standing there in the darkness. When a few heads turned to get a second look into the room the figure was gone. From there, there was another adjacent hall turning left where two more servants hid in their rooms quivering.

"The way should be clear for you to make your escape now," Lynn said informing the servants of the situation.

The two servants ran down the hall passing the mid-wife's room. When the second servant was about to pass the room, she was suddenly dragged into the room. They ran to the room where the servant was just dragged in to see the servant on the floor with the mid-wife sucking vigorously at her neck.

The mid-wife peered up from her feast with those yellow feral eyes. "A thrall. I knew they were here somewhere," Gaia said stepping further into the room.

Lilander notched an arrow and let fly. The mid-wife spun under the arrow and swept Gaia off her feet on to her back. The mid-wife moved to one side of the room away from the fallen servant looking like an animal trapped in the corner.

Verne stepped forward with his blade drawn stalking the thrall. With everyone's attention taken away from her, the servant jumped up and lunged at Verne's neck. Verne turned in surprise but was saved when Uri's blade came down through the servants neck.

Verne remembered the mid-wife and quickly spun with his blade to take her head as she attacked. Verne finally exhaled as they helped Gaia up and left the room. Upon exiting the mid-wife's room, they saw the head servants door slam shut. They immediately ran back down the hall towards the room with Verne screaming, "When will they get it through their heads, it's dangerous up here!"

They burst into the room with weapons drawn but the room was empty. Lynn sheathed his katana and everyone else followed suit. They turned to leave but the door was slammed shut by the head servant who was on the wall above the door. His eyes had a linger of crimson but still retained the yellow feral tint.

He smiled and said, "Of course it's dangerous, but for whom?"

At that moment, three thralls, two females and one male, came climbing in through the window. The thralls attacked them with their teeth bared to inject their venomous bite or kill, it didn't matter to them just eliminate the prey and feed their hunger. Like all other thralls, these lost their sense of comprehension and rushed to their true deaths.

They left the room a tad bit exhausted from fighting in the small room. Lynn lead them back to the stairs to go down. Their progress was halted when a wind out of nowhere shut the door. They all turned and their eyes fell on the head chef who now sported crimson eyes. The chef went into his room without a word spoken.

"We know what must be done," Lynn said leading the way to the room. When they stood in the doorway the chef stood by the window with six thralls each crawling out the window and up to the roof. The chef smiled a sinister grin before saying, "You will pay for abandoning us."

The chef then quickly crawled out and followed his thralls. Lynn didn't have to inform people on what to do because they were already in action. Lilander was climbing along the wall with Gaia leaping from nook to nook with a nimbleness that wasn't known that she had. Uri transformed and took Verne's shoulders in his talons and flew up carefully so to not dig into Verne's flesh.

Lynn put his hands together to concentrate on bringing his ancient power to the forefront of his psyche, grabbed Maria and levitated out the window and up the wall to the roof. They all arrived one after the other. Lynn released Maria from his arms just as Uri was reverting back to his human form.

"Welcome to my castle. As you can see, King Ganon is no more!" shouted the head chef.

"Baron, what has happened to all of you and what did you mean by I was going to pay for abandoning you?" Lynn asked.

"You abandoned the kingdom for your own selfish gain. You were not here when the **vampire** came. Now I have eternal life. Or undead life, however you want to look at it."

The thralls attacked them and quickly fell upon the blade. All that stood on the roof now was Lynn, Maria, Gaia, Uri, Lilander and Verne with Baron smiling like he had no care in the world. "Now try my power, no, not some ordinary thrall but a vampire Lord!" was all Baron's evil sounding voice said before attacking.

Baron's speed was unlike the thralls and he used his manipulation over the shadows to move closer for his attacks. Every time one of their attacks fell on target, which was barely, Baron's undead body would heal it. Before long, Lynn began thinking that it just might be impossible to beat a true vampire Lord. Out of nowhere, a familiar thrall leapt on to Baron's back and began plunging his teeth into Baron's neck.

After a brief struggle, Baron grabbed a hold of the thralls neck and said, "King Ganon, I should have did this before instead of letting you survive."

Baron carried Ganon by his neck toward the edge of the roof. Lynn impaled Baron through the back, immobilizing him and making him drop Ganon on the roof. Gaia attacked, leaping over Lynn just as he relieved Baron's back of his katana, to take Baron's head with her two blades.

"King Ganon, are you alright? You're a vampire," Lynn said reluctantly looking at his age old, now a bit younger, friend as he slowly rose to his feet.

"What happened my king," asked Lynn.

"It was quiet," he began, "almost too quiet. They came in the stillness of the night with malice and the intent to kill and devour. It started on the outskirts of the city and moved in like water being poured into a bowl. Death followed in their wake and even more undead followed. It seemed like nothing would stop their tide."

"They eventually made it to the castle walls and that was not enough to hold back their might. The broke down the doors with their strength and scaled the walls with their agility. They were among us like a swarm of locust consuming any living thing that crossed their paths leaving only a few alive because they knew more would come. They saw my messenger flee and never cared to apprehend him."

"They didn't act alone though. they were lead by one who calls herself Ursula," the undead King Ganon finished.

Everyone heard the name spoken and immediately started conversing amongst themselves. Then King Ganon intruded on Lynn's conversation with the others, "Remember the day you swore oath to me?"

Lynn turned to him, "Yes. I will never forget."

Ganon looked into Lynn's eyes and said, "Well, as your King, I request that you relinquish my body of this parasite."

"But there's only one way to-" Lynn stopped when he realized what Ganon was asking. Lynn knew he would do anything for King Ganon, but could he do this. "Is this an order my lord?" asked Lynn.

Ganon shook his head, "No. Just a friend asking another friend to have mercy. Listen, find my son and retrieve him from the darkness that has taken over the city so that he may live out my legacy."

Ganon took Lynn's katana and placed it in Lynn's hands then nodded. Ganon closed his eyes so that the vampire in him couldn't try to preserve itself by attacking Lynn. "I will carry out your last wish," Lynn said as he separated Ganon's head from his body, "my king."

They re-entered the castle by making their way down to the royal chambers. "Let's try the dungeons. Vampires love cold, dark places," Gaia recommended.

Everyone nodded to the notion and made their way back down to the throne room. Upon arriving at the bottom of the tower to the throne room, a cry pierced through the air and sounded terrified and vibrated to the bone. They started for the tower leading to the dungeon when Lilander and Uri stopped.

"Can you feel it?" Lilander asked, "It's as if the room has grown extremely cold."

Lynn let his mind go blank and felt through the darkness. The hairs on the back of his neck began to prickle but he was too late to warn anyone. Numerous thralls came out of the shadows with a few dao-tug emerging from the dungeon door. The fiends overwhelmed Lynn and the others like a wave hitting the beach and sucking what ever it caught back out to sea.

The thralls and dao-tug seized Uri, Lilander and Maria and drug them kicking and screaming to the dungeon. Once Lynn, Verne and Gaia got their bearings back Verne shouted out, "Why couldn't they take her? That way I don't have to worry about her attacking us from behind."

Gaia sneered at Verne but Lynn interceded, "Not now. We have friends that need our help."

Gaia angrily went through the door leading down to the dungeon. Lynn shot a glance over at Verne as if saying, what were you thinking. All Verne could do was shrug and follow Lynn and Gaia as they went down the stairs. When they reached the bottom, the three cells looked to be occupied by their friends but there were too many thralls blocking the cells.

Once the door shut behind Verne, twelve thralls rushed at them with growls resounding off the walls and teeth gnashing. Verne swung his blade at the thralls attacking him but failed to connect. These thralls were a bit different and seemed to battle as one mind. After a moment of blind fighting Verne relaxed and flowed like the wind through the valley he once ruled.

One thrall approached from behind but Verne ducked and arose quickly swinging his blade out to his right to take the head of another incoming thrall. Three more thralls attempted to charged him this time. Verne did a splits while swinging his blade around his head in a clockwise motion slicing through their legs. As they fell to their knees he swung his blade a little higher in a counter-clockwise motion to lope off their heads.

Gaia wielded both her blades, which were angled back at a ninety degree angle on the tips, and waited for the four thralls to come within striking range. One thrall attacked out of rage and Gaia brought her left blade down on the head but had it turned so that the angled tip impaled the thrall. Gaia brought her other blade tip up into the thralls mid-section.

The other thralls, thinking Gaia was off balance, soon found out otherwise. Gaia swung the impaled thrall around in a circle, hitting the other three thralls. She then tossed the thrall into the air with ease and before the thrall hit the ground, its head was no longer attached to its body. Gaia took up her battles stance and gestured for the remaining thralls to attack.

They did, all swinging and clawing at Gaia. She was able to dodge a few of them but then the barrage of punches began to connect. Gaia went to one knee and before being beaten any further she swept all their legs from under them.

The thralls simultaneously leaped up off their backs to land partly crouched. Gaia was already up with her blades slashing taking all three thralls heads as soon as they were up.

Lynn stood on guard with his katana held in one hand behind his head readying to attack while Gaia and Verne battled on beside him. Four of the twelve thralls slowly inched forward hesitantly feeling Lynn's hidden power flow within him.

All four thralls dropped the facade of confusion and attacked as one unit. Lynn ducked and dodged between the four while with inhuman speed, slashing at all four thralls. When the thralls realized Lynn was behind them, they spun around but not fast enough since their undead bodies were to busy trying to heal from the damage Lynn had inflicted.

By the time the thralls turned fully about, Lynn had decapitated three and was just taking the fourth thrall's head. No sooner did they finish with the thralls, three female dao-tug warriors stepped forward. The three dao-tug averaged their height at six-foot-one with that skin tight armor gleaming eerily in the dark.

They carried different swords than the others. One armed herself with a kriss style blade, another had a curve blade, and the last juggled a scimitar between her hands. The dao-tug attacked with a vivaciousness that Lynn seen only the dao-tug could use. The dao-tug with the kriss style blade attacked Lynn that evidently surprised him remembering their warrior blood.

Her blows were powerful enough to throw Lynn off balance but never lose his katana. She delivered a slash at Lynn's torso but he parried and forced her blade out of her hand. Still she came with hands trying to pound on Lynn. As she rushed forward, she felt Lynn's katana enter through her stomach and out her back. They both fell to the ground with the dao-tug straddled on top of Lynn.

She froze for a second to look down at the sword sticking through her stomach. She began pounding on Lynn's chest but this time without much force. Lynn twisted his katana and brought it up further just below her sternum and breast. The pounding stopped and she died still on top of Lynn. Lynn saw something on her that he never thought he would see on a dao-tug before.

. . . A tear.

Lynn wiped the tear from her dead cheek and wondered why would such a warrior shed a tear just before dying. When Lynn got to his feet Verne and Gaia were just finishing up also. They went to the cells but found only servants huddled together along the back wall. "Where did they take our friends that were just brought down here?" asked Gaia harshly.

All the servants seemed frightened except one young female of about the age just before womanhood. She pointed at the small window just big enough to fit a body through and said, "The same place they took the prince, to the dining hall for supper."

Lynn, Gaia and Verne flashed each other looks and ran for the dungeon door to go back up to the throne room. Lynn paused just before going up the stairs, turned to the servants and said, "Get out of town for now. Head north through the valley until you reach a large encampment and tell them Lynn Thrax and Verne Wingo sent you there for a temporary place to stay until we rid the city and castle of these fiends."

The young female nodded her head and directed everybody up the stairs. Lynn took up the rear and followed up the stairs. They made it back to the Throne room and watched as the servants left the castle. Lynn then lead Gaia and Verne to the door leading up to the Dining Hall. They entered the Dining Hall to see Lilander, Maria and Uri unconscious on the three middle tables and the prince in the same state on the head table.

There were a dozen thralls and a dozen dao-tug sitting at the three tables with their menacing glare locked on the three new intruders. Lynn looked at the head table to see Lady Ursula and a noble dao-tug beside her. Ursula brought her attention to the three new additions and said, "I see you've made it to our little feast."

"Why are you doing this Lady Ursula?" Verne asked her.

She shot Verne an evil glance from her crimson eyes that made Lynn's blood run cold.

She said, "You know something about Dante and you're not telling me. If you continue to hide him I will destroy everything in my path!"

The dao-tug noble snapped his fingers and just that quickly the thralls and dao-tug were drawing down on Lynn, Gaia and Verne. They kept inching their way stalking like a tiger in the brush. Gaia and Verne sensed Lynn's intentions. Just then as Verne nodded to Lynn, Gaia pressed each of her rubies together to bring about her white and gold armor in place on her body.

Lynn placed his hands together and let his ancient power spread over him. With their abilities enhanced and powers activated, they made short work of the thralls and dao-tug. When the fighting ceased, Lynn could tell the noble dao-tug was no warrior because he started fidgeting as their plan fell through.

"Dante will be mine!" yelled Lady Ursula.

She grabbed the nervous dao-tug and snapped his neck with one hand then created a mist around herself. When the mist cleared, she was gone. Lynn, Gaia and Verne were alone except for the unconscious prince, three unconscious friends and a load of dead bodies. Lilander, Maria and Uri began coming to so Lynn directed Verne and Gaia to cut them loose of their bindings while Lynn went to rouse the young prince.

"It's really not fair," said Verne, "you all get to sleep while we play hero."

Maria, Uri and Lilander all looked around confused like they didn't know what happened. Lynn roused the young prince, of about sixteen years of age, out of his sleep. The prince instantly knew who Lynn was and began weeping.

The prince asked, "Where is my father? Is he . . ."

Lynn looked down and the prince already knew his answer. "They changed him and before the beast could take over, he asked me to let him die human. You must take over his kingdom as your own," Lynn told the prince.

Lilander asked, "Well, prince, uh?"

"Aurelius," answered Prince Aurelius.

Lilander finished, "Well Prince Aurelius, do you think you can handle it?"

"I will gladly take the throne as the new king of Maru and bring my kingdom back to its former glory," said the new king.

King Aurelius.

"Dante! Who the hell is Lady Ursula and why is she interfering with my plans?" yelled Niccolo telepathically through the aerie.

Dante entered his fathers chamber and said, "Father . . . Master she was one of my toys at a time that I forgot to dispose of properly."

Niccolo closed the distance between him and his son in a blink of an eye, "Don't you know she is delaying my quarry because of my cowardice sons stupidity?"

Dante gritted his teeth and was about to speak until Niccolo cut in, "You don't like being called a coward? Then get out there and get my prey here!"

Dante nodded and was on his way out the door then stopped and turned on Niccolo. He stared at his fathers back and advanced on him with one of his knives drawn. He was so close but as soon as he blinked, Niccolo was behind him.

He spun Dante around and caught his throat with one hand and his knife hand with his other one. "Son, you will have your chance to rule, but not being as weak as you are. Now go and do what I commanded you to. Bring Lynn Thrax to me now!" Niccolo said showing his beastly features.

He released Dante and moved to the side to allow Dante to leave. Dante moved past his father this time without the thought of coming on his father again. Once outside the chamber Dante showed his frustration by punching a hole through the adjacent wall.

Dante growled with fury, "One day all of this and more will be mine and everyone will bow to my might." He then formed his mist and vanished into the night.

The castle began to look how Lynn remembered it, beautiful and full life. Lynn walked around the castle dodging servants and cooks as they carried out orders for the preparation of the castle for Aurelius' coronation. Maria, Verne, Lilander, Uri and Gaia were running around between the city and the castle on a self given tour.

Lynn decided to go to the royal chambers and check on Aurelius and make sure he wasn't having any butterflies in his stomach. When Lynn arrived to the royal chamber, Aurelius was still being tailored and didn't notice Lynn's entrance.

"Do you think that the kingdom will accept me as their new king?" Aurelius asked.

The tailor kept quiet not giving his opinion and continued at his trade.

"Well, go ahead you're free to speak," Aurelius told the tailor.

The tailor began to voice his opinion hesitantly, "I-I think you will make a just and great king. If not like but maybe even greater than King Ganon."

Lynn then interrupted the conversation letting his presence be known, "Of course you will, and like the gentleman said, maybe even greater than your father."

Lynn could tell by the look on their faces that he surprised them but Aurelius quickly changed his facade to a smile.

"Godfather, I didn't hear you come in."

The tailor looked at Aurelius, at Lynn, then back to his work with a kind of confused look that Aurelius would hold Lynn so high on a pedestal.

"Come and have an appetizer before the feast and see how my garb is coming along," said Aurelius invitingly pointing towards the table of fruit and wine.

Lynn did so not wanting to disrespect him especially in front of his tailor and said, "Of course you'll make a fine king. The people and servants watched as you grew into a man and love you for still being that humble child you were a few years ago."

Aurelius had a skeptical look on his face so Lynn added, "These servants raised you since you were born and now that your mother and father are no longer here, you're the only link they have."

Aurelius nodded his head and accepted the answer. Lynn took a bite of an apple and resumed, "You also need to find you a suitable wife so that you may still carry on your line."

"I'm glad you're here godfather. Where would I be without your advice? Please stay and be my second," Aurelius said surprising the tailor.

Lynn expected that Aurelius might have wanted someone that he could go to without much criticism and Lynn knew he was the obvious choice.

This time Lynn had to turn down Aurelius request, "Sorry, but I really can't. Me and my newfound friends are on a journey that might as well decide the fate of everyone living and dead."

The tailor looked more scared than surprised now by Lynn's remark. He gathered his took and made to leave now that he was finished.

"Wait," commanded Aurelius, "I would like an opinion on your work from my godfather."

Aurelius looked at Lynn and he could only say, "You look marvelous. Anyone who doesn't know who the new king is, will now."

Aurelius smiled and nodded to the tailor. Just as the tailor was leaving, Aurelius said, "Oh, and Sir William Baggert?"

The tailor stopped and turned to face Aurelius with his head down, "Yes my lord."

"No need to hold your head low when speaking with me" said Aurelius.

Baggert lifted his head showing his red embarrassed face as Aurelius finished, "But if any of this conversation with me and my godfather leaks, I will have your head."

Lynn thought, "He looked more and more like his father when he said that."

Baggert let out a breath he never knew he was holding and rubbed his neck as he was escorted out of the castle.

"Well, shall we go and introduce Fawn and Maru to their new king?" Lynn asked holding the door open for Aurelius.

Aurelius took one last look in the mirror and could see the mixture of emotions playing on his face. He eyed himself up and down and thought, "Too soon. My father is supposed to still be here and still be my king."

Aurelius looked from Lynn then to himself in the mirror one more time then he walked over by his godfather. Lynn held the door open for the soon to be king. Aurelius took a deep breath and went downstairs to be crowned.

Lynn and his friends watched along with thousands of others as Prince Aurelius was formally crowned King Aurelius and afterwards ate a mighty feast in his celebration. Lynn approached King Aurelius during the meal and whispered in his ear, "I'm sorry but me and my companions must be off, my king."

King Aurelius raised his arms to quiet the crowd and then spoke, "My godfather has just informed me that he must take his leave now."

The crowd began to talk a little but was quickly quieted again. King Aurelius finished, "I'm announcing this cause if not for him and his loyal friends, we all would have perished. Thank you for now and for helping us many times in the past."

He bowed his head to Lynn so Lynn bowed at the waist in response. The guest roared in applause. Then Aurelius turned to Lynn's friends and bowed his head and they bowed to him also.

Aurelius escorted the six heroes to the city gates himself and bid them farewell. "Godfather, are you certain you can't stay?"

"Sorry, but this is something that must be done. Though keep me in your thoughts that I may return and maybe be what you need."

"So be it. I wish you a safe journey and return. We will await word of your success."

The two hugged and parted ways. Aurelius watched from his chariot as Lynn and his friends made their way toward the Forest of New Life. Aurelius' guards lead the way for him back through the city of celebration to his castle for some well needed rest for tomorrow will be a busy day. His official first day as King Aurelius.

Chapter: 10

They emerged out of the Forest of New Life to come upon the Valley of Verne. Uri and Gaia were looking all over the valley expecting trouble and if necessary, stop it. Suddenly bodies appeared from behind boulders and on top of the high rock walls.

Uri and Gaia took up their weapons and defensive postures but Verne held up a hand to halt them.

"What are you doing, Verne? They have us ambushed and you just stand there holding your hand up," Gaia demanded through clenched teeth.

He responded, "We're not being ambushed. These are my people."

One of the young men who came from behind the boulders approached Verne. Lynn saw the three gold armbands the young man brandished in the heavy sunlight. The young man spoke, "We have been sent here to escort you to the encampment sir."

Verne informed his fellow travelers why the men showed up. They took the escort in good spirits and made it to the camp the next day. Sir Peter Macdowl met them as they came out of the valley.

"Welcome back. We've been waiting and watching for your return everyday and—"

"Sorry, but we still have a long way to go before I can return to you," Verne said cutting off Macdowl.

Macdowl nodded, "Come tell us everything that's happened since you left and rest a few days before you must be off."

Everyone followed Macdowl into the camp and prepared for the night to come.

"So all this happened, you came back around full circle, yet no one lost a limb. Amazing for any feat but I expected no less from your group," said Macdowl over the bounty of cooked deer and rabbit stew.

Verne nodded and said upon finishing his meal, "If you'll excuse us, we need to rest for a long day ahead."

Macdowl smiled and shook his head, "This is still your settlement. Your free to do as you please. Tomorrow, I will be more than happy to pass the reigns back to the rightful owner though."

Verne acknowledge this and took his new friends to one of the guest tents and decided to stay with them. All of them and the camp, except for the sentries, fell into a nice cozy sleep. Lynn slept well through the night without any interruptions from either allies or enemy attacks.

In the morning Lynn woke to Verne's nudges. "It's dusk. Wake everyone and let's move quickly. Don't ask questions just move and stay quiet," Verne said in a whisper his lips almost touching Lynn's ear.

Verne left the tent like a cat lurking through tall grass. Lynn got everybody up and relayed Verne's message or warning he knew not which it was. Verne stuck his head through the flaps of the tent a few minutes later and motioned for everyone to follow him. When they stepped outside the tent, Verne put his finger to his mouth for silence and led the way.

Verne led them to the back of the tent where the horses were being kept and away from the camp. Two bodies lay stretched out in the open but were unconscious. Maria made to ask Verne but he held his finger to his lips to keep the silence. When Verne had them a good distance away from the camp, Maria ran ahead and snapped at Verne, "Why did we leave like that?"

He stared at her for a moment with some intensity and turned to keep walking but she grabbed his arm. "I asked you a question," she demanded.

He took a deep breath and began, "Yes, my people need me but my place is with all of you. Macdowl was ready to give the leadership back to me. I can't have that now as long as these creatures are roaming the world. So please, let's get back to Nospherat and help Lilander bring his brother back."

She started to look as if she understood and allowed them to keep moving toward The Great Woods.

Macdowl awoke thinking, "I finally get to give these people back to Verne and be on my way."

He smiled to himself as he knew what would happen when Verne took over once again. Verne would be stuck here and he would be free to leave and pursue his own power. He would have the chance to become somebody revered by everyone.

"Sir Macdowl," one of his men yelled into the tent, "we have a situation."

Macdowl dressed quickly and followed the man to the clearing just behind the tent that kept the horses to see two of the sentries just being roused.

"What happened here?" demanded Macdowl angrily.

The man who came and retrieved him answered, "We are stuck in the same dense fog as you are sir. No horses have been taken and everything else of value seems to be in place."

Macdowl contemplated for a second then snapped, "Not everything of value. Check on our guest."

The man turned to leave but Macdowl halted him, "No! I'll accompany you."

They made their way through the camp to the guest tent and entered to see the tent vacant. Anger boiled up inside of Macdowl as he caught hold of reality.

"What do we do sir?" asked his escort.

Macdowl thought quickly never once showing his anger. He could not believe that his opportunity slipped between his fingers. He quickly grabbed the dagger from his side and plunged it into the neck of the man beside him venting off most of his anger, but, not all of it. He wiped his blade clean on the dead man's clothing and went to retrieve another guard.

"Prepare some horses and a small handful of men, we're going on a hunt," was all Macdowl said as to not bring any suspicions to himself.

He called to one of the higher ranking officers, "Dalimir, I'm off on a hunt. I have reason to believe that Verne was kidnapped by his so called friends. Even after we welcomed them in they have stolen our leader away and I aim to bring him home to us."

Macdowl let the lie flow from his mouth like the poisonous saliva of a komodo. He knew the officer would abide. He had no choice. Macdowl was still his leader and he would obey his commands. The officer snapped to and went about getting ready for his chance to prove himself.

Macdowl thought, "Now we'll see how fast you can run."

Lynn and company came upon The Great Woods with its giant trees and birds singing all around. Lynn peeked a gander over at Lilander and could see him hiding his excitement but was giving it away with the corners of his lips upturned into a barely noticeable smile.

"I feel like I'm at home on my training grounds in these woods with so many shadows to dodge behind. Where are we on our way to now?" asked Uri.

Lilander answered, "We're going to my home, Nospherat, the elf city in the woods."

Uri nodded and resumed following everybody. They came upon that weird tree and stopped to look down into the now empty ravine.

Uri peered into the empty ravine and asked, "Where's the city you were telling me about Maria?"

Maria looked at him and put her finger up to her mouth to silence him. He obliged and watched as Lilander stepped forward and placed his arms out in front of him then spreading them outwards. Everyone watched as the city revealed itself like an invisible veil was being pulled away from it.

When the city was fully shown, the wind that rushed into the ravine gave them natures signal to step forward. Everyone stepped forward to surround Lilander as he grabbed the hanging tree branch and teleported them to the city gates.

"Who goes—" the guard paused, "alert King Ravenholme. One of the Chosen Ones and Prince Lilander has returned."

Elves from all over the city gathered around to see what all the commotion was about. The guards escorted them to the palace helping to keep the building crowd out of the travelers' way. As they were making their way through the streets Uri was surprised by the excited faces of children and adults alike. Some even went as far as to reach out to touch the passerby's to cement that they were actually real and here.

King Ravenholme was standing in the entrance of the palace. He rushed Lilander and hugged him tightly then released his embrace and asked, "Was it a success?"

Lynn held up the staff and smiled. Ravenholme smiled in acknowledgement. "I wasn't sure if you would have a safe return after—" Ravenholme began to say but cut off abruptly.

"After what . . . after what father?" Lilander demanded.

Ravenholme began, "Your brother broke loose and said he must find your company and stop him," he paused, "he killed three guards in his escape."

Lilander asked, "Who is he trying to stop?"

"He didn't say who, just him." Lilander's face went blank as all hope fled from his face.

"So, he's gone and we can't save him," said Lilander looking like the world just let him down.

Ravenholme softly grabbed his sons shoulders to comfort him and said, "You must find him and bring him back."

"But where do we began to look for him? Lilandro could be anywhere by now," Verne said to Ravenholme.

Ravenholme looked toward him and said, "He said something about going the route of your ultimate destination where yours and his own life will end."

Lilander approached Lynn and said, "We must be off now if we want to stand a chance of catching my brother."

Lynn looked around at his friends to see them nodding their heads in agreement.

Before Lynn could say anything, Ravenholme said, "No. First feast and rest up, then be off in the morning at first light."

"No father, we leave now."

Lynn held up his hands to caution Lilander and said, "Your father is right, let's feast and rest then we'll be off before the morning dew can dissipate."

Lilander looked as if he was going to say something but thought better of it when Lynn crossed his arms aver his chest and Lilander caught sight of the markings on his hands.

Lilander gritted his teeth and clinched his fist then relaxed a bit, "Yes, Chosen One, I'll say no more about it."

Lilander was hurt and angry as he walked off to his room to prepare for the dinner. Lynn knew how his elfish friend was feeling but it had to be done this way.

After the feast, and after the guest went home, Lynn stood outside the palace just admiring the clear night sky. Verne and Maria walked up on both sides of Lynn and stood quiet for a few seconds. Neither of them said a word to Lynn. They just waited looking out at the sky along side Lynn. Lynn smiled at the two friendly faces who began this journey with him.

He asked, "How is Lilander? Is he still upset with me for not going after Lilandro?"

Verne sighed and Lynn smelled the wine on his breath before saying, "From the way he was eyeing you and since he said nothing to anyone the whole feast, yeah, I think he's still upset."

"Verne, you're not helping, go inside and get some sleep," Maria said with a scold in her voice.

She pulled at his arm to ease him on. Before leaving, Verne smiled and winked at Lynn. To Lynn's surprise, when Verne was gone, Maria came behind him and put her arms around his waistline and asked, "Do you really think we will find Lilandro?"

"I know we'll find him or he'll find us for sure. The question is how will it end."

"What about defeating Niccolo?"

"I strongly believe we'll hold together and see him to his end."

Lynn turned in her arms and placed his around her. He stared into her eyes and saw the moon and stars reflect in hers as she stared back. Lynn broke contact first but Maria pleaded, "Lynn, why won't you let me in?"

Lynn wasn't too surprised by her question. He could somehow sense her want for him but also a wall there that couldn't be scaled. Lynn answered her question after taking a second to think, "I've lost too many people close to me to lose anyone else. Whether its from leaving them or them being taken."

She looked at Lynn as if she was going to cry. Her lip trembled before she turned and quickly went into the palace. Lynn sat there for a moment longer trying to catch a glimpse of the stars as he blinked his brief tears away. Lynn felt a new menacing presence around him that he hasn't felt in Nospherat before. Something was missing but Lynn couldn't put his finger on it since his mind was on what Maria had just asked him. He turned quickly to find nothing there or anything moving in the shadows.

"I must really be exhausted. I'll get me some rest after I go talk to Lilander," Lynn said to himself as he went into the palace.

"What the hell is going on!?" screamed Niccolo, "Why are they worried about an **elf**!?"

One of Niccolo's top followers, Christian Cova, the last and only survivor out of the three men sent to deliver Lynn a message at his home those many years ago, stepped through the chamber doors and stopped a few paces behind his back.

"Well!?" demanded Niccolo rounding on Christian giving the big man a glance that made him look away. Christian said not daring to look back at his master, "The elf is Lilandro, twin prince of Nospherat. He was changed into a dao-tug by your follower. Stratton is his name."

Niccolo stared at Christian for a moment and let the name roll off his tongue like sap, "Stratton, Stratton?"

Christian interrupted, "Yes Master, James Stratton."

Niccolo became very angry just then for being interrupted and changed to his vampiric beastly form. He seized Christian by the neck with one hand and lifted him easily off the floor even though Christian was at least more than a couple inches taller than Niccolo. "I know who Stratton is. The question is where is he and why he hasn't reported?" Niccolo said with a slight growl in his throat.

Christian tried to answer while gasping for breath, "Ly-Lynn battled him in the—in the dao-tug city and—and we haven't—heard—anything about him yet—Master. We think he's dead."

Niccolo released Christian letting him fall to the floor and gave him some room to breathe. Niccolo walked to a basin on his table which held about half an inch of his own blood inside and asked, "Christian, are you ready to partake on the journey to be one of my children?"

Christian stood to his full height with his chin held high, "As you will me Master."

"No!" Niccolo screamed, "are you ready to partake?"

"Yes, yes Master, I-."

Before he could finish, Niccolo was already behind him biting down on his neck, killing him slowly. Niccolo stuck two fingers in the basin of blood and smeared it on Christian's lips. The blood immediately disappeared on his lips and he began writhing on the floor as he made the change to be a true vampire.

Niccolo knelt beside Christian, "Christian. Christian, I know you can hear me."

Christian looked at Niccolo through the pain surging through every inch of his body. "That's more like it. Now, when the change is complete, your energy will be greatly drained. One of my maidservants are here to watch you. You know what to do, then bring me Lynn," Niccolo patted Christian on the head before leaving the chamber to take a walk around his aerie.

The maidservant didn't know it but Niccolo just sealed her fate and sentenced her to death by leaving her to a newly born true vampire.

Lynn knocked on the door leading into Lilander's bedroom. Lynn heard the invite and let himself in but didn't see Lilander anywhere. Not wanting to be surprised like he was the last time when the others were with him he decided he would call out to the elf prince.

"Lilander, where are you?" Lynn said with some inflection.

Lynn waited for an answer and knew Lilander was still angry with him from his pause in answering. "On the balcony," Lilander finally answered.

Lynn went out on the balcony and joined Lilander there. Lynn felt awkward just standing there while Lilander watched the night sky.

Lynn broke the ice first, "Lilander, you know I had to agree with your father on us staying. Right now, *you're* his only hope."

Lilander stared at Lynn with a blunt look only an elf can give. Lilander let out a sigh, "I know. I was just being stubborn and was so excited about having my brother back to normal. When we were informed of his escape, it was as if nothing or nobody else seemed to matter. It was a fatal blow to me. It seemed like everything we went through to get the staff was for naught."

"Don't worry, at first light we'll be on our way and we're going to find your brother even if I have to put Niccolo on hold."

Lilander smiled and looked back at the sky. "Funny how the stars and moon are just like me and my brother right now," Lilander said.

"What do you mean by that?" Lynn asked wanting him to press on.

"You know they both occupy the same celestial plane, but, tonight is different. Tonight, the stars shine bright as ever but there is no moon in sight."

"What do you mean, 'no moon in sight?' I saw-" Lynn stopped when he saw Lilander look at him in all his confusion.

Lynn looked up but could see no moon in the distant sky anywhere.

"Lynn, are you alright?" Lilander asked.

"No, I'm tired that's all. I'm going to go get some sleep."

Lilander nodded and Lynn made his exit. When Lynn made it outside the room, he thought, "Either my mind is playing tricks on me or the moon is really not there."

But Lynn knew he saw the moon reflect in Maria's eyes. He couldn't quite figure out how he saw it but he knows he did. It was as if the moon was there then it suddenly decided to call it a night and leave the sky to fend for itself against the dark.

"Lynn. Lynn, get up so that we may be on our way," Uri said in Lynn's ear.

"Where is everybody else?" Lynn asked while rubbing the sleep out of his eyes.

"They're all getting ready. Lilander sent me to wake you out of your sleep."

Lynn got up and followed Uri out to the main hall to see everyone waiting. Lynn checked to make sure they had enough food to make it to Kamma. They turned to leave but was halted when King Ravenholme called for their attention.

"Once again, safe journey. And Lynn, Chosen One, please bring my sons back safely. If something were to happen to them, I don't know what I'd do," he said.

Lynn looked at Lilander then at the rest of his fellow adventurers and said, "I think we're all in good hands as long as we take care of each other. Yes, we will see this through and come back alive and more than what we were before."

King Ravenholme smiled and bowed his head as they left the palace.

Chapter: 11

Lilander closed the invisible veil over the ravine, and they were on their way through The Great Woods with a few complaints from different members of their party. Every now and then, Lynn would look over at Lilander and see his intensity to press on for his brothers sake.

Lilander would sometimes forget that humans don't have as much wind or tracking ability as an elf, yet, they all aren't human, but they still needed a little rest for their feet. They finally made it to the meadow a little after dark which meant they were half way to Kamma. Their spirits picked up briefly until they saw a body, with what looked to be an expensive but tattered emerald color cloak with ivory trimmings, lying face down in the ankle length grass.

They took off in a sprint towards the body. Maria spoke while running, "I wonder what could've happened to that person for 'em to just lay there like that."

As they made it a few paces closer, the wind that was blowing at their back died down, Uri abruptly stopped quickly followed by Gaia. "Do you smell that?" Uri said, "It's a—It's a-"

"Well what is it?" demanded Gaia.

"Stop, it's a-" Uri tried to scream but it was already too late.

Lilander stopped a few paces back also but Verne was already checking the body. "He's dead," Verne said looking back over his shoulder at everyone.

Suddenly the once dead body came to life and seized Verne with amazing strength and threw him at Lynn, Maria and Lilander about twenty feet away. The figure went straight for Maria but stopped short when Lynn and Gaia blocked his path with weapons drawn.

"Wait," screamed Maria, "that's my son . . ."

"Dante."

Everyone looked at Dante for a moment. He stood there heaving and glaring back at them. Dante's face shown his grotesque beastly features. His pupils formed to cat-like slits, were dancing around looking at everyone and catching any sudden movements.

Gaia was first to speak, "Your son is no more. All that there is left is that beast."

"No, he was born a vampire," explained Maria.

Gaia looked at Maria skeptically.

"What?"

It was more of disbelief than a question. Dante's features relaxed so that his human features could surface and his cat-like pupils turned back to those crimson orbs of a true vampire. He made his unusual polished fangs recede before speaking.

"M-M-Mother, is that you?" Dante asked while slowly walking toward them with his hands outstretched to them as if wanting an embrace. They couldn't tell but Dante had a slight smirk flirting on his face.

"Once I get a little closer to Lynn, I will strike," he thought to himself.

Just then a familiar shiny black gelding with a gray mane and tail rode up with a familiar but unexpected dao-tug straddled atop its back. Lynn remembered the gelding and even though he hasn't physically set eyes on Lilandro the resemblance is unmistakable. Dante was immediately back on his guard fronting his beastly looks.

"Lilandro, its you," said Lilander in shock to his twin brother.

"Dante, now is your only chance to run. If you don't and would like to try me, your time will come much earlier than you predicted," Lilandro spoke with a hissing sound to his words almost like he was a snake whispering.

To everyone's astonishment, Dante looked frightened behind his cat-like pupils. "Soon, all of you will be mine to harvest like the cattle you were meant to be," Dante said before forming his mist and disappearing.

"As for you six . . . your time is nearing also. We shall see which of you will prove yourself to me and see if I'll allow you to go on with your miserable existence," said Lilandro before turning his bareback gelding and riding off.

"No! Lilandro you can't leave! Let us help you," begged Lilander.

Of everyone that stood there, Maria was the only one who was uneasy about the situation. "What was Dante doing here," she thought, "Either Niccolo sent him or he's striking out on his own."

"Let's go. We'll run across him again. One things for sure, he can find us at anytime," Lynn told Lilander as they began to walk the rest of the large meadow.

Macdowl rode through the Great Woods with a company of ten well trained men and women. There were two trackers which were the only two women amongst the men. Two more out of the group were the scouts who rode with the two women since they were the lightest and fastest. The last six were deadly warriors known as the Warrior Blood that were never beaten in battle. These warriors were only called upon from their training in times of war or in times of great need. Times like when they believe their leader was kidnapped and they were sent to retrieve him . . .

Alive.

The Warrior Blood were trained since the age that they could start walking and were so adept and precise at their art that not even if it were ten to one could you hope to beat them.

"How they our Warrior Blood, I still can't understand but it won't happen again as long as I'm apart of the onslaught," thought Macdowl.

Macdowl is going by the information that he received from his prey's story. The one thing they didn't tell him was that the city, Nospherat, was inaccessible to anyone but the elves and their guest. Macdowl and the six warriors disliked the conditions by which they were currently traveling. The trees seemed to close in around them as if attempting to plunder them for their lives.

The branches caught on to any article of loose clothing or jewelry that their long skeleton like fingers could grasp. At times those finger like branches were dangerous enough to catch bare skin and draw blood as Macdowl or his men tried to jerk away. Unlike the warriors, the trackers and scouts enjoyed the circumstance they were in.

The former believed it made the hunt more exhilarating, while the latter enjoyed the so many shadows, trees and underbrush to hide in and watch. One of them was lucky enough to move silently enough to sneak up on a doe and watch as a panther took her for its prey.

One of the scouts brought back knowledge of the ravine and its whereabouts but saw no thriving city. Macdowl showed his anger at the notion. The scout lead them to the ravine and they saw the truth in the scouts story and the lies in Verne's. The two trackers agreed that people have been here more than once but the scent they're searching ends here but picks up on the other side.

"Sir Macdowl," one of the Warrior Blood spoke, "the scouts and trackers says that there is no safe way down into the ravine."

"So they could still be in the woods if they went around," Macdowl said but didn't mean it as a question.

He watched as the trackers squatted and talked amongst themselves. The sun shown bright here since the trees no longer could hold the gloom or blot out the suns rays. The trackers suddenly jerked their heads up, which caught Macdowl's attention and began looking around in confusion. One of the scouts came back with a look on his face and a pale color to his skin like he had seen a ghost or that he could be an apparition himself.

He ran to the trackers and began sputtering. Macdowl seen the look and immediately went to where the trackers and scout were standing by the ravine. "What is he saying?" Macdowl demanded while cutting the scouts words short.

"He says, he's seen a grisly sight-" one tracker said but the other spoke as if they knew each others thoughts and words. "-and it killed his companion-"

"-whatever it was-"

"-it saw him-"

"-and we sensed it."

Macdowl looked from the trackers to the scout then back to the trackers again.

"You said it. Doesn't he mean animal or something?" Macdowl asked of the trackers.

The trackers shook their heads simultaneously.

"No-" began the second tracker then the first picked up where she left off, "*it*, is all he-"

"-could call *it*."

Macdowl looked over his shoulder at his six warriors and said, "Men, we move now. Be on guard with weapons drawn. There's something out here."

Just as Macdowl turned away from the two trackers and lone scout; he caught their sudden movements and also seen a face in the trees before the massacre began. Before he could turn back to his trackers they were already getting the life sucked out of them by a monster of a humanoid with yellow feral eyes and he knew that they were thralls in that instance.

He turned again to his men to see them being dealt the same fate also even though they put up more of a fight. Eventually they were overcome by the sheer numbers and strength of the thralls. When he turned halfway again, a young man who looked as if he could be no more than a teen, stood before him. He stood there with a dreadful grace and a look of serenity upon his face. Macdowl noticed the rich but tattered looking emerald cloak with ivory trimmings and the graceful look of the way his black hair is free of tangles or loose strands.

He also noticed how his hands looked so perfectly manicured but still held the perception of being deadly. He seemed perfect in the eyes of Peter Macdowl. Finally, Macdowl looked into his eyes and saw the crimson color as if hell was staring him in the face and breathing down his neck.

Dante spoke with a calmness of a Caesar in his own palace, "Now, what do we have here? It seems now that me and my thralls have feasted, we are too full to drain you. Luckily for you, I hate killing and wasting a good lunch."

Macdowl stood there unable to speak in the presence of such power. "Where were you and your entourage traveling? You were well armed. You were not hunting my kind, were you?" Dante said as he stepped so close to Macdowl that their lips almost touched.

"N-N-N-No," stuttered Macdowl, "I was tracking Verne and the man he follows, Lynn."

Dante's face immediately changed to the twisted face of a rogue beast and almost seemed like he grew two or three inches in his transformation. When Dante spoke this time his voice sounded like a baritone, "That name. You say you're after Lynn?"

Macdowl nodded his head not knowing if it was good or bad.

"You maybe of some use to our cause. In return for your services," Dante said as he took Macdowl by the shoulder and began walking.

The thralls melted away with the shadows of the trees. Macdowl knew, he was about to be made a deal with the devil. In the end, the result of him accepting or declining would mean his death.

As they approached the city known as Kamma, all they could see was the radiant brightness of the city emanating from it. Their faces were in awe of the various structures with their well placed jewels and gems to make up the bulk of the buildings. It was almost as if when the sun shined upon the gems the whole city seemed to have turned a light on.

"Wow, it's beautiful. There's some kind of positive energy here. Just walking into the city, I feel like a weight has been lifted off of my shoulders," said Maria.

Lilander complemented on her statement, "The city is known for its wide variety of crystals and the artisans who are adept enough to work with them. The windows and roofs are all made of different kinds of crystal, the latter is domed and usually green or blue colored crystals in various shapes and sizes interlocking like a perfect puzzle. No two roofs are alike."

As they made their way through the city, cheerful faces and waving hands were aimed their way with a few specific greetings for Lilander. Lilander greeted them in kind with a smile none of his friends have seen except for when they were at the site of the new coliseum when he was in the presence of Le'Anne. Lilander greeted everyone as if he knew them personally by name and like not a day has passed since they last spoke.

"Why do they seem so happy to see you?" Gaia asked Lilander.

Lilander kept looking forward as if in deep concentration and produced a barely noticeable smirk. "Kamma and Nospherat are really good friends. We always get together for a lot of events," he said.

The buildings looked extremely beautiful with the blue sky reflecting in the windows. When they entered the center of Kamma, Lilander pointed north down a long street and said, "That's the way to Iggarius Ports."

Instead of going north, he lead them east. Lynn looked around at everyone else and they gave him questioning looks, so he asked, "Lilander, where are we going if the ports are this way?"

Lilander answered, "I'm going to see King Augustus. You can go look for us a nice ship to cross the Grand Straight on if you want."

Lynn nodded in agreement with Lilander and said, "Verne and Maria, go with Lilander and announce our coming."

Maria agreed but Verne voiced his opinion, "I'm supposed to protect your backside."

"No, go ahead. I'm sure I'll be alright with Gaia and Uri beside me."

Lynn turned and walked off towards the ports with Gaia and Uri in tow. They walked past shops with merchants screaming into the streets, advertising about their different merchandise and wares. Some were offering to sell or fix swords for a good reasonable price; others were selling rare and copious metals and other items; others had armor and new boots for sell. Yet of all of them there was one claiming to have rare crystals for sale caught Lynn's attention.

"I don't think there are any *rare* crystals in this city, Lynn," Gaia said trying to get Lynn back on track.

"Oh but madam," commented the merchant, "this crystal was found buried in the heart of the volcano known as the Caves of Moorya."

He then tried to seal the deal.

"As you can see there's some sort of fire buried within the crystal and if you know the legend, then that could be one of the twelve crystals that holds the dragons at bay," he said with a fox like grin on his face.

Uri laughed at the notion and said, "Dragons. Yeah, and I'm just your everyday regular human."

The merchant looked at Uri as if his face was searching for an exclamation. Lynn handed the merchant, what he thought was a fair amount, three hundred gold pieces for the crystal. After pocketing the money he said, "I would've gladly given it to you since its been nothing but a curse since I came into possession of it. It scares my customers away so my sales are down. The darn thing even has me stressing. I'm only in my late thirties and I look like I could be a great-grandfather."

Lynn looked the merchant over and could not believe that this old man is truly not old. It is pretty convincing seeing as the man was hunched over with ice white hair and skin like crumpled parchment paper. The merchant looked so brittle for is age.

"No, I insist that I buy it. Especially after all the trouble you've been through," Lynn said taking the crystal, placing it in his pocket and leading Uri and Gaia away from the shop.

Gaia jumped in front of Lynn to block his path and asked, "Why did you fall for that hype? A crystal to hold a dragon at bay?"

Lynn shrugged his shoulders and said, "I don't know. His story was intriguing and if the crystal did that to him then there must be some truth to it. Then, I don't know if anyone else felt it but there's a dormant power calling out to me from deep within the crystal. The power doesn't seem the least bit human either."

"Whatever, let's just find us a vessel to cross the Grand Straight. We're going to have to worry about that crystal when we find the time."

They resumed their walk down the Iggarius Ports and saw plenty of crews going into pubs, inns and places of the like. Every now and then, but not a lot, a few men would stumble out of the pubs drunk off their feet. Some would engage in little bouts while others would walk haphazardly down the large port district.

A few even went as far as to try their luck with the ladies ... yes even Gaia wasn't spared from the onslaught of courtships. Lynn would stop every few minutes and inquire about any ships soon to set sail. That turned out to no avail seeing that the people they asked were either too drunk to talk, they were not the captain of the ship or they just wasn't setting sail anytime soon.

They were ready to cut their losses and go see Lilander until Lynn remembered something that happened back in Cinlae. If he could find some help in one of the pubs like the help they received from Chakran, then it would really change their situation from dire to manageable.

They decided to enter a pub with a painting of a large black wave over the name, ironically enough, Black Wave. Upon entering, all conversations ceased and all eyes fell on the three new faces.

"We're looking for a ship," Lynn started and noticed that he still held everyone's attention.

"A ship and crew to take me and my friends across the Grand Straight to Draconus City," Lynn finished.

Every head turned away showing that no one was interested in taking up their task. Seeing their reaction, Lynn added, "We are willing to pay any amount."

Still no one seemed interested so they decided to have a seat at the bar. Before they had a chance to order a beverage, a young looking sailor approached them and said with a voice to match his looks, "You don't go around saying stuff like 'we'll pay any amount.' You never know who's listening, watching and waiting to catch you three at a disadvantage."

Gaia turned to him and snapped, "Do you think we are helpless?"

The young sailor shrugged, "No, but do I look helpless? I've bested many to be respected by just about every man that passes through these ports. Now since your outsiders, all these sailors will stick together if you decide to rally something."

Lynn turned to him, "Do you know someone with a ship that we can catch a ride with?"

He shook his head and said, "Sorry, if my captain wasn't constantly on call, I would be more than happy to ask."

"Don't worry," Uri said, "we'll manage."

They stood up to leave. Uri and Lynn shook his hand but when he offered it to Gaia, she turned away. Before they were out of earshot, Uri screamed back, "What ship might we be able to find your captain on?"

He responded, "One of the biggest ships docked. Its name is 'The Pablo,' but, like I said, my captain is constantly on call."

Uri thanked him with a bow quickly left the pub to catch Lynn and Gaia.

"Let's just find King Augustus estate and Lilander then see if we can get us something to eat," Lynn said to his companions.

They walked back to the place where they split up with Lilander, Maria and Verne and started walking east in search of King Augustus estate. They asked plenty of people on the streets where they could find the estate. Just about everyone that was asked, pointed them in the same direction. They went as far east as they could until they stood in front of a large gate of at least ten feet high.

There were two guards standing just inside the gate. Uri went to ask them if this was the estate, but before he had a chance to ask anything, four servants came outside and opened the gates. Three were males and the other a young lady who looked around somewhere in her early twenties.

She stood about five-foot-nine with a petite frame. Her hair was brown and, to Lynn's surprise, straight and tangle free. She wore a royal blue uniform to match the other servants uniforms which all resembled business attire.

She spoke with a dainty voice, "King Augustus is aware of your arrival. He awaits you with Prince Lilander, Lady Maria and Sir Verne Wingo in his office."

Lynn, Uri and Gaia all looked at each other with a clueless look on their faces. Lynn turned back to the girl and said, "Sorry, but where-"

"I'm sorry Sir, follow me. I forgot, you've never been to King Augustus estate before," she said cutting Lynn off.

Lynn and Gaia were walking off following the young maiden but stopped when they noticed Uri wasn't by them. They looked at each other then back at the front gate to bear witness to a hilarious sight. The servants had their heads bowed, but, Uri was bowed also in respect. Neither moved and neither looked as if they would dare move first.

"You three, back inside, we have work to do," said the young maiden.

Lynn watched in amazement as the men who accompanied the maiden to see them in, fell into compliance. Out of curiosity, Lynn asked, "You're fairly young, so why do you have so much authority over the other servants?"

She smiled at Lynn with a flirtatious look and said, "Well, if you have to know, my mother is the estate mid-wife and my father is head chef," she shot a glance to Uri and Gaia then finished, "Also, me and Princess Le'Anne grew up here as best friends. So, King Augustus allows me a little immunity and the same education as Princess Le'Anne."

Gaia then asked, "So, King Augustus is allowing you to better yourself?"

"He allows us to pursue our dreams but most people are too scared to ask him," she said while resuming her formal self.

"Why would they be scared?" asked Uri.

The maiden smiled again before saying, "Oh, you'll see soon enough why."

They followed her in close pursuit. As she lead them down a straight walkway, Lynn looked at the couple of two story buildings. One sat on the left and the other to the right. These were connected by another building running between them at the end of the walkway. The maiden looked back over her shoulder and caught Lynn taking in the man-made scenery.

"Those are our guest rooms. They can house twenty people each building," she said looking forward once more.

"Wait. Before we go any further, may I inquire on our guides name?" asked Uri.

She stopped in front of the three guest, turned and said, "I'm sorry I haven't mentioned my name before, but, it is usually not required for us to present our names only our services. You are only one in a handful that has ever asked me and I think you're very polite in doing so. My name is Loraine. You may call me—Loraine."

She turned back to lead them inside but Gaia caught the small smile that played on her face. They entered the entrance hall and straight ahead was another hallway leading into a circular room. They had to be careful as they followed Loraine dodging other servants on their errands. Before Lynn went through the hallway he turned around to get one more look at the hall.

The entrance hall was adorned in ivory lining and beautiful lotus flower pots along the wall. Two guards stood in each corner facing the front door but still able to look down into each of the guest buildings. Lynn noticed two identical statues of a woman by the entrance doors that he didn't see upon entering.

"Loraine?" Lynn called out to her.

"That's Queen Iana. She passed away after a severe head injury while horseback riding ten years ago," said Loraine catching sight of what had Lynn hypnotized.

Lynn turned to follow Uri, Gaia and Loraine through the hallway into the circular room ahead to see four throne chairs in the middle of the room which were currently vacant.

Loraine stood by the lone door and said, "Behind this door is King Augustus' office. He should be in there waiting for you along with your friends." Loraine curtsied and left them to themselves.

"Well, lets go see King Augustus," said Gaia.

Lynn nodded his agreement, looked at Uri to see if he could read something, anything in his expressions, but he just nodded back in agreement also. Lynn turned back to the office door leading to his first meeting with the king of this great estate with Gaia and Uri still close behind.

They slowly walked around the throne eyeing the four chairs with blue velvet back cushion, seat and arm rest and once again with ivory trimming. Hanging from the walls were the velvet draping also. There were portraits of past kings that have lived and died. Lynn read the print under a few of the portraits and wasn't surprised that he was born before some of them.

"Lucky for them, they don't have to feel the pains of losing someone anymore," thought Lynn.

They stopped in front of the door and was amazed at the crystal knob and knocker. The knob was perfectly cut to resemble a round gem of the sapphire persuasion. The knocker was some how molded out of the same crystal and rested on a metal plate with a small metal cap on the back of the knocker to prevent it from being easily broken by someone's brash knocking.

Uri reached past Lynn to grab the knocker and knocked three times slowly. A few seconds passed then the door opened and they were instantly relieved to see a friendly face they knew. In the doorway stood the elf Lilander with at first a curious look which quickly converted into a smile.

"You've finally arrived. King Augustus is waiting inside to meet you," said Lilander escorting them down the short hall into the kings' office.

They came through the threshold to see Maria sitting in a chair in front of a giant semi-oval desk. The desk contained a golden balance beam on one corner with small pieces of crystal in and around it. The desk also contained a scepter laid across it with a blue egg shaped crystal on one end with, to Lynn's surprise, his markings at both ends of the scepter.

Verne was along the left wall skimming through the many books in the miniature library. He looked up and snapped to attention when he saw Lynn standing there. Lynn waved him off, so he smiled and went back to his reading.

Lynn looked over at Gaia and Uri standing wide-eyed next to Maria looking at a spot over Lynn's right shoulder. Lynn turned to look at the right wall to see what had Gaia and Uri captivated but his sight couldn't get past the burly chest directly in his line of sight.

The figure in front of him stood at least six-foot-ten, probably an inch or two more. Lynn moved his eyes up to the face looking down at him and saw an aged face but still portrayed some youth at the mid-forty mark. His face was clean shaven except for a goatee and mustache that he obviously kept neatly trimmed.

His hair fell a little over his face but was pulled loosely back into a braid. "Hello, I'm King Augustus, and if I'm correct, you're the Lynn Thrax one of the Chosen Ones," he said in a soft voice that sounded as if the wind whispered in your ears.

"Ye-Yes, I am. It's an honor to hold your company," Lynn said bowing to King Augustus.

King Augustus lifted Lynn upright effortlessly and said, "No use bowing Lynn. It should be I who shows you the respect for you are the one we've been waiting for."

He squinted his eyes while saying, "Yet, if you're finally here then there must be some powerful evil out there?"

Lynn looked at the rest of his companions then back at Augustus and said, "I don't know, I'm just here to help these fine people defeat Niccolo and get our lives back."

King Augustus laughed a hearty laugh that shook the room and showed two different spectrums of where his voice can go. He then said,

"Lynn, you don't understand, the times and nature have told of your coming for as long as I've been alive. It was always said that when the darkness begins to engulf the light, twins would come, stand and fight and return the light and make the world once again right. That's the way it was told to me as a child."

Augustus moved off to his seat behind his desk. Before sitting he asked, "Lilander, if you would please step outside and have someone bring in five chairs for you all?"

Lilander bowed his head and walked to the office door, stuck his head out and repeated the message. Within a few seconds, five men brought in chairs and placed them in front of the big desk all in line with Maria's.

Now that everyone was seated, Augustus pointed out, "I've won many battles but if this Niccolo has eluded you this long then I would stand no chance in a duel with him."

Lynn was about to comment but Gaia shot off first, "So, I see so far that all of your servants are well dressed and look content. You must be treating them right?"

Augustus chuckled merrily then said, "I treat them how I would want them to treat me if I was in their position."

"That's good, because if you wasn't, I could easily take everything from you."

Augustus then turned very serious, "Oh, so you think?"

"I know, not think."

"Easily?"

"Easily."

Gaia was sitting on the edge of her seat now as well as Augustus.

"Gaia, why do you always have to act so immature when you meet someone?" Maria asked angrily.

Gaia looked at Maria and saw something in her eyes because she relaxed and sat back in her chair.

Augustus did also and smiled, "I understand why you would ask. I'm a big man, but, they don't call me Augustus the Just, just for show. You know Gaia, I've heard a lot about you from Verne, Maria and Lilander. I know with Lilander's words backing theirs that they had to be true. You may not know, but I instantly liked you and I still do. Probably even more."

Gaia looked at Maria, Verne and Lilander as if to enter into their minds and inquire on what was said about her. All three were like a blank canvas that she just couldn't see the picture of their minds on. She looked back when Uri raised his hand bringing all attention to himself.

Lynn proceeded with the question he was going to ask before being interrupted by Gaia, "Excuse me sir, but do you perhaps happen to know of any ship that isn't in use right now?"

"About that," said Augustus, "I have-"

Just then he was cut off by someone barging into his office. From the sounds of the voices Augustus didn't even flinch just smiled as they made their way into his office.

Lynn thought, "It has to be someone of importance if he's holding a big bright smile."

The laughter of two females became louder while making the current conversation inaudible. "Sorry father, we were (*giggle*) just talking about . . . Oh! Lynn Thrax," said Princess Le'Anne accompanied by Loraine.

Le'Anne and Loraine both did curtsies and came back up. Le'Anne said while both her and Loraine rounded the desk to get behind her father, "Father, this is the man that saved my life at the new coliseum. I hear he is actually one of the Chosen Ones."

She put her hand on her fathers' shoulder like a child that truly admires their parent.

"I wouldn't exactly say 'Chosen One'. I'm just another person who has an enemy out to get me and plunge the world in chaos. I guess it was just my luck that his hand can reach out far enough and do great damage to everyone's future," Lynn said sarcastically to the group of people around him.

Loraine tapped King Augustus on his shoulder, "Sir, everything is prepared for the opening of the new coliseum."

He shot a proud glance to both girls and said to the others, "I'm so sorry but if you could accompany us, we can finish this conversation there."

Lynn looked around to everyone and they all seemed excited to go.

"We'll gladly accompany you to this historical event."

Augustus rose to his feet quickly and made for the door with everyone in his office in close pursuit. He looked over his shoulder and spoke very quickly, "I'm glad you all can join me. This will be one of the greatest ceremonies I have ever thrown."

"You always throw the greatest ceremonies," Lilander said enthusiastically.

They followed Augustus out to the circular throne room. He stopped, turned around and said, "I'm going to get ready, take a walk around the estate if you like."

With that said he went through the hall immediately to their left. Lynn decided to go to the hall just on the other side of the one Augustus went through. When he came to the end, there was another hall, but longer, with rooms in it, upstairs and downstairs. There was a guard standing in the corner to Lynn's left across from the stairs which was to Lynn's right.

"Which building might this be?" Lynn asked the guard.

"These are the barracks for the kings guard," he said with a straight face without even blinking an eye.

Lynn started into the barracks but stopped when he heard a woman calling his name. He turned to see Gaia coming toward him in full stride. Lynn backed up slightly because it seemed as if she would run him over. "Come with me, I want to show you a new battle technique," she said as seriously as Lynn has ever known her.

"Ok, but what technique might that be? If you'll permit me to ask," Lynn asked her amusingly knowing that he could best her at sword play.

She began walking off back toward the circular room with Lynn behind. She stopped dead center and unsheathed her two swords then signaling for Lynn to do the same.

"Wait, are you crazy, we can't train in here. Augustus would have our heads," Lynn said hastily trying to get Gaia to put away her swords and relinquish this idea until an opportune time.

"I've already had some one talk to King Augustus and he has had his servants move the throne chairs out of our way. He said anything that would help you is more than welcome to be tried," she said with a smirk.

Lynn unsheathed his katana and took his stance. Gaia dropped her blades to her sides and said, "Take out both of your swords. I'm going to show you how to fight using the dual wielding technique."

"You know what happens every time I strike with the Staff of Locked Souls," Lynn tried to reason.

She countered with, "Don't give me anymore excuses. you can control its effects and you know that, now pull it out."

Lynn obliged and no sooner than he did, she attacked him with a miraculous speed and prowess that he has only seen the dao-tug display. Lynn dodged her fast coming slashes and her thrusts.

"How will this help me?" Lynn asked her while never ceasing to stop his dodging.

"It will . . . strengthen your arms . . . and allows you to . . . battle better against multiple opponents. Ahh!" Gaia said while attacking after every few words.

"Try to parry or strike back so you will get the hang of this dual wielding technique," she told Lynn while allowing him to catch his breath.

He did, attacking with both blades thrusting at Gaia. She easily parried them to the side and threw an elbow right to Lynn's face but stopped a mere inches away not making contact.

"Never commit both blades unless you're sure there is an opening without room to counter. Always have one ready to defend unless like I said there is an opening and your thrust is sure and true," she told him pulling back her elbow.

They went at the training for about another twenty minutes letting Lynn get the technique down correct. They each went to freshen up and by the time they returned to the throne room, King Augustus and Le'Anne were entering dressed and ready. Loraine was close behind and to Lynn's surprise, dressed really nice also.

"Well, I assume that everyone is ready?" Augustus asked of Gaia and Lynn.

"Yes," Lynn said a little exhausted but made every attempt to hide it, "let me go find everyone else."

"We have two coaches out front Mr. Lynn. We'll be waiting for you and the others," Loraine said with that same shy smile that Lynn encountered in Augustus' office.

Lynn knew that it would take forever for him and Gaia to find the others so he decided to ask a passing servant to put the word out that they were ready to depart for the new coliseum. Within a few heartbeats all were assembled and ready to go.

All six of them walked out the front doors to see two huge coaches that were a pearl white and adorned with blue crystal shards all over them and drawn by six beautiful white quarter horses. Everyone jumped in the second coach except Lynn.

When Lynn went to enter the coach Augustus threw his head out the door of the first coach and said, "Lynn, if you would be so kind as to join us up here please?"

Lynn looked at everyone's face in the second coach and didn't see any awkward or jealous looks so he accepted and boarded the coach holding Augustus, Le'Anne and Loraine. During the ride, Lynn remained quiet while Augustus Le'Anne and Loraine laughed about things that they would love to see at the new coliseum opening.

"Where am I?" Lynn asked of no one but his surroundings.

He only saw a plain white landscape and knew that he wasn't on his way to the coliseum. "You are in a safe and familiar place," said a light and omnipresent voice that sounded very familiar to Lynn.

All there was as far as the eye could see was white light, so Lynn asked, "Where might this safe place be?"

Just then, Lynn's childhood home and the surrounding lands came roaring into view with everything he remembered still in place how it was when he was a youth. Everything was the same from the vintage home to the stables on the side of it. He could even see where he loved to watch his father chop wood for the fireplace.

Lynn looked at the enormous house in front of him and wanted to go inside but his legs wouldn't move for him. Lynn noticed the front door open very slowly and his sister came running out. It just wasn't the sister he helped send to the true death but the sister from when they were six and content. She ran to him and jumped into his arms with a big hug that felt so real that for that one moment Lynn began to cry.

She leaned back in his arms and said, "Brother, why are you crying? Don't cry. I came to help you."

Then Dania kissed the tears off his cheeks with those same lips that would make his bruises feel better. "Mother and father are inside. They sent me out with a message for you. Oh, you can't go inside either. It's not your time yet. Well, are you ready for the message?" Little Dania said with a childish smile.

At the mention of their parents, Lynn felt nothing but sorrow wash over him as he looked down away from his sister's eyes. Dania placed her little hands under Lynn's jaw right behind the chin and raised his face back up to hers and said, "Father and mother said be careful of who you surround yourself with. You can't expect to change everyone to good because a lot of the time, temptation rules. Everyone has a hint of evil in them but it takes will of mind to overcome it and see it to its end. They also said something about your enemy having a trump that he doesn't know about and could easily go your way or his."

Lynn asked his sister, "But, what are they talking about? What trump?"

"I don't know. I'm just telling you what they told me to. I'm only six years old, bear with me," she said and began to wiggle to get down out of Lynn's arms.

Lynn bent over to put her down and while still bent down, she kissed his cheek. She pulled the red crystal Lynn bought from the merchant in Kamma out of his pocket and said, "I like your crystal. It looks even better with some of the other colors."

Dania turned and ran back inside the house. Lynn began calling after her, "Dania, wait, I have to know something."

She didn't return and all Lynn could do was cry tears of happiness to know that his sister, mother and father have made the journey and are together.

"Lynn are you alright? You've been crying since I asked if you would escort Le'Anne inside," said Augustus catching Lynn's attention.

Lynn quickly rubbed the tears from his eyes and said, "I'm sorry, its just I was thinking about my sister, Dania," Lynn looked at Le'Anne and finished, "I would be honored to escort such a beautiful young lady, but, I think she would prefer to have Lilander be her escort."

Princess Le'Anne's smile seemed to have brighten at the mention of Lilander's' name and that's when Lynn noticed how beautiful Le'Anne and Loraine actually were. Princess Le'Anne's hair was pulled back in a braid but brought up in a chignon to show the back of her petite neck.

She blushed her cheeks to bring out her very light green eyes. Every time she smiled, her precious dimples would show and being a brunette brought that out even more. Her dress had an open V-back to show her slender petite back. The bottom fell loosely down her legs to show off her nice accentuated hips. She wore light green crystal heels to show off her beautifully pedicured toes with their green painted toenails to match her green dress.

Loraine could easily pass for being Le'Anne's sister seeing as how close they are and that they closely resembled each other in appearance and personality. Loraine wore a midnight blue dress almost like Le'Anne's as far as the bottom was concerned. The top had the front open in a V-shape covering just over her breast and stopping just below her navel. It also covered her shoulders and back and came up to her neck in a stiff collar.

Her brown hair, the same color as Augustus', was long down to her buttocks and worn loosely over her right shoulder. She also has that petite figure and dimples like Le'Anne's except her eyes are a subtle hazel.

Augustus wore a white shirt with loose hanging ruffled and embroidered lapels and cuffs. His trousers were the same in color and stopped and bulged at the knees. His long stockings were blue to match his cape and scepter. His spirit was so high that it brought out the colors in a more vibrant aura.

Lynn saw the sword hanging on Augustus' right side ready to expect trouble. The sword stretched to just below Augustus calf. The hilt was made of leather with an orb containing red liquid, about as big as Lynn's fist, in the hand guard. The pommel was made of onyx.

"Well, we're here," Augustus said and waited for Le'Anne and Loraine to exit.

"Lynn, what about Loraine? Will you escort her?" Augustus asked after the two ladies were out of the coach.

Lynn looked at Augustus for a second and was about to answer but Augustus said first, "I ask because I would like to be sure that my daughters both have an escort."

"How is that possible? What do you mean 'daughters'? I thought they were just friends," Lynn said in a hushed tone with a look of confusion playing on his face.

Augustus peered outside to make sure there were no prying ears around and said, "Indeed, I was married to Le'Anne's mother but she knew Loraine's was my love from childhood," he took a long sigh and continued, "So, she said she would like for her child to have a sibling but she wasn't blessed to give birth after Le'Anne. The physicians said she was messed up so bad from the birth that she would not be able to go through another birth. So, while she was recovering, I took up with Loraine's mother."

"But what about her father, the chef?" Lynn asked trying to sort out what was just told to him.

"Ah, he is just her stepfather and he knows it. Le'Anne don't know because we don't want any controversy over the throne but they've become such good friends," he answered quickly as if he already knew Lynn's question before he could ask.

"So, Loraine knows about this?" Lynn asked.

Augustus nodded and just stared into Lynn's eyes as if he just told someone that he was a wolf in sheep's clothing and not really the king. Lynn knew he was just entrusted with a secret that could be dangerous if too many people knew.

"Well, I think Loraine has her eyes on my companion, Uri," Lynn said to bring the original subject back to the topic while looking out the window at Loraine and Uri through the coach window.

He followed Lynn's gaze and asked, "You think?"

"Father, come on, we can't start the celebration without you," called Le'Anne from outside the coach holding onto Lilander's elbow.

Lynn and Augustus exited the coach and no sooner as they did, Uri and Loraine went their separate ways. "You tell your friend and I'll tell Loraine who's her escort," Augustus whispered to Lynn.

Lynn went to Uri and took him by the shoulder off to the side a little and said, "Me and Augustus think its best if you escort Loraine."

"Really?" Uri asked with anticipation and excitement like a happy pup.

Lynn nodded and looked over at Loraine to see her hug Augustus around the waist and then look at Uri. Maria came to Lynn's side, he offered her his arm and she affectionately accepted. Gaia tried to force Verne but he kept insisting that the king needs an escort. She eventually went but shot Verne an evil looking glare before taking Augustus' arm.

Verne ran to Lynn's side and said, "You're my excuse. I'm supposed to protect you, remember. It's my duty after all and there is no time for rest."

Verne was so witty like a fox that Lynn couldn't help but laugh. They entered the coliseum with Augustus and Gaia in front, Lynn and Maria beside them, Verne was off to Lynn's left side but falling behind a little. Following behind them were Lilander and Le'Anne with Uri and Loraine on their right all walking in a single file side by side.

They took their seats in a designated box area that was in the middle of a section surrounded by the wealth of Kamma. Guards sat in each of the four corners in the royal section. Maria nudged Lynn drawing his attention and pointing up. Lynn looked up and saw one of the most beautiful sights he has seen since beginning his journey.

There was a brown and white peregrine falcon flying in circles and performing flips around the top of the coliseum but couldn't touch the blue abyss of the sky above because of the crystallized dome. The falcon made a magnificent corkscrew dive straight to the royal patrons in their section.

The falcon made a slight change in direction to go just below the box. Maria almost lost her breath until everyone looked down and saw the trainer below with the falcon perched on his wrist. He put the falcon on its wooden perch and then took a bow to King Augustus.

Augustus clapped his hands with enthusiasm and gave the trainer an approving nod. Just then from an entrance below them came two pair of tumblers with the back two repeating the front two like a repetitious wave. Behind them came a parade of men and women dressed in scandalous and exotic revealing garments and adorned with different color feathered crowns and crystal necklaces, wristbands and anklets.

Their dancing and parading around went on for some time until those same tumblers that lead them in, lead the parade back out through the entrance below the royal section. Augustus then stood up and raised his arms to quiet the crowd. Augustus gave a quick look to a young lad who did some quick gestures with his hands and recited an incantation.

Lynn deduced in a heartbeat that the teen was in fact a wizard in training but experienced enough to be trusted by the king. The spell the teen used was an inflection spell on Augustus so that he could be heard across the whole of the coliseum.

"Welcome," he said, "to the grand opening and naming of this fine construction!"

He paused allowing for his voice to carry throughout the arena. "I know you would like to be on with the amazing show that we have planned for you. Well, I won't hold you much longer. From here on out, this will be known as the 'Crystal Coliseum'. We as a people have strived long and hard to have this remarkable structure developed and built. This is in no way for me, but, for your pleasure and entertainment. So enjoy, this is your day!"

The crowd erupted into cheers and whistling as they brought on the entertainment. Augustus looked at the young wizard and he immediately did a counter spell. The show consisted of criminals battling for freedom. Only a handful were victorious.

The audience cheered for the spectacular show that the gladiators were putting on. Now close to the end of the entertainment, there were three criminals that Augustus pointed out were ex-soldiers in his regime facing two huge gladiators. One of the gladiators held a double-headed axe while the other used a spiked mace.

Lynn decided to ask while the combatants were sizing each other up, "What crime could be so heinous that you would put your own soldiers in there to fight for their freedom?"

"Those soldiers wished to attempt regicide and usurp my throne. They even tried to conspire against my kingdom and throw it into chaos. They will be an example to any who comes after them and wish to follow in their foot steps," Augustus said keeping his eyes on the action below.

Lynn took that as his cue to watch the rest of the show. the ex-soldiers broke from a huddle and took their chosen target. Two of the smaller soldiers surrounded the gladiator with the spike mace while the larger of the three soldiers had a standoff with the other gladiator.

The gladiator with the mace began swinging his weapon from side to side keeping the two ex-soldiers at bay. The larger of the ex-soldiers saw his opening on the gladiator fighting his two mates and made a run for him.

The other gladiator screamed to get the attention of the other to warn of the oncoming attack. the endangered gladiator swung the spiked mace around to have the ex-soldier stop in his tracks just inches out of reach. The gladiator readied his mace for another swing but never got it off because the two forgotten ex-soldiers took him down.

One cut the back of the gladiators left knee, the other took his head as soon as he went down to one. Now there were three on one with the crowd going crazy. The three ex-soldiers surrounded the lone gladiator, stalking him like the lionesses do their prey.

Just then a dense mist fell over the coliseum and seeped down into the arena. Lynn knew something was wrong when the mist rose up out of nowhere. Lynn, Maria, Verne, Lilander and Uri all looked at Gaia to make sure if their suspicions were correct.

She nodded at them and mouthed, "Vampire."

The mist began rolling into the center instead of just thinning out. When the mist finally cleared, there stood in a circle around the combatants were two dozen thralls to Lynn's count. Surrounded by the three ex-soldiers was the gladiator being held fast by the neck at arms length by a towering figure.

Lynn looked into the fiends eyes and saw the crimson blaze in the irises that only a true vampire has and he noticed something familiar about the vampires features. Lynn flashbacked to the time when three messengers attacked him at home on his family's land. The fiend was the last and biggest of them except now he was void of any facial hair as if he never even had one stubble.

He pointed up at the one person he could want, Lynn, then took a bite out of the big gladiator, raping out his throat. The crowd went wild with fear trying to get out of the coliseum but every exit had thralls coming through them to create blockades. The three ex-soldiers tried to run but the thralls surrounding them kept throwing them back in the center to their master.

Lynn rose to his feet and the rest of his companions knew it was time to take action. Lynn, Verne and Lilander all leapt out of the royal section to the arena floor. Uri took hold of Maria in his arms and followed suit. Gaia pulled out her blades, looked around to make sure the guards were ready, then turned and jumped down to the arena floor along with her companions.

"Ahh, Lynn Thrax, we meet again. I can sense your power. It has grown miraculously, but, as you can see, I've changed also. I have seen what lies in the light and in the dark. Of course you can see from my spectacle which side I finally decided to dwell in. But, there will be no show when I destroy you all," said the big man that was about the same size as King Augustus.

Maria stepped forward and said, "Christian, what do you want here? Why did you let Niccolo damn you? Do you truly think you're on the winning side?"

He grinned showing his white stainless fangs then said, "You of all people, showing your traitorous face and asking me if I chose the right side. I chose no side, I chose power, and the man who gave it to me has my allegiance."

Christian then looked at Lynn and with a scary grin and said, "Did you know . . . Maria was sent to spy on you and if she could . . . destroy you?"

They all looked at Maria, their expressions asking, pleading for an explanation. Christian then said, "The way she kept her eyes on you Lynn, she was only keeping you in my masters' sight. Her eyes were the windows to keeping tabs on you. Now she has some kind of, hmmm, power that is some how blocking his link to her."

Gaia seized Maria by the throat from behind with one of her swords at the ready to slice through the thin muscle of Maria's neck. Lynn turned back to face Christian and saw that he had that wolfish grin back on his face while backing up allowing his thralls to step forward.

"Have fun with your new friends. Play nice!" Christian said as his thralls closed up the hole in their formation where he made his exit from.

Lynn spoke keeping his eyes locked on the feral eyes in front of him, "Gaia, let her go and help us fight. Let her decide her own fate."

"But, she has already decided her fate by-" Gaia was saying until Lynn cut her off with a stern look.

He then repeated, "I said let her go! Her life is in her hands and if she is any the least bit wise she would do right to leave this place unless she wants to be on the end of my blade."

Lilander asked, "Lynn, can you feel that?"

"Not now," Lynn said through gritted teeth. Gaia released Maria just as the thralls drew down on them. Lynn quickly took down two thralls but more came out of the stands. Lilander killed a few with his daggers but quickly sheathed those and began shooting pinpoint accurate arrows up to the box where Le'Anne and Loraine sat in fright as thralls approached the box from all directions.

King Augustus, blade in hand, battled along side his guards trying to keep the vampire thralls at bay. There were screams of fear as chaos raged in the arena but through all the noise, Lynn heard her voice while he was being overwhelmed.

"Lynn, use the new battle technique I taught you!" Gaia screamed just after she took out four thralls.

Lynn pulled out his Staff of Locked Souls blade and saw the faint green glow to it. He began slashing away, taking down more thralls faster and faster, while making a beeline for Christian. Christian kept on going to Augustus' royal section not even acknowledging Lynn killing thrall after thrall.

Lynn kept running toward Christian, slashing and cutting up thralls by the dozen, all while Christian was halfway up the stands to the royal box section. Lynn thought quickly trying to assess the situation then remembered and yelled out, "Lilander, over there, take him down!"

Lilander looked to Lynn then to Christian's big form he was pointing out. Lilander acknowledged and let loose three arrows in close succession. The arrows flew briskly through the air and looked as if they were going to hit their target dead on. Christian showed his new enhanced speed and unsheathed his sword and cut down two of the arrows and then caught the other in his free hand all in one motion.

With the arrow in hand, Christian turned his neck to face the immortals and smiled that same wolfish grin again. He broke the arrow with his thumb and forefinger then resumed his progress to the royal box where Le'Anne and Loraine sat hypnotized by their fright. He climbed into the box and made his way to Le'Anne and Loraine smiling sadistically as he went.

Augustus barred Christian's way with his sword on guard and asked, "What do you want with them?"

Christian took in Augustus size looking dwarfed by the king. Christian swung his own sword into Augustus' own blade throwing him off balance and over the edge of the box.

"Uri, the king!" Lynn screamed but saw that he was tied up fighting some seemingly unending thralls.

To Lynn's surprise, Maria caught Augustus, with their hands interlocking in each other, while she clung to the wall. She pulled him back into the box in time to see Christian holding Loraine's limp body in his arms and said, "I'm done here."

He smiled and formed a mist and vanished just as Maria leapt at him. When Christian disappeared, a loud crack like lightning sounded from outside the coliseum and his thralls that were blocking the exits descended into the arena. Lynn looked around and saw his friends and the guards being overwhelmed.

He didn't know what to do first, help here or chase down Christian. As his world began to crash down around him, he felt an intense heat energy radiating from his pants as if he was on fire. He pulled out what was causing the sudden energy burst and found it to be the red dragon crystal pulsing like it was alive and feeding off Lynn's desperation.

Lynn concentrated on the crystal willing the power to flow over him and wishing for a miracle. his body went rigid as a celestial light erupted from his core with cleansing power and sounding like rolling thunder. When the light died down, all the thralls were burnt up leaving their bones which turned to dust at the slightest touch. Lynn met back up with everyone in Augustus' royal box section where Augustus stood staring wild eyed at Maria. When Maria turned to face everyone, Uri, Gaia and Verne all gasped to see the Black Widow mask on her face.

Chapter: 12

Everyone stood there looking at Maria as she pulled the mask off with ease and stared into Lynn's eyes. "Lynn, I-" she began to say but was cut off by Lynn's upheld hand.

Lynn asked with a stern defensive look on his face, "Is it true? What Christian said?"

She nodded and the affirmation of the suspicion broke Lynn's heart into a million pieces, possibly scattering them across different universes unable to be retrieved.

She spoke, "Yes, it was true."

Gaia advanced on Maria and grabbed her wrist making to restrain her. Lynn stopped Gaia with a gesture and asked, "You said it *was* true?"

Maria nodded, lowered her head and took a deep breath then exhaled while looking back into Lynn's eyes and said, "I fell in love with Lynn and even though he wouldn't give himself to me I saw the truth in him."

She had no tears running down her face as she spoke, "Niccolo spread so many lies about Lynn that I believed every bit. That was until I found out Lynn was prey turned predator to stop Niccolo's evil. If I would have succeeded in my mission, I would never have opened my eyes in time to figure out the truth."

She broke down to her knees and that's when Lynn broke his own defenses and moved to her side to comfort her. "Now that we have settled that," Uri interrupted, "we have to bring Loraine back."

Augustus added input, "Yes, please bring my daughter home."

Le'Anne caught wind of her fathers words and went directly to him and asked, "What do you mean by 'daughter'?"

Everyone present looked at Augustus for either an answer or correction to his statement. Augustus looked at Lynn then to Le'Anne then said, "I mean daughter as in my 'flesh and blood'. She is your sister and always has been and always will be."

Uri asked, "Maria, do you know where Christian took Loraine?"

Maria shook her head and said, "No, I messed up Niccolo's plans. Now he's doing just about anything. He's desperate and changing his course of action probably as we speak."

"Let's go. We need to get the king and Le'Anne back to the city. Its not safe for them out here for now," Lynn said to everyone while walking toward Augustus and Le'Anne who were comforting each other.

"Lets get you two home," Lynn told Augustus and Le'Anne as the rest of his company came to stand by him.

As they exited the coliseum from one of the upper exits, everyone saw two riders on horseback head for 'The Advent'. Lynn asked the one person who had the greatest eye-sight out of any species present, "Lilander, who is that?"

He smiled and let relief show in his features and said, "Two of our targets. Lilandro and Christian, and yes Loraine is still with Christian."

"Why is Christian still around? Why isn't he back with Niccolo?" Uri asked of no one in particular.

Lilander smiled and said, "So that is what I felt."

Everyone looked at Lilander puzzled and Verne asked, "What did you feel?"

"Lilandro put a spell on the coliseum to stop any unnatural travel in or out of the coliseum," Lilander answered the question.

"He's weakened by the spell. It sapped his power and would've killed him if it wasn't for him being a vampire," Lilander said also.

Verne asked, "Well, if the spell was able to stop entrances and exits, how the hell did he get in?"

"He didn't activate the spell until he was in the coliseum. I guess Lilandro had plans of his own."

"Looks like we have a new destination. Augustus, take Le'Anne home and wait for us there," Lynn said to his companions then to Augustus.

They made their way to 'The Advent' as Augustus was escorted back to Kamma by what guards were left from the battle. Lynn and company entered quietly, ducking and dodging behind years of fallen debris, hearing faint swordplay getting louder as they made their way through the corroded coliseum.

They entered into the arena area the way they came in when Gaia was trapped there to see Lilandro and Christian in a duel. Loraine was unconscious on the ground a few feet from the two combatants. The two battled hard, Christian attacking with hard and heavy powerful strikes, Lilandro using his smaller and limber frame and speed to avoid the attacks with the vigilance of a hawk.

Christian took a swing at Lilandro's legs but he jumped on the big man's shoulders then flipped off behind Christian about ten feet. They turned and faced each other, put their swords down to their sides, and looked each other in the eye.

Christian spoke, "You foolish elf. You know since you interfered, you will never stick your meddlesome nose in our affairs again. I hear that elf blood is almost as sweet as the nectar of a vampire. Its time I feed."

Lilandro grinned and looked even more sinister and sadistic than Christian and said, "I'm sure your blood is tasty, but, I just thought I would kill you instead. After all, your union with certain powers is what makes you my enemy."

That remark upset Christian and almost sent him into a rage. Both warriors raised their swords and charged. Both performed a side slash and paused for a brief moment. They both stood straight up and turned to face each other as if neither one made contact. They both grinned that same grin but Lilandro went down to his knees then fell back as the cut in his chest showed itself and began pumping blood out.

As Lilandro lay there gasping for breath, Christian began walking toward his fallen foe as his chest wound was healing over but his steps were brought to a halt by an arrow placed right where his next step would have been.

Lynn looked at Lilander still holding the bow ready with another arrow pulled back taut with a look on his face that reminded Lynn of a dao-tug.

Christian looked their way and gave that tireless grin, "Thank you for showing up."

Everyone charged except Lilander, but their road was soon filled with obstacles of thralls stepping out of the shadows. They battled the thralls while Lilander used the rest of his arrows then joined in the fray with his daggers cutting away like a savage.

Lynn finally stood face to face with Christian again after so long. Christian brought his sword up on guard and said, "So, finally I can repay you for my two friends you killed. They were meant to be here with me and wallow in the power of a true vampire."

Lynn pulled out his second sword and said, "The only way I see you repaying me is the same way your friends did . . . with your head."

What Lynn said seemed to anger Christian but he gained control of himself and his composure before letting his animalistic side take over. Before they engaged in battle, Lynn took one look over his shoulder to see Lilander doing a healing spell on Lilandro's inert body.

Christian charged Lynn, his blade up for an attack and all Lynn could do was brace himself for the blow. Christian swung his sword down like a heavy mace down onto Lynn's waiting blades almost making Lynn lose his swords.

"Lynn, one for defense, one to attack!" Gaia screamed in Lynn's direction while she battled with three thralls.

Lynn began attacking with his katana, lunging and slashing then switching it up with his other blade, the Staff of Locked Souls. After a few rounds of attacking, dodging and defending, they both paused a second to admire the others progress in power.

"You know, I can't allow you to win?" Christian said after a while.

Lynn put his guard back up and said, "Don't worry, I'll just take this victory."

Christian charged first and Lynn began to charge but two pair of hands threw Lynn onto Christian's protruding blade. Christian flashed his wolfish smile again as he twisted his blade in Lynn's gut bringing him to his knees.

"It is over," he screamed, "with your death it will bring me kingdoms from my mas-"

He couldn't finish because right then his eyes glazed over for a few seconds then caught focus again. He looked down upon Lynn from his full height and said, "My master says he would rather he be the one to kill you. You're a very lucky creature. I could've taken you to the true death but he requests your presence."

Christian pulled his sword free of Lynn's body, allowing him to began his healing, and walked over to Lynn's Staff of Locked Souls and picked it up. He turned the blade over in his hand then turned to Lynn and said, "I like this blade, but, since I didn't kill you, I can't activate its power. If you wish to attempt at retrieving this precious item then come to my lair in the caves of Moorya."

Lynn stretched out his hand to Christian trying to speak but couldn't because the wound was so bad that it still hasn't healed all the way over yet. Christian struck out at Lynn wit his nails bared cutting a deep gash in Lynn's cheek. Christian disappeared taking his thralls with him, leaving everyone including Lilandro and Loraine.

Lynn awoke on his back with Loraine, Lilander and everyone else except Lilandro standing over him smiling as he came to. Lynn sat up, looked around and asked, "Where is Christian and Lilandro?"

"They're both gone and Christian has taken your Staff of Locked Souls," said Lilander while giving Lynn a decent look over.

Lynn felt over his shoulder trying to feel for the handle of the staff but felt nothing but air. Lynn got to his feet quickly, but too quickly because he stumbled dizzily only to have Uri catch him.

"Please Lynn, take it slow so we can think for a moment," said Maria pleading with Lynn, holding his hands.

Lynn looked Maria in her eyes and said, "I remember now, what's in the caves of Moorya?"

Maria took a second to think and said, "Nothing important that I know of, especially for a vampire seeing as there's a volcano in there. Why?"

"That's where he has taken the Staff of Locked Souls," Lynn said walking towards the exit with everyone falling in behind him.

They made their way back to Kamma via 'The Crystal Coliseum' route. When they entered into Kamma, there were cheers all throughout the city for returning Loraine safely. The group finally made it through the crowded streets to King Augustus estate to walk in on a heated conversation.

Princess Le'Anne was in her father's face even though she's about an inch shorter than Lynn saying, "How could you not tell me? After all these-"

She stopped to see Lynn and his friends walk into the office with Loraine in tow. "Loraine, sister, are you alright?"

Le'Anne asked looking as if she changed personalities. Loraine nodded and took a seat to rest her weary body and mind. Le'Anne looked at her father then from him back to Loraine and asked, "Did you know that we are blood?"

"Yes, but, we had our reasons for not bringing it to your attention yet," Loraine said reluctantly.

Le'Anne seemed surprised as if she just received a slap to the face and it wasn't the answer she expected and started shedding tears. Loraine went to hold and comfort her sister.

Le'Anne asked, "Why? Why have you never said anything? Why keep this from me?"

Loraine placed her cheek on top of Le'Anne's head and said, "Father didn't want us to fight over the heir when it was time."

Le'Anne pulled back just enough to look into her sister's face and said, "I'd never fight you but for you."

Loraine smiled at Le'Anne and escorted her to her room. Augustus rose up out of his seat and proceeded to leave also until Uri asked, "King Augustus, sir, about your ship. May we use your vessel?"

Augustus answered, "I'm sorry but through all this drama I can't recall the ships name, you know age and other matters of the city burdens me so. What I do know is the captain's name is Admiral Jo Cutthroat, my cousin."

He then returned to his desk and wrote on a piece of parchment. "Show Jo my signature and my insignia and the whole crew would be glad to oblige," said Augustus.

Lynn took a peek at Augustus insignia as he received it from the king. The insignia was a crested shield divided in four parts. The upper left and lower right quarters had Lynn's birthmark in white writing on blue background. The upper right quarter had a blue stallion rearing up. The lower left quarter had two swords in blue crossed over each other.

The latter two were on a white background and in a ribbon over the top was a name 'Versecon'. They thanked Augustus and left after he took up in his quarters. Lynn and his companions made their way to the ports of Iggarius to find this captain.

They asked around and people kept pointing them further down the dock in the direction to a large ship until they came upon it. Seeing as it was dark out, it was hard to see the name until they were right under the massive vessel and the water reflected the torch light up to the ships side.

"This is it," said Lilander, "The Pablo."

They walked down the pier to the ramp to board the ship when Lynn, Gaia and Uri saw a familiar face. "You there! Young sailor, where is your captain?" screamed Gaia.

The young sailor came down the ramp with a surprised look on his face. He looked Lilander, Verne and Maria over then looked over to Lynn and spoke, "So, I see you aren't helpless."

Lynn smiled. "This is Maria Maccio, Lilander Ravenholme and Verne Wingo," Lynn said pointing to each in succession.

"Well, you can call me, Tommy Hawkeyes."

"Why are you called Hawkeyes?" asked Uri.

Tommy chuckled and said, "I have eyesight like a hawk and can see great distances."

Lilander then said in the elfish tongue, "I knew I felt something unique about you. You're half elf, am I correct?"

The young sailor looked wide eyed at Lilander and responded, "Yes, you are correct. Is it that obvious?"

"Only to another experienced elf or a human adept. What is your true name?"

"Tomare'n Eeillodor is my given elf name."

Lilander started rubbing his chin taking in the information and contemplating over it. He came out of his trance and said, "Your father is one of the greatest archers in Nospherat."

"I heard, but I never showed too much interest in archery. I guess because I was raised by my human mother," Tommy said in the common language while signaling for everyone to follow him onboard.

Uri asked, "So where is your captain?"

Tommy looked over his shoulder and said, "She's in the briefing room."

Verne sped up, stopped Tommy and asked, "Did you just say **she?**"

He nodded and said, "Yes. Can't a woman be a captain?"

"Yes, its just **her** name is Jo Cutthroat," said Verne looking a little confused.

Tommy kind of chuckled and said, "It's short for Josephine."

He showed them the briefing cabin below the helm at the stern of the ship. Tommy knocked on the door then entered and waved them inside. They walked into the cabin with a large round table situated in the center and some stairs leading up into a trapdoor. There was a pole about four feet from the stairs that lead down into a hole where the next deck was located.

There were three people seated around the table, one of them was a woman with the bars of a captain emblazoned on her shoulder. The bars shined like they were newly polished and never experienced a stain but everyone knew that those bars have seen much and will see even more.

Lynn thought, "She must be the captain seeing as she wears the bars proudly."

She rounded the table and asked, Which of you is your captain?"

Lynn was stuck admiring her beauty. It was weird to him seeing a woman of the seas as beautiful when he knew that there was a lot of work she has done to get where she is at.

Her eyes were hazel with thin eye brows. Her brown hair was pulled back into a ponytail but looked like it stopped just short of her shoulders. Her body, you could tell just by looking, was tone. She wore brown slacks with knee high brown cow hide boots, a white long-sleeve shirt with the sleeves rolled up to her elbows showing off more of her tan.

It took Lynn a few seconds to just go over her features while everyone in the cabin was staring at him in all of his frozen stupor. The captain smiled showing her perfect teeth and dimples and said, "Well! Maybe we might need to let him get a taste of sea water."

Lynn snapped out of her hypnotic beauty when someone nudged him from behind. Lynn took a step forward, extended his hand and said, "I'm Lynn Thrax and these people are my good friends."

He went on to name off each one then finished with, "We've come to ask of your service in crossing the Grand Straight."

She took her head making the ponytail swing from side to side like a pendulum while walking to the pole leading into the hole, "I apologize for your time being wasted but I'm on call and no amount of gold can change that."

When she finished, she slid down the pole before Lynn could say anything. Lynn stood there with a flustered air about himself and desperation in his quick step toward the pole. He stopped short not knowing what to do. Follow her, wait or just go back to King Augustus.

"You should've showed her the parchment with King Augustus insignia on it," said Lilander.

That's when Lynn remembered that he even had the parchment and went down the pole after her.

"Don't worry, he really has great people skills," Verne told the first and second mate.

Chapter: 13

Lynn made it to the bottom of the pole to set his eyes on the dining hall. There were twenty round tables with four seats about them. The kitchen area was along the starboard side of the wall on this deck facing the bow. A few handful of sailors were sitting at some tables talking and laughing but all ceased when they saw Lynn emerge from the upper deck.

Lynn caught sight of his target as she slid down another pole in the middle of the dining hall. Lynn made his way briskly through the tables and was almost at the pole until a sailor sitting at a table accompanied with two others stuck his foot out trying to trip Lynn up.

Lynn unsheathed his katana and swung the razor sharp blade at the sailors hand on the table, stopping the blade just as it broke flesh to show a small incision and letting the sailor see how close he was to losing his hand. The sailor jerked his neck down to look at the blade then up at Lynn with a mixed look of surprise, frustration and anger on his face.

Lynn took that chance to say, "I don't need or want any of your problems. I just need to speak with your captain."

Lynn pulled his katana away from the hand and sheathed it back in the scabbard on his left hip. No sooner than he did that, the two at the table stood up and rounded the table. Lynn spotted a fist coming from his left side and stepped back before the blow connected with his jaw.

Two more sailors at another table were now standing with the other three wanting anxiously to join in the little dance. The other sailors around the room were jeering and taunting Lynn. They wanted to see this new face dealt with and dealt in the manner that they were accustomed to.

Good old fashion beating.

The sailor who almost had his hand severed asked, "Who do you think you are coming onto our ship starting trouble?"

The sailor was at least twice Lynn's size in mass and a few inches taller. His bald head turned red along with his face as he became angrier. His eyes were now darting around seeing all of his fellow mates waiting for him to make a move. Lynn shrugged and tried to walk past the sailors but the instigator swung at Lynn.

Lynn ducked low and caught him with a punch square in the diaphragm forcing him to fold over. Two more stepped forward but halted as Lynn put his guards up. Feeling a little better that they came to their senses, Lynn started walking towards the pole until he heard Maria say, "Lynn, what the hell did you do?"

Lynn turned around to see one of the two sailors from the briefing cabin helping up the downed mate. It was barely noticeable but while helping up the downed sailor Lynn could see a small smile on his face.

"Great people skills, I like him already," said the sailor from the briefing cabin helping up the downed mate.

"I'm second mate, Pappy Jones, and him over there helping the idiot is first mate Byron Bull," said the second mate.

Lynn took in their features at a glance. Pappy Jones' face had a dainty appearance to it. He was a thin looking person who stood about six-feet with a white long sleeve shirt on. His eyes are gray and alert but for all his young features, his hair was white as snow.

Byron Bull stood about six-foot-three. His belly protruded over his waistband but it wasn't loose blubber. His arms were as huge as an ox with hairy forearms. His face is chubby with a thick beard braided in two French braids hanging down from his chin. The one thing that sets him apart from everyone else is that he has one of those nose rings like a bull. His brown eyes were stern but they had crow's feet in the corners giving him away to the trained eye.

"This one may be a hard ass but he loves a good time when he sees it," thought Lynn.

The second mate took Lynn down the stairs, two levels to the bunk deck where the captains cabin sat in a corner in the bow of the ship. "Admiral Jo, Lynn has something that you might want to check out!" Pappy said after knocking.

She opened the door and pulled Lynn in and shut the door before saying, "I see that you are very persistent, but it will get you no where. As I said before, I'm on call and no amount-"

Lynn said nothing but presented the parchment to her from Augustus. The sight of the insignia was enough to stop all protest. She looked at Lynn like this couldn't be true then sat down on her bed and tore open the seal.

"King Augustus said to render your services," Lynn told her as she was opening the parchment.

She read it, seen the signature and said, "How could my cousin do this to me?"

Lynn knew the question wasn't directed at him so he waited in silence allowing her to sort things out. "I'll go topside and await your answer," Lynn told Admiral Jo readying to leave.

Lynn opened the door and was almost through the door when she called out, "I can't and I would never deny my cousin, my king anything. Tell B.B. to prepare the crew for a trip."

Lynn had no idea of who she meant so he asked, "I'm sorry, but, who is B.B.?"

She smacked her forehead and said, "I'm talking about my first mate, Byron Bull. Never, ever call him B.B. He only lets me call him that and that is with great tolerance."

Lynn nodded and made a mental note to never call the first mate B.B. He didn't want to find out what happens when some one called Byron B.B. Hell he didn't even want to see what might happen to a stranger or even Niccolo for that matter.

Lynn began to walk off but stopped, "Be warned, we are no ordinary individuals and that there is an even more unusual evil looming before us."

Her look was a nervous one, unsure to even let them board her ship for the safety of her crew but she knew she would help them seeing as they were the ones that the people have been waiting for. Lynn left and made his way back to the dining hall to see his friends talking at one of the tables waiting for him to return. The five sailors that tried taking on Lynn were sitting close by at another table eyeing Lynn carefully.

"She'll take us," Lynn told everyone, "so, where is the first mate?"

"They said that we can find them in the briefing cabin," said Verne.

Lynn asked, "They?"

Maria intervened, "He's talking about both the first and second mates."

They made their way back up to the briefing cabin to see the two men talking. Lynn interrupted, "Byron, your captain sent me to tell you round up the crew, we weigh anchor soon."

They both stood up and Pappy already had on a different shirt but the exact same as Byron's. The long sleeves surely deceived a couple people because his arms were almost as big as Byron's but with more tone.

Pappy took off down the pole to tell the crew that they now have some work commanded directly from Augustus. Before Byron was able to leave and ready the ship to leave, Admiral Jo stepped in and said, "Lynn, you and your friends can go on land and get some rest. I'll forewarn you now, we leave in the morning at dawn."

Lynn nodded and replied, "You will find us at King Augustus estate."

Before they left, Lilander turned and said, "When you're ready for us send Tommy Hawkeyes."

Jo waved them off then they made their way down to the ports. They walked past the pubs while trying to avoid the drunken sailors either just docking or getting themselves liquored up before weighing anchor.

There were a few fights that broke out but they didn't intervene since they were trying to attend to even more important business. The city began to die down as merchants made their last sales and as patrons made their way home to rest for another day of browsing. Lilander abruptly stopped and began looking around suspiciously.

"Lilander, what is it? What do you sense?" Gaia asked him.

He stopped looking around and focused on a figure on top of a roof looking down upon them. "Lilandro," he said in a very low tone.

Lynn went to Uri, "See if you can follow him."

Uri jumped to a wall and kicked off the wall to land on the roof but Lilandro had already seen him coming and took off.

"I'll meet you at Augustus' estate, leave him to me!"

Lynn nodded but Lilander called out, "Do not confront him, please, he is too dangerous!"

Uri nodded back and took off after Lilandro. They made it back inside the estate with no problems from any of the late night wanderers in the streets. One of the servants that greeted Lynn upon his first trip there escorted them to their rooms. Lynn's room was the last to be escorted to.

When he made it inside, the servant called out, "Master Lynn, King Augustus said that when you return he would like your company alone one more time."

Lynn sighed, "Alright, I'll be out in just a few seconds."

Lynn took off his cloak and hid his katana behind the headboard and hung the red dragon crystal on his katana. Lynn stepped out into the hall to see a different servant awaiting him. He looked fairly young and new to the job.

"Well, lead the way," Lynn said.

With a bow of the head he took off like one of Lilander's shot arrows. The servant lead Lynn back to the entrance hall then to the circular throne room. He then lead Lynn down the same hall he seen Augustus go through the morning before to get ready for the opening of the 'Crystal Coliseum'.

At the end of the hall it opened up just a little with a door to Lynn's left, right and directly in front of him. The servant knocked on the latter one. The knocker used was an exact replica of Augustus' insignia.

"Come in," is all that was said from behind the door so the servant opened the door and moved to the side to allow Lynn access to the room.

"Yes, yes, Lynn, please come in," Augustus said as Lynn stood there in the threshold of Augustus' door admiring the massive room.

Lynn has seen so many different royal chambers, yet, they never cease to amaze him. Along the right wall was adorned different types of swords and daggers. His bed was along a semi-circle wall. His bed had ivory post with a white silk curtain hanging over it.

It looked as if it could fit all of Lynn's company plus a few more. His spread was navy and emerald color halves. The wall behind his bed had portraits of what looked like to Lynn was Augustus, Le'Anne, Iana and what looked to be younger portraits of Loraine. The left wall had an outline cut out to fit his gold and white celestial looking armor into it with barely an inch between the compartment and the armor.

"How did it go down at the ports with Admiral Jo?" Augustus asked while sipping on some fresh wine.

"You never told me Jo was a Josephine," Lynn said looking at him with and exhausted smile on his face.

Augustus had a hard time swallowing while laughing and said, "I'm sorry, but she is lovely, isn't she?"

Lynn nodded his head in agreement with a chuckle that followed and then Augustus said, "Yes, that's my adventurous little cousin and I have to make sure she's well taken care of."

Augustus signaled for Lynn to sit on his bed by him. When seated, Lynn asked, "Are you sure about sending her with us?"

He looked at Lynn like he didn't just ask that and said, "It's what she loves to do. The sea is an unpredictable and dangerous force, yet, that's what she loves to do."

"I'm not talking about the sea. I'm sure she can handle anything nature throws at her on the water. I'm talking about the things nature has lost control over."

"Oh," Augustus said.

"So, what did you need to see me about?"

Lynn asked to change subjects and steal another glance around the room. Augustus pulled out his sheathed sword and held it in his lap. He cleared it of its scabbard with the ringing of the blade echoing off the walls.

It was about the same length as Lynn's katana. The hand guard had a clear orb about the size of Lynn's fist with some red liquid in it. Even though its seen many wars and deaths, it still shined like it was just forged.

"This sword belongs to **you**," he said to Lynn.

"What?" Lynn said while taking a long look at the blade.

Augustus held it out to Lynn so he took it and held it up to examine the clean blade like a brand new toy.

"That sword was given to my ancestors and past down the line, "Augustus took a sip of wine and finished, "by your father if I'm correct."

Lynn looked at him confused and asked, "What do you mean by, '**my** father gave this to you'?"

Lynn became captivated by the red liquid in the orb. As it sloshed around in the orb Lynn almost felt enamored by the red liquid. It was thick and a dark velvet like blood but it flood like milk infused with honey.

"Exactly what it sounds like. Your father gave that sword to my ancestors to protect it from the wrong hands at the same time it would protect us. That orb contains your life blood, including some of your essence. If my memory is correct, your father siphoned your blood into that orb with the help of some mystical knight."

"The same was done to your sister but to whom he entrusted the orb to, I don't know. I was told that in the wrong hands both orbs will do nothing but chaos then armageddon would soon follow," Augustus said looking calm all the while.

Lynn still captivating by the weapon asked slowly, "Do you know what object or region the orb might be in?"

"As I said before, I only know about the orb, not its whereabouts."

"How will I know if the other orb is near?"

"The orbs will summon each others powers when nearby. That is when you will know."

Lynn bowed to the king, "I thank you and your ancestors for protecting the orb and returning it safely back into my hands."

Augustus was about to speak when a loud frantic knock came from the door. Lilander said, "Lynn, King Augustus, come quick, it's Uri, he's hurt!"

Lynn and Augustus exited the room and followed Lilander through the estate. They ran past the circular throne room across to a hall Lynn has yet to explore. When they stepped outside, Lynn could hear the horses were frightened by something while the grooms tried to keep them calm.

Lynn looked toward the grass between the stable and dining hall to see Le'Anne, Loraine, Maria, Gaia, Verne and about four servants standing around Uri's motionless body. Lynn ran through the circle with Lilander and Augustus stopping at the edge.

"Uri, what happened to you?" Lynn asked while going over the many wounds on Uri's body.

Each slash bled freely as if it were a fresh cut. Lynn ran his hands over the cuts inspecting them. He began adding what pressure he could hoping it would staunch the flow but it was to no avail.

"Why haven't you healed?" Lynn asked.

"Li-Lilandro is (cough) very powerful. I tried to speak with him but he attacked me with a blade and chain made of sil . . . ver," Uri said in an almost inaudible whisper.

Lynn still searching for ways to help said, "I don't know if there is anything I can do."

Lilander then intervened, "You have to force him to change. If he changes, his wounds will heal, if he doesn't he's lost to us."

Lynn looked into the faces of everyone around him and thought, "How could I possibly make him change, I'm no moon, my powers are not lunar."

Lynn asked the crowd, "How do you expect me to make the change if I don't possess lunar powers? Why can't he change on his own?"

"This is how it works," said Lilander, "You and him are-hell all of us are connected to you. You don't need lunar powers as long as we are loyal to you."

"Your powers can force his beast forward the same way you brought his human conscience to the surface in his beast form," Gaia jumped in, "Also, he's too weak and too far gone to change on his own. You have to be his beacon and his source."

Lynn nodded and took a deep breath then placed his splayed hands over Uri's eyes the same way he did back when they first met in Cinlae's battle arena. Lynn pulled his hands back a few inches from Uri's face.

Still focused on Uri's face, he asked, "Now what do I do?"

"Focus on his animal form and pull or coax it to the surface. Be careful, this could be very taxing on you," Lilander spoke so low that it sounded like wind whispering past the ears.

Lynn peered between his hands into the depths of Uri's eyes to search for his hybrid-beast that was somehow hiding. For a split second, the beast showed himself by flashing his mighty fangs. Once Lynn locked all his conscious thought onto the beast, he began pulling with his mind and using his power to lure it closer.

Then the beast began to withdraw from Lynn as it began to understand what was happening. That's when Lynn closed his mental hands around the beast and pulled forward even harder. The power of the beast seemed to lash out at Lynn as the apparition fought to stay inside. Suddenly the beast did something unexpected and unprepared for.

With all of Lynn's mental guards down it leaped into his body trying to merge with his mind—or usurp it. Lynn knew if he didn't act quickly and place the beast back in Uri, then Uri would fade deeper into the collective unconsciousness and be lost to them forever.

He reversed the flow of energy and directed it back into Uri but just enough so it wouldn't be pushed back deeper into the depths of Ur's mind. Lynn knew it was working when he saw Uri's brown fur began to engulf his cut and bruised flesh.

His arms became twice their original length as his feet changed into talons. Gaia reached down to remove his mask while his face made the metamorphosis. Lynn rose to his feet dizzily to have Augustus catch him by the elbow to steady him.

Uri blinked his now feral eyes and jumped up quickly. He looked around the circle, roared and took flight. He stayed aloft for a few seconds then landed in front of Lynn. He bowed low before Lynn and King Augustus. His bow was noble but also looked kind of twisted and provocative in his were-animal form.

"Thank you Lynn, for saving me once again," he said while reverting back to his human form. Lynn smiled wanly at his healed friend as darkness fell over him.

Two figures stood in the fiery depths in the caves of Moorya. They conversed in the seclusion of the dark cave illuminated only by pulsing magma in fissures and cracks in the stone walls.

"I overheard you tell my father that you have a present now and one soon to be retrieved. Is this true?" asked Dante.

Christian turned to face Dante who he dwarfed easily. Christian couldn't believe that Dante would bring him here to ask him a question about something of this caliber, almost like testing his loyalty and his ties. He knew even though they were both true vampires, Dante surely was much stronger seeing as he was basically born into vampirism, while Christian himself just came around to the quintessence of being undead.

Christian's powers were blossoming well and fast but he can almost sense the strain in Dante holding back a powerful beast. It kept Christian wondering how powerful Dante truly is. Christian tried to shield all these thoughts but little did he know, Dante plucked them from his mind as easy as taking grapes from their vine.

Dante admired the big man for his efforts and decided not to say anything and let Christian think that he succeeded. "Everything that I told your father, my master, Niccolo, is true," said Christian choosing his words very selectively.

Dante smiled at Christian and said, "Show me."

Without saying another word Christian turned and lead Dante through and around the heated walls of the cave. After walking around many twist and turns they finally came to an opening where down below lay nothing but ever moving magma looking like a crimson lake being disturbed.

Across the void was the prize, the Staff of Locked Souls but to keep up the charades, Dante asked, "That is your prize? What the hell is that?"

Christian annoyed by the little prince took a deep breath and said, "It is the Staff of Locked Souls. It belongs to Lynn, but, I can't access the power of the staff unless I kill him. So, I decided to bring him here on my grounds where the opportune time will present itself."

Dante cuffed the big man on the shoulder and said, "You are truly unique and maybe I can help you in your goal. Just remember when the time comes, I could use allies like yourself. What do you say?"

Christian looked into Dante's eyes and thought, "What could he possibly need that I can help with. Then again, a chance to kill Lynn once and for all is too tempting."

"Alright, what do you plan to do?" asked Christian.

"This is how I'll bring him to you and what I'll need," said Dante taking Christian by the shoulder and leading him back through the cave to leave out.

Chapter: 14

"Lynn, Lynn . . . finally your coming around. Are you alright?" asked Maria sitting in a chair next to his bed.

Lynn sat up, rubbed and focused his eyes then asked, "What happened?"

Maria smiled and reached out to hold Lynn's hand, "You used your powers to save Uri. He's doing fine, it's you we're worried about. Admiral Jo said she and her crew are ready to weigh anchor as soon as you can make it down to the ship."

Lynn got up steadily out of bed and retrieved the katana from behind the headboard. Maria handed Lynn the sword that Augustus returned to him. Lynn looked at the scabbard and noticed that it was same type of reptile hide, green fading into a pearl color at the bottom.

Maria left out the room with Lynn soon to follow. Lynn stopped as he felt, not seen, the red glow from behind the headboard. He reached down and caught a hold of the thin cord attached to the red dragon crystal. Lynn peered into the crystal and was captivated by the once little flame inside that grew some.

He put the crystal around his neck and tucked it away under his tunic and made his way to the entrance hall. He rounded the corner and made for the front doors. The male servant there opened the door so Lynn didn't have to slow his stride. Lynn crossed the threshold to see Augustus, Le'Anne, Loraine, Lilander, Verne, Gaia, Uri and Maria standing in a semi-circle facing him with smiles on their faces.

They were clapping and congratulating him on returning to the land of the living. Uri stepped forward, "I'm not sure if you heard me before but thank you for saving my life. King Augustus has two coaches for us to ride in down to Iggarius Ports."

Lynn smiled at him and embraced him tightly then said, "You know, in some way we're all family and I won't let you or anyone else go that easily. Now, lets go ride this Grand Straight and stop this taint called Niccolo before he turns into an epidemic."

Everyone began clapping again when Maria went to Lynn and kissed him passionately not allowing him the chance to rethink this moment. Maria started crying when they finally decided to separate for some air.

Lynn asked, "Why the tears? Am I not standing in the arms of someone I love?"

Lynn wiped away her tears with a brush of his thumbs. She rested her head on his chest and said, "You just don't realize how close we were . . . I was to losing you."

"We are not out of the fire yet. We still have Niccolo after us. Are you ready to go?" Lynn said to her.

She nodded her head in response. They walked into the group of their friends. Lynn took Lilander's hand to shake it, but to Lynn's surprise, Lilander pulled him in close to embrace him. Maria followed suit, then Uri, Verne and lastly but not reluctantly, Gaia.

They held each other for a few seconds like a tree with the vines suffocating its trunk. Lynn got everyone to board the coaches. Uri, Gaia and Lilander rode in the rear coach while Verne and Maria waited on Lynn to board the lead coach along with them.

Lynn went to Augustus, Le'Anne and Loraine to bid farewell only to have them bow and curtsy to him. "Please, please don't, I'm not really that important," Lynn tried to reason.

Augustus spoke first, "Oh, but you are who we have been waiting for. You're the light in the darkness, the warm house in the middle of a dense forest, you are the living legend that has been foretold for aeons."

Le'Anne began, "Please Master Lynn, bring Lilander home safe. We have been betrothed practically since birth, but since the hunt to cure Lilandro began, we have been put on hiatus. It is time that he quit running from his duties."

Lynn saw the grin on her face when she said that. Loraine then said, "And my Uri. We have fell deeply in love and I will take no other man. No other man can match up to his stature of love in my eyes."

Lynn looked over at the coaches then back at the royal family and said, "I promise."

Lynn walked to the lead coach, stopped and looked back behind himself. Augustus, Le'Anne and Loraine were all smiling and waving. The coachman opened the door for Lynn so he could enter, closed it and started the horses on their destination.

"So, what do we do when we cross the Grand Straight?" Verne asked Lynn.

Lynn shrugged and looked out the small circular window and said, "As of right now I don't know. First, we have to make it over the waters safely. First that is."

When Lynn was finished speaking, Maria, who was sitting on Lynn's right, reached out and held his hand the rest of the ride as they rode in silence. They arrived in front of 'The Pablo' to have Tommy Hawkeyes waiting for them.

As the coaches came to a halt, Tommy ran to open the first coach door. After opening the door he turned for the second coach and said while walking to the coach, "Admiral Jo is in her cabin. She said to inform her of your boarding."

He opened the second coach door for Lilander, Uri and Gaia to step out. They all fell in together and bid Tommy to lead the way into the ship to see the Admiral. He did without hesitation.

They followed round the back of the briefing cabin to a trapdoor in the deck with stairs leading down into the vessel. They followed their lead through the dining hall to the other side where some more flights of stairs descended down into the ships bowels. Those stairs lead down to the storage level.

"These boxes were not stacked this high when first I came down this way with Pappy," Lynn said as they walked around large boxes and barrels.

"That's because now we are ready to depart. Before we were just sitting in port but once we have orders to depart we stock up on rations and other supplies," Tommy said enlightening Lynn.

When they rounded a few more they were stopped by the same five sailors who gave Lynn problems in the dining hall on his first visit down there.

"Now what do you want?" asked Tommy but they just moved him out the way.

The one who initiated the first ordeal spoke, "You," he said pointing at Lynn, "how did you do that the other day?"

Lynn relaxed after hearing him inquire about Lynn's battle tactics. "It's just second nature to me since I was taught at such a young age. You could learn it easily if your mind is willing," Lynn told him as they followed Tommy past the sailors.

They came to the stairs at the other side and descended to the bunk deck. They made their way to Admiral Jo's cabin in the bow without any interruptions or problems. They didn't have any problems until Tommy knocked and she didn't answer.

Tommy opened the unlocked door and peered in, brought his head out and said, "She's not home. I don't have any idea of where she could be. I mean she didn't tell me to meet at any other part of the ship."

Just then the second mate, Pappy Jones, came up from the stairs to the left of the Admirals cabin and said, "I thought that was you. Tommy, you did a good job and yes she was in there but we had a problem with the pipes on the boiler deck below. Follow me."

They followed Pappy and Tommy down the stairs and set their eyes on pipes lining the walls, going this and that way, turning and disappearing into more tangles of pipes. Along the walls were large black furnaces that were roaring with fire in their bellies. Halfway down the deck stood Admiral Jo talking to the one in charge of the boilers.

She stopped what she was talking about with him when she noticed their presence and said, "Oh, hi, this is Burner Pontello. Burner these are our guest, Lynn Thrax, Maria Maccio, Verne Wingo, Lilander Ravenholme, Uri Tanko and Gaia . . . um?"

"Just Gaia if you please," Gaia said shaking Burners' hand after everyone else.

"Ok Burner, back to what we were talking about," Admiral Jo resumed, "are we for certain that those pipes will make it through the Isle of Trapped Songs to the Ports of Weider?"

He nodded and said with a raspy choked up almost whispered voice, "Yes, as long as nature doesn't give us too much of a problem on the water."

Lynn was guessing that his voice was like that due to the working conditions down on the boiler deck. From looking at him anyone could tell he was serious about his work. He never drinks the night before or during a trip so as to be in top condition to face the ever unpredictable waters. His shirtless body was pale from spending so much time down on the lowest deck but the soot on his skin more than made up for his lost pigments.

No one who hasn't seen him clean could tell the true color of his auburn hair because of the mixed in soot. His hair had a close crop haircut to allow his muscular jaw line to stand out. By the look of him you could tell he was very muscular and athletic with scars adorning his body. Even Admiral Jo don't know how he got those scars. He stood about the same height as Lynn and made Lynn think he could be a challenge with his vigor and athletic looks.

"Keep me informed on the status of those pipes. We set out this hour," Jo told Burner.

He nodded and walked off to the stern of the deck. Admiral Jo turned to her guest, gave a relaxing sigh and smile then said, "Shall we go topside and get this beauty going?"

"Lead the way, Admiral," said Lilander as they created a hole for her to pass through.

No one really uttered a word as they made their way topside. Admiral Jo would occasionally call a sailor who looked like he wasn't busy and assigned him a job for the moment. When they finally made it to the briefing cabin, it seemed that Jo had just remembered she had guest following behind her.

"As you can see, this is my vessel and I run it in a sensible manner and order. You are my guest while aboard this ship. I'm not telling you to help out, but, if you feel the need, go right ahead. If you don't know the safety procedures, then at all cost, follow one of my men's lead. That will be all," she finished and went upstairs to the helm.

Lynn knew he was—but couldn't speak for the rest of his friends—shocked at her quick personality change from a really laid back almost gullible type to a vain, narcissistic person. But the love wasn't for herself but for the love of her beautiful ship and its passengers.

"You haven't even seen why they call her 'Cutthroat' yet," said second mate Pappy leaving the briefing cabin to go outside on deck.

Everyone followed him outside to see that the ship looked even more alive now that they were ready to weigh anchor. Smoke bellowed out of the stern where pipes protruded and the anchor was raised up to the bow. Tommy climbed to his post in the crow's nest.

They released the mooring line so that the ship was finally set free. The propellers stopped and the three sails were released simultaneously to catch the wind as they moved into the Grand Straight. As 'The

Pablo' set out along the Grand Straight, Lynn knew that there was no turning back.

It took nearly two days to reach the Isle of Trapped Songs. Darkness began to fall as they approached the Isle of Trapped Songs. It seemed almost surreal because the wind ceased which in turn stopped the melodies from the Isles leaving nothing but the sound of water splashing on the side of the ship and the neighboring Isles.

Everyone onboard became quiet as a mouse because they sensed something was wrong. Byron spoke to Lynn on the top deck, "Something isn't right. The wind has never stopped passing between these Isles. The wind just doesn't stop blowing on the open sea."

Tommy was in his crow's nest when he yelled down but tried to make it sound like a whisper, "Lilander, there's something out there. Whatever it is, it's on all the surrounding isles moving, wait more like creeping."

Lilander stood by Lynn in the middle of the deck looking around, "Do you see them?"

Lynn shook his head still looking for the current unseen presence. The wind suddenly picked up and blew an unnatural mist onto the ship extinguishing all lanterns topside leaving them in total darkness except from the eerie light of the moon. Then Lynn saw them coming over the sides of the ship, those yellow feral eyes.

"Vampires! Vampires are aboard the ship!" screamed Tommy from up in his nest.

Lynn spoke to Lilander, "Go up there and help Tommy out. You know as well as I do that he's easy prey up there, but–"

Lilander cut him off, "A great vantage point for me and my bow."

Lilander took off for the crow's nest and released three arrows at three targets up the pole. The arrows flew silently through the air and hit almost simultaneously as out of the darkness three vampire thralls hit the deck. Lynn beheaded a few thralls that had dared to attack him.

As Lilander made it to Tommy's side, Lynn screamed up to him, "Lilander! I'm going below deck to help the others and the sailors!"

Lynn didn't wait for a response but took off to the briefing cabin and slid down the pole to the kitchen deck to come up on Gaia fighting off some thralls. Lynn started slashing away with both blades taking heads in his onslaught to help his friend.

"I was just on my way to look for you for some help. Maria, Uri and Verne each took a floor to help defend. They just seeped through the cracks like the mist. Where is Lilander? Shouldn't he be here helping us?" Gaia bombarded Lynn with information and questions while still dealing damage to the thralls.

Lynn kept hacking away like a butcher in his art while saying, "He's topside with his bow and hopefully enough arrows in his quiver to take down any thralls coming his way."

They cut their way through more thralls to the next descending pole. Even as they slid down the hole more thralls showed up and began to follow pursuit. Their feet hit bottom on the next deck and they heard grunts of battle. The grunts were the familiar sounds of Verne fighting off some thralls.

"Verne, where are you? I have Lynn with me! We're coming to help!" yelled Gaia.

Gaia soon realized her mistake because no sooner had she finished speaking, vampire thralls came hurtling and snarling over the boxes at Gaia and Lynn.

"Let's show these abominations what four blades could do wielded by two deadly experts," said Gaia unsheathing both her blades.

Lynn unsheathed his katana and his Blood Sword then crossed them over his chest. Lynn lashed out at the next thrall in the air as it came at him. As the female thrall hit the ground, the gashes Lynn put in her chest and abdomen were already healing but not quick enough before Lynn took her head.

More thralls came over and around the boxes and were easily ran through. Lynn and Gaia quickly went around the boxes toward the bow by the ascending stairs. Lynn and Gaia froze in astonishment to see Verne holding his own, no, more like toying with four thralls. Gaia broke her trance first and roused Lynn out of his to help Verne.

The thralls seemed to have unaccountable endurance while Verne was tiring faster and faster. A thrall grabbed Verne's neck from behind, readying to break it until his hands fell to the floor separated from his body. Lynn and Gaia stood on each side of Verne with their swords bloody from the separation of the thralls hands.

As Lynn caught the exhausted Verne under the arm, Gaia took the handless thralls' head and followed the two men to the next descending pole. They made their descent to hear growls of frustration coming from around various bunks. In the blink of an eye they caught sight of Maria running, ducking and dodging between bunks to avoid the clutches of oncoming thralls.

Verne, Lynn and Gaia started mimicking Maria's movements, moving around the bunks trying to catch up with her. After a few moments of running, they finally caught Maria but it wasn't the one they knew and if they didn't know about her new weapon, they would have been even more frightened at the sight.

"Ahh!" Maria screamed and was about to attack until she realized who it was.

"I didn't know it was you guys. I've been trying to hold them off as best I can but they keep coming," she said with that demi-god like voice.

With her voice still ringing in Lynn's head, he looks at her intently and says, "You're still wearing the Black Widow mask? Don't answer, we'll have plenty of time later to talk. Right now, we need to go and help Uri then we can start our extermination."

They took up their weapons and made these thralls on this deck into the dead corpses they were meant to be. Head after head was taken and rolling on the floor releasing the thralls of the monstrous virus in their body, the hell-born curse placed on their souls. The descending pole was only a few feet away when Gaia fell to the floor.

"Go on down and help Uri, I'll get Gaia," Lynn told Verne and Maria motioning for them to go down the pole.

Lynn ran to Gaia's side with both blades drawn and ready. He saw that a thrall had caught hold of Gaia's leg and was attempting to pull her under and around a bunk but she held on to one of the legs of the neighboring bunk. Lynn first threw his Blood Sword then his katana soon followed.

The former impaling the thrall in her forehead, the latter slicing through her neck eviscerating her head. Lynn stopped by Gaia's side and picked her up. "Do you have any injuries? No bites?" He asked her.

Gaia shook her head while looking over her body. While she did that, Lynn retrieved his weapons from the floor and joined her at the descending pole. Gaia waited till Lynn stood beside her then descended with Lynn immediately behind.

The scene resembled a star and moonless night with fires spread out amongst a sleeping camp. These fires were actually the bellowing boilers.

Both Uri and Maria were on the ceiling and walls dodging pipes and battling thralls that followed their lead.

Verne, Burner and Pappy were taking on the attack from the floor. "Uri, down here, I have a plan but I need you for it to work!" Lynn screamed up to Uri as himself and Gaia began helping on the floor.

Uri ran across the wall slicing through three thralls disorienting them and causing them to fall to the floor stunned. He then leapt off the wall and landed by Lynn's side. He kept battling while asking, "What's the plan? They seem to be coming from everywhere."

"I need you to change. Your scream can drive them back," Lynn said while dodging one attacking thrall.

Uri and Lynn now stood back to back fending off the snarling thralls. Uri asked, "And how will that help us?"

A female thrall dressed in peasants clothing with blood still fresh on her cheek lunged at Lynn. Lynn sidestepped the thrall and impaled her through the back with his Blood Sword then proceeded to take her head with his katana.

"Vampire are supposed to be supernatural creatures of the night with heightened senses," Lynn said when they were close enough again.

"And?" Uri said concentrating on his fighting, "I still don't understand where you're going with this."

"They can see in the dark like an owl in the night. They can smell with the uncanny sense of a wolf," Lynn paused to let it register in Uri's head while his pupils turned to little white dots.

His arms grew double their original length and sprouted that silky membrane known as wings. His brown fur emerged just as his talons and ears grew out. When the change was finished, he flapped his great wings and let out a piercing scream sending the thralls fleeing for the stairs. Lynn only heard a slight high pitched sound like a whistle.

Everyone followed Uri to the next deck and did the same there. They did this until they finally emerged topside trapping the vampire thralls. The thralls could choose their demise between the wanted warriors and angry sailors or the ever flowing waters. The thralls growled and lashed out in frustration not attacking but shifting uneasily where they stood.

Uri took flight and circled the ship in stealth in the night sky. The thralls knew that their only chance was to fight or go overboard. Vampires were never known for their cowardice. They started forward going in for the kill. Everyone braced themselves for the strike but it never came.

The thralls were instantly cut down by dozens upon dozens of arrows impaling them through the chest.

"It's Lilander and Tommy. They're still in one piece," Lynn said looking up into the night towards the crow's nest.

"So that's where he's been hiding all this time," Maria said with that voice she only has when donning the Black Widow mask.

Lynn looked Maria over and said to Gaia and Verne, "Stay here. Maria, come with me, we have some heads to take."

Lynn pulled out his Phase Spider mask and donned it also. Lynn and Maria ran along the rails, one to each side, to come up behind the thralls and began their attack. As they attacked from behind, Lynn screamed to the others, "Now, deal them the true death."

The sailors and his friends came forward at Lynn's command taking heads. Uri would swoop down and rip heads off with his talons or slice through the necks with his wings. They eventually killed all the thralls on deck and let out a mighty cheer.

The cheers quickly died down as everyone set their eyes on Admiral Jo on the helms roof battling another vampire. The only difference between this vampire and the others is that he wore a red cloak with a white long sleeve dress shirt and some black pants and black loafers. His hair fell brownish blonde to his neck in a ponytail and looked awfully familiar to Lynn.

"Dante," Maria said adding a little bit of a hiss to her voice.

Lynn phased himself to the crow's nest just above Lilander and Tommy, rephased and said, "Lilander, see if you can hit Dante down below you."

Lilander nodded but Tommy almost fell out of the nest when he set eyes on Lynn. Lilander caught hold of Tommy's collar and steadied him. Lilander and Tommy pulled their bow strings taut and let fly two arrows at Dante's back while he battled Jo.

Dante swung his blade behind his head and stopped the arrows with the broad side of his blade. Uri swooped down just a little over Dante and prepared to unleash his sonic scream until Dante threw a splayed hand up and forced Uri to the bow of the ship.

"Telekinesis!" said Tommy.

Lilander asked, "Lynn, did you feel it?"

He looked up to see that Lynn no longer occupied the spot above them. when he looked back down he saw Lynn crawling down the pole towards Dante and Jo. Lynn lurked down the pole but had his progress halted when Dante shot his sword in front of Lynn using his telekinesis.

Lynn phased from where he was to a few paces behind Dante. When Lynn rephased back to the material plane Dante already had Jo, held fast around the throat, smiling at Lynn with those needle point cuspid.

"Isn't this a surprise, me anticipating your movements. The one my father is going mad over. What is it that you have that he wants so bad?" Dante asked but didn't expect Lynn to answer.

"I have already ended Ruffio's miserable existence and I will finish your father's also along with your whole line," Lynn said with that demi-god like voice.

The remark caught Dante by surprise and angered him, "You? You're mine."

Dante summoned his sword to him but made it go for Lynn before returning to its master. Lynn back flipped onto the blade and rode it to Dante. Dante tried to stop the sword before it reached him but Lynn already had enough momentum and jumped free with both his swords out to his sides.

Lynn slashed at him as he passed over Dante's head but Dante ducked and avoided Lynn's attack. When Lynn turned to face Dante he had his sword by his side with Jo still in his vise grip.

"Dante, go ahead and kill me like you killed my sister," Jo strained the words out.

Dante threw her at the ground at Lynn's feet. "Oh, but she isn't dead. She walks the earth just like you and . . . hell just like me."

Lynn helped Jo to her feet as Dante laughed vigorously. Jo spoke, "She might as well be dead, prince of lies."

Dante smiled, sheathed his sword and began forming a mist, "I feel flattered that you hold me in such high regard, but, I could never hold a torch to Him. In time you will share the same fate as your sister, little Jo. Lynn, you know where the caves of Moorya are. Christian awaits you there with your staff."

He finished talking and dissipated. The wind mysteriously picked up like a cork was pulled from a wine bottle and expunged the aroma causing the sad melodies to began again and once more becoming the Isle of Trapped Songs. Every one on 'The Pablo' were on edge for the rest of the night. No one slept not even daring to give those animals another chance to surprise them.

Chapter: 15

Niccolo paced his private chamber, thinking of different ways to torture and skin this cat named Lynn. Every time he tried to put his mind on something more productive his mind would some how drift back to Lynn. The name that he was finally able to put a face to with Maria's help has been plaguing his every waking moment. How he convinced Maria to turn against him Niccolo still didn't know. Her mind was cut off to him.

"Where have I been going wrong," he thought to himself, "my eyes to Lynn are now gone. My son is changing in more ways than one and it seems that my thralls are becoming second rate to this group of warriors"

"You still haven't killed him yet?" said that old wise voice with a tinge of youth in Niccolo's mind.

Niccolo at once brought up a mental picture of his grandfather, Ruffio. His grandfathers sinister smile appeared in his minds eye. The person who started Niccolo on this path paced around in Niccolo's mind awaiting an answer from his heir.

"Well," He demanded.

"Do you feel him on that side with you?" Niccolo asked his grandfather.

"No," came the answer.

"Well, then that means I am still pursuing it."

"Let me know if this simple task is too difficult and daunting for you and I would be more than happy to see your arrogant son," Ruffio threatened.

"No, you showed me the mysteries and I in turn showed him. There is no need for Dante to be in your grace, only I am worthy or have you forgot, you sought me out. Only I opened my mind and accepted you without hesitance."

"You flatter me grandson but it won't work with Lynn."

"You've mastered going into the past and witnessed the first vampire created and how to alter the characteristics. You taught me these things and for that I am grateful. Yet, you still haven't mastered the future travel. Why, if I may ask again?"

"I have told you once before, the future can not be controlled or altered. The future may be open to a select few like a book, but, what is written can't be changed. Enough talk about what I can do, you need to do with Lynn what I instructed or someone else will be brought into the fold," Ruffio threatened again before breaking connection.

Niccolo was seething and showed his frustration by picking up one of his sofas and hurling it at the door causing it to burst into pieces. The tumultuous noise was followed by a quick knock. The door opened slightly as the splinters and broken chunks of wood fell to the floor.

"What?!" Niccolo screamed at the door.

Two thralls that both stood a few inches taller than Niccolo loped in and stopped just inside the door. They looked around like there was a fight that they just missed out on.

"Well?" It sounded like venom oozing from Niccolo's voice.

The thrall to Niccolo's left spoke, "Master Niccolo, your prey, the one you call Lynn, has crossed the Isle of Trapped Songs. He would've arrived on land sooner but was momentarily delayed."

"Who," Niccolo didn't mean it as a question but searched the thralls mind, "Dante."

The thrall to his right then spoke, "For what reason, we don't know. Every thrall that attacked with him perished."

Niccolo turned away and squinted his eyes into a sinister glare then said after plucking their minds again, "Dante escaped."

The thralls stood there until Niccolo waved them off. Niccolo thought, "What is my son trying to do? Why attack when Lynn is already on his way to meet his demise? Why attack him when he is on his way to me?"

Niccolo decided to ask Dante himself and reached his mind out to his egotistical and narcissistic son. He made the connection and Dante said, "Father, I don't have time for this right now."

"Oh, why is that? Does my son have to go lick his wounds. Let the grown ups handle this you bumbling idiot."

"If I were to let the grown ups handle this, I will be dead before I reach a millennium," Dante snapped then broke the connection and blocked his father out.

"How powerful are you?" Niccolo asked no one in particular.

'The Pablo' pulled into Weider Ports the following morning in one piece. The sails were torn and battered from the battle but it was still able to make the trip to port. It creaked along in the waters as it crept into the ports.

"Secure the mooring! Drop Anchor!" Jo yelled to anyone who heard.

Verne walked up to Jo with a message, "Jo, Admiral Jo, Lynn would like to speak with you before we disembark."

Jo followed Verne into the briefing cabin to see Lynn and his company standing on the other side of the circular table.

Yes?" She said with a smile but couldn't hide her restlessness in her tone.

"What is the condition of your men?" Lynn asked.

"Five casualties who are truly dead and not one of **them**. Almost half of my sailors are injured but not too bad. Byron has a broken arm from trying to protect me from Dante. I'm sure he won't let that stop him from lending a hand. He's really stub-"

Lynn held up his hand to stop Jo's mumbling. "I want to talk about what Dante said last night," Lynn jumped to the point.

"What are you talking about?"

"The incident with your sister," Lynn responded.

Jo took a seat then a deep breath and began telling the story of how her sister met Dante.

"One night when I was young when it was just me and my sister. Our parents had passed due to some unknown illness. She would work the farm while I handled matters inside the house. One day Dante appeared and it was a surprise and exciting because we never had any one come out that far to the farm."

"He immediately liked my sister and she fell for him in no time but she always resisted hi charms to a degree. One night she gave in and went with Dante and I had an eerie feeling so I decided to follow them.

I stayed hidden and witnessed the one thing a sibling should never be allowed to see."

"I witnessed his beastly side the demon that dwells inside him. He bit into her neck and cursed her that night with the disease of the undead. She lay there clutching at the last thread of life she had left. Dante left her there for dead and the last words he spoke to her were 'sleep now for your gift comes with a curse'. He left her lying there bleeding out like a child that was bored with its toy."

"I stayed there with my sister, holding her, crying for her but there was nothing I could do but watch as she lay there lifeless. I was surprised he didn't come back as loud as I was screaming. then miraculously she opened her eyes like she was coming out of a refreshing nap. I knew it was impossible what I was seeing. What was scary the most was that her eyes had a tinge of red to them like there was a blood lust lurking beyond them."

"She looked at me and told me one thing . . . run. That's all she said was run. I knew she was lost to me forever and that there was nothing I could do. It must have been a game of cat and mouse because not long after my sister was upon me throwing me to the ground readying to bite into her first meal. I don't know what stopped her but the last thing she told me was to tell everyone she died in an accident. I didn't know what to exactly tell everybody but I took them to her souls final resting place. The only thing that was there was her necklace she always wore that our father gave her on her tenth birthday," Jo finished the story not being able to hold her tears back any longer.

Maria went to comfort her but Lynn had to be sure and inquired some more.

"What was your sister's name?" Lynn asked.

"Tina Crow," she said through a sniffle.

Lynn released a breath he didn't know he was holding and relaxed a little. Then Jo said, "Of course she no longer goes by Tina. She is a very powerful Lady vampire so she goes by the name Ursula."

Everyone present shot glances at each other.

Jo asked, "What, why the surprise?"

Lynn resumed his inquiry, "How do you know that's her?"

"Well, there are a few sailors I listen in on in the pubs and they describe her to each other and exchanges her name. Those are the survivors but after a few days or weeks, their bodies turn up dead with the vampire teeth marks. Why do you want to know so much about Tina?"

"We've met with your sister before."

"What do you mean 'met with my sister'?"

Lilander answered, "We have met with her before and I know we will see her again."

Lynn and his companions left the briefing cabin with Jo in tow behind them. Before they made it to the ramp, Jo jumped in front of them and asked, "What are you going to do if you see her again?"

Lynn took a deep consoling breath, more for himself rather than for Jo and said, "She is a part of this taint that threatens our very existence. There are some vampires that are worth saving. Yet, if she crosses me, I will deal her the true death."

Jo let one tear fall down her cheek, "Thank you. I'm glad that her suffering could come to an end. She would be better off dead than cursed for eternity."

Everyone walked past her, hugging her in turn. They made it to the bottom of the ramp to see Tommy there waiting with a bow and quiver strapped to his back also with a smile as big as the former.

Tommy spoke in the elvish tongue, "Lilander, thank you for everything. Will I ever be able to come see you in Nospherat?"

"Of course, only if I come back alive. If Lynn dies, we're all dead," Lilander said and turned to face Lynn.

Tommy stepped forward and stood face to face with Lynn and smiled then hugged him tight around his waist and said in the common language, "Thank you all. We would've been food for the waters if you were not there."

"If we were never on your ship, you never would have been attacked," Lynn said while holding Tommy out at arms length.

"Yes, that's true," Tommy said, "but, you helped bring Lilander to show me a passion I didn't know I had and a part of a family I never expected to see again."

He held up his bow to Lilander and in return Lilander bowed his head to him. Maria and Gaia both kissed him on the cheek. Verne shook hands with him then Uri bowed in respect.

Before Lynn walked away he said, "Tell Admiral Jo to make for Kamma. If we don't return she will just be waiting in vain. If we survive, I can't say if we will be in a hurry to make it home. Also tell her thank you for allowing us passage aboard such a beautiful vessel. We will always be in her debt."

Tommy nodded and ran up the ramp to deliver the message. Lynn and his party left the port to enter the city, Draconus. They walked down the streets to see that the city wasn't very lively with only a person here or there. Draconus was the exact contrast of Kamma. The merchants shops were open but made no attempts to attract the attention of any potential customers.

No children played in the streets. Shutters to windows were closing as they passed by. Lynn stopped a passing lady, who's age looked to be in her forties or fifties, to ask why the city was so lifeless. When she raised her eyes from her short frame and looked into their faces she quickly backed away, turned and tried to run but was stopped when a gang of eight thralls surrounded her.

Seeing what was about to happen, everyone began to walk towards the group while Uri ran ahead of them on the walls of nearby buildings. Uri jumped into the center of the thralls, grabbed the woman up by her waist and jumped back to another building then behind his friends for safety.

Uri let the woman go and she instantly ran in fright but Uri couldn't tell who she was frightened of, them or the thralls. The thralls eyes had followed Uri back to where everyone now stood in the street. He snarled bearing his fangs.

"How dare you int-. Lynn Thrax, the one Master Niccolo seeks," said the thrall in the immediate front of the group.

He stood about six-foot-three with brown curly locks falling to the middle of his neck. His build was an average build for someone his height. His face was gaunt as if he just came out of the desert. He wore a vest with long black snake skin pants.

On his left shoulder was a mark that no one in Lynn's company knew what it meant. Lynn smiled and unsheathed both his swords letting that send the message to everyone else. The lead thrall shot a glance over his shoulder and one of the other thralls took off running from the scene. When he was gone there were only seven thralls left for Lynn and his friends to decimate.

"I feel cheated some how," Gaia said humorously.

The thralls began to flank out trying to get a good position to attack from. Three of the thralls began climbing the walls of the buildings going towards the group of warriors. A noise erupted from behind them. It was people running away from and making way for what was to come.

"Lynn, behind us," Maria said nudging Lynn to get his attention.

Lynn turned his head to see more thralls coming up behind them. The lead thrall was now smiling when Lynn looked back at him and said, "As you can see, I sent my friend to gather up some artillery. Now you have to deal with a gang of hungry vampires."

Lynn showed a sly grin and said, "Did you actually think that by more of you coming that you would actually be able to take us? You must have only heard the name and not the feats we have performed against your kind."

"I know what you can do, but, that means nothing when you stand in front of Dillon."

"You do know that by you summoning more thralls, you only shorten our trip from hunting all of you down?" Lynn said while taking his battle stance as did his friends.

The thralls rushed them like a tidal wave crushing down from all sides attempting to overwhelm them with numbers. The six warriors began their fight with the thralls taking a few heads as soon as they came in range. Lilander was demolishing thralls with is elegant daggers. His movements were swift, precise and smooth as moving water. Ever flowing freely in and around everything never being contained. Every time a thrall managed to grab Lilander he would slip loose and strike like the mongoose plays with a cobra.

Verne fought with what seems to be almost like he was possessed or driven by a hatred and vengeance. His face was battle worn but looked as if his physical shell knew no bounds. Verne brutally cut, slash and hacked through the pitiful creatures.

Gaia had her armor activated and slicing through thralls like a dao-tug warrioress. As she overwhelmed more and more of them with her prowess they seemed a bit hesitant to go into battle against her. Uri constantly kept flipping through the air, dodging the thralls that were on the ground and the ones leaping at him in the air.

Every time he touched ground by a thrall he would whip out his sword lightning quick, take the head, and move on before the thralls ashes hit the ground. To the thralls, it seemed that Uri chose his targets at random and was unsure of where to be when the blue clad ninja landed.

Maria was doing fine for a time but started getting overwhelmed as more thralls came from within the city. She kept trying to reach for her

Black Widow mask but the constant barrage of thralls interfered with her attempts every time. The thralls choice was clear, be taken or die. Seeing this happen, Lynn placed his palms together bringing about his ancient power once again.

Lynn felt all of his abilities at a thought now: the ability to slow time, levitate, telekinesis and telepathy. Lynn decided to slow time down this time around. Everyone moved a fraction of their speed in Lynn's eyes now. Lynn did a spinning attack with both of his swords out to each side of himself. Starting low and coming higher he took the heads of the thralls surrounding him.

He then flew to Maria's side and made the thralls relinquish their pressure by taking their heads also. Releasing his hold on time as the stress fro using his power began to strain, Lynn held Maria close as the fire burned from his completely white eyes while he surveyed the battle field. The others went and stood by Lynn and Maria and readied themselves for another attack.

"They seem to keep coming from everywhere. Does anyone have any ideas on how to get out of this one?" Verne said to the group but not daring to take his eyes off of the lurking thralls.

"Everybody, stand down," Lynn said sheathing his swords and retrieving his dragon crystal from around his neck.

"What?!" The group said as a whole.

"Just do as I say and trust me. Its time we sent them on their way," was Lynn's reply to them.

They hesitated for a moment then reluctantly put their weapons away. The thralls started coming even faster seeing the weapons sheathed. Lynn raised his arms above his head, levitating the crystal just in between his hands. A few thralls advanced on the ground while a good handful leapt through the air at the surrounded prey.

The crystal felt the power Lynn was feeding it as it pulsated then released the celestial light from within itself. Blinding light filled the area forcing everybody in the vicinity to close their eyes except Lynn. The light felt warm against the body's of Lynn's friends. They could hear the damned souls of the vampires as they succumbed to the power of the dragon crystal.

When the light returned to the dragon crystal just as fast as it came, Lynn's powers had receded to the depths of his mind also from the strain.

Maria, Gaia, Uri, Verne and Lilander still stood there with their hands covering their eyes.

"Lets move. We are still in the thick of things and we need to keep moving," Lynn said to them while looking around at his surrounding.

People and faces started showing up and looking out windows curious of what the warm light was. Lynn didn't have time to explain so they quickly made their way to a local inn. They had a hard time paying for some rooms but eventually convinced the owner to allow them to stay. The inns lobby had a few tables here and there with three booths along the wall by the front door.

The counter stood adjacent to the hall where the dwellings were. From what they could see behind the counter, the place served drinks and hot meals. The proprietor was fairly short about five-foot-six, with a potbelly. His face was about as stout as a pig with a nose to match it.

The bald spot on his head is probably what upsets him every morning when he awakes and realizes that its not a dream but reality, its really his hair leaving him to face the world alone. They had a hot meal then all retired to there respective rooms.

Later that night, Lynn lay alone in his bed facing away from the door unable to sleep when he felt a small draft of air. Goosebumps formed on his skin as the cold touch of night sent chills all over his body.

He didn't hear it but he knew it was his door opening and closing without the slightest sound. Lynn made no sudden movements as he waited for whatever phantom was there to make the first move. Lynn crept his hand under his pillow and almost had his hand around the Blood Sword until a soft cool hand barely touched his face.

He still didn't move.

The hand went from his cheek down to his neck then to his chest. He instantly grabbed the hand and held it there feeling the tender softness of the little hand in his.

"Lynn," Maria whispered, "it's me. I came to offer myself to you."

"No," he said in an even, stern tone.

She continued her caresses, "Please Lynn, I need you."

"I said-" he was cut off by his own groans as she started to fellatio him.

The sensation that he felt when being in that moment with her overcame all of his reasoning. She felt him become even more aroused and knew he wanted her when he started feeling her firm breast. He lifted her mouth to meet his then he pulled away and whispered, "Now you."

Before she could utter a word he licked the rim of her depths teasing her with every touch. She became short of breath as she began to feel herself feel something within her that she hasn't felt in what seemed a lifetime and she knew that he knew she was ready. She started moving her hips in rhythm with his oral stimulation. Lynn then took Maria and laid her down on her back and steadied himself in between her thighs just above her precious flower like a bee ready to pollinate.

"Please," she begged pulling at him with all her need and want for him.

He obliged and entered into her moist fiery chasm making her breath catch up in her throat. They kept going back and forth using each others energy to go the distance neither has ever gone before. Finally she exploded in climax on him as he greeted her with his own finale to the show. They fell asleep tangled in each others arms and legs and still joined together the way they felt they were destined to be. Lynn could dream of no better place to be and neither could Maria.

When Lynn awoke the next morning, he awoke naked and alone in his bed. He tossed and turned in the sheets trying to fight his way out of the tangle he found himself in. He looked around the room for any sign of her. He saw not one thing that could have left a clue as to whether she was actually with him last night.

"Was it all just another one of my dreams," he thought.

He pushed the thought aside, leaned up on his elbows and yawned as he began to get out of bed. He got dressed and made his way down to the lobby for breakfast. The short fat proprietor was in the lobby sweeping dirt and dust out the door when Lynn showed up. Lynn peered around the lobby looking for any sign of his entourage.

He didn't see any of them but he let his eyes fall upon a cloaked figure sitting in the booth closest to the door with his cowl shadowing his face. Lynn acknowledged him with a small nod but the cloaked figure made no movements to respond in kind. Lynn felt that it was kind of awkward but quickly let it depart from his mind.

"Excuse me sir," Lynn called to the owner, "has anybody from my party been through here this morning?"

The owner stopped sweeping, looked over at Lynn and thought for a second. His dingy white shirt was moist from sweat and even wetter under his armpits. His red overalls were even more worn out and stopped just above the ankles. Probably from his belly. He scratched the bald spot on his head and said, "That one elf guy."

"Lilander," Lynn said so that the owner knows his name and that Lynn holds him in high regard as should the proprietor.

"Whatever," the owner said blowing away Lynn's notion, "he said some tin 'bout goin's fur uh walk 'round duh city. Said he's gots ta look inter some tin."

The owner sucked his tooth one time then went back to is sweeping. Lynn was about to tell him something about his rudeness until a soft cool hand landed on his own forearm. Lynn turned to whoever wanted his attention to see Maria smiling at him. Uri, Verne and Gaia were sitting further down the counter talking amongst themselves about what they were going to eat.

"I enjoyed last night," Maria whispered to Lynn as she pulled him by the hand to join the others.

Now Lynn knew it was no dream. Everything that happened the night before wasn't an illusion. That night spent in a moment of bliss with this woman that he met on the outskirts of the kingdom he served. Never thinking that they would actually fall for each other at a time like this but they did and they both enjoyed the company. After long nights of wanting to hold each other, Lynn knew that it was real.

"How are you? Are you alright?" Gaia asked Lynn in delicate manner that was rare to her.

She sort of surprised Lynn with her gentleness so he replied, "I've been better, but, I'll make it through the day."

Uri and Maria began talking on a subject of their own. Lynn decided to not pay attention to their conversation. Gaia immediately dove into her plate of food when the young maiden brought their breakfast to them. The maiden shot a flirtatious eye at Lynn. He smiled and gave her a friendly wave.

She was fairly young but of marrying age. Every time she smiled it was as if she had not a care in the world. She had freckles just under her hazel eyes by her thin nose that seemed to dance on her face every time she smiled. Her hair was brownish blonde that extended loosely to the middle of her back. Her hair looked so soft and free that every time she leaned forward it would hang down in front of her and get in the way.

Her body was blossoming well and Lynn wondered why this beauty has not yet wedded. The dress she wore extended to her ankles and was beige with a white sash around her waist and brown sandals on her tiny beautiful feet. Lynn let his gaze fall back on the cloaked figure in the booth by the door and was captivated by him but didn't know why. Verne started waving his hand in front of Lynn's face struggling for his attention.

"What?" Lynn snapped at him.

The look on Verne's face made Lynn realize where he made his mistake and who his company was so he apologized. Lynn pointed to the cloaked figure trying to put Verne's focus where his was. Verne took a peek at the cloaked person in the booth then back at Lynn. The look on his face was and inquiring one.

"Forgive me Verne I was just-"

"Lynn, what's wrong with you? I know yesterday was pretty draining on you and I wanted to make sure you was alright," Verne said close to Lynn so no one else could hear.

"Last night was draining also," Lynn thought.

"Don't worry, I'm alright. I just had a few things on my mind, that's all," Lynn said instead.

Lynn looked back at the booth to see the figure was no longer there. Lynn quickly looked at the door to see it just close. Lynn rushed to the door, but in a way as to not bring suspicion to himself, and exited out into the street. He looked to the left, nothing but people coming and going, then to his right, and the same as before.

Lynn heard something from his left he didn't hear or see before, the thud of galloping hooves. He ran to his left and paused just at the entrance to the alley and saw the cloaked figure on horseback bearing down on him. Lynn took a few hesitant steps back thinking that the horse would run him into the dirt under his feet.

Out of nowhere a mist appears and takes a hold of man and beast then disappear as quickly as it came. Lynn started to walk into the alley but was halted by a stern but smooth hand gripping his forearm. He spun around to see a cloaked figure with his cowl on his head.

He pulled off his cowl and said, "What's wrong? Has something happened?"

"I'm fine, Lilander, its just that-" Lynn was cut off as Lilander escorted him back into the inn.

"No, no, nothing happened. It's just that rider looked out of place somehow," Lynn said after taking a seat in the exact booth where the cloaked figure just sat.

Lilander sat across from him and said, "I noticed him watching me also as I left earlier. I didn't want to approach him alone so I figured I could go for a walk and hopefully he would still be here when you and the others woke up."

"Good. I'm glad you didn't approach him. He just didn't seem right. So, what did you have to go look into?"

"Well, I took a walk around few parts incognito so as to get the whole story."

"What whole story?" Lynn asked impatiently.

Lilander held up a cautioning hand, "I've not seen nor heard of any vampire activity going on in the city. There are a lot of people who are grateful for what we did, also, there are people who want our heads for what we did. I think our little scuffle destroyed the bulk of them and however many were left in the city got out quickly."

"That's all good news to hear but why would some of the people want our heads?"

"Well, there are some people who liked their presence and literally dying to be one of them, I guess."

The proprietor delivered two drinks to Lynn and Lilander. "Yurr friends o'er der," he pointed at Verne, Maria, Gaia and Uri who were sitting at the counter eating breakfast, "send you d'ees. Dey also ordered yous some break-fast which should bees out shortly."

He walked off before Lynn and Lilander could thank him.

"That guy really is rude. He acted that same way when I was leaving for my walk," said Lilander after taking a sip from his mug.

They busied themselves by talking about their journey until the young maiden brought their plates to them. The sausage cakes still had steam rising from them with freshly baked rolls and scrambled eggs. The young maiden leaned over the table showing off her cleavage and said, "Please excuse Papa, he kind of liked the vampires being around. Me and Mama kept tellin' him he was signing a death wish by 'liking' their presence."

"Why is that? Him liking their presence, I mean," asked Lilander.

She looked at him with her hazel eyes, "He thinks that they've been keeping robbers and looters out of the city but if you ask me, I think they just convert them and then feed on the law abiding citizens."

"What about the city's commerce?" Lynn asked getting her attention back on him.

She shrugged her shoulders and before she walked away said, "Our only real profit comes from the other side of the Grand Straight since the cities to the north have been put off limits by a force even more powerful than the vampire Lords."

When she was gone, Maria went to the booth and sat beside Lynn. "Maria," Lynn said, "I've been wondering. If vampires are children of the night then why can these specific vampires be out in the daylight when it should be safe?"

Maria began the story about how Niccolo's rise to power came into fruition, "When Niccolo was young before he learned of his grandfather Ruffio and his deeds Niccolo was always wondering when Ruffio would return. Eventually the loneliness turned into worry. From there it blossomed into the need to investigate the disappearance of Ruffio because he knew there was no way he would leave him alone."

"After much searching he soon found that his grandfather had succumb to the one known Lynn Thrax, or you." She looked over at Lynn when she said that.

She continued, "After finding out who took Ruffio's life he soon found where that village buried his grandfathers' remains. He retrieved the body and took it home for a proper burial in the family plot. Not knowing that his grandfather dabbled in the black arts he soon found out when he entered the family burial that Ruffio didn't just go there to honor his ancestors."

"From there he found his grandfathers' secret library but that was not the only thing he found. Ruffio some how left a piece of his spirit, his psyche in one of the books of the black arts. Niccolo began a long close relationship with his dead grandfather on his studies and how the curse known to man was actually a gift given by the Prince in the darkness. The curse we know as vampirism is actually a gift."

"Wait," Gaia interrupted, "how is it a gift? They are the reason why the immortals exist right?"

Maria shook her head, "No, the immortals were first but not as a natural enemy to the vampires. The immortals were created not to eradicate the vampires but to watch over man. They were meant to maintain the peace between nations. The vampires were once immortal also but they were created by the Prince of darkness and not by the King of creation. The Prince wanted to make them in his own image as his father did with the immortals. His father being upset that his own son would step out like that in defiance he struck down the Prince and his creations. One of those creations were his immortals who were turned into vampires."

"But why is it that vampires can kill an immortal and become stronger?" Lynn asked Maria.

"It's not that they become stronger. They become whole again. Yes, they maintain their vampiric powers but they once again become whole and that's why their weaknesses seem like they are no more."

"So Ruffio was a day walking vampire when my ancestor fought him?" Lynn asked her.

Maria shook her curly reddish blonde head and said, "No, he became an immortal after the fight with your ancestor. He supposedly already had a scheme on how to become a normal vampire but he had his future told to him. The medium who had once told his fortune told him if he kept going down that path then his adversaries seed will strike him down. Not understanding the future, he decided to go after you and in return, was struck down."

"He didn't fully understand that you were not the fighting type. He only knew that you had escaped when your ancestors perished. Instead of taking into account that you may have been frightened he figured you two were of the same mind and that you desired revenge. Truthfully you wanted peace. Like I said he went after you and in your sisters time of need you aided her."

She dug into Lynn's eggs before speaking again, "Now he showed Niccolo his secrets and made a pact with his grandson."

"What type of pact could that be?" Lilander asked after washing some of his meal down.

"Well, after Niccolo retrieved his grandfathers remains and then dispose of Lynn the pact would be set. He was successful in finding where that village hid and condemned his body. Now the last piece of the puzzle is you, Lynn."

"Why me?"

"Niccolo plans to resurrect Ruffio with your blood and life force," Maria finished explaining.

The young maiden came and removed their plates, offered to refill their drinks but Lynn declined and informed her and the owner that they were taking their leave the next morning.

They split up for the day and did what little shopping for rations they might need. Lynn and Maria went out in the town to gather some supplies. "So, the vampires are not whole and we are?"

"No, immortals are not whole either."

"What do you mean we're not whole? We don't have to consume blood to stay alive."

"No, you don't need blood but you do need the essence of a dying person. You see, the immortals were made that way by the Almighty King so that there would be balance. Your kind were meant to watch over man but not reign. Which is why when you go years without taking in an essence you began to age like every one around you."

"How did you know about that?"

"There is much lore in Niccolo's stronghold about your kind."

"Oh, so I guess that's why he knows how to kill us."

"Yes."

"Hmm, well now I know how he knows that taking my head will kill me."

"Yep," Maria's attention was now elsewhere. Lynn looked to see her checking out the produce on the fruit stands. Lynn dropped the conversation and began to shop around the wares with her. They returned to the inn after a day of shopping for more rations for their journey and more medicinal herbs.

At the end of the day before retiring, Verne consulted Lynn, "I found out why the owner's daughter isn't wedded."

"Oh, why is that Mr. Sleuth?"

"I hear she's a nymph. She can't be satisfied with one mate."

"Verne, leave it alone and go get some sleep."

"Ok, but if she visits me tonight, I won't turn her down."

Lynn left Verne in the hall and went to sleep with no nightly visitors this time around. The next morning they greeted each other in the lobby. Verne looked whipped and tired like he was up majority of the night. Whether it was Verne waiting or him engaging Lynn didn't know and he didn't ask. They paid for their rooms then left. They made it through the city, which seemed a bit more lively now, without any problems from anybody or anything. In the distant horizon sat the volcano that housed the Caves of Moorya.

"Behind that volcano is Niccolo's stronghold," Maria said out loud for everyone to hear.

"Well, lets go destroy this small epidemic before it spreads too far out of control," Lynn said tightening up his gear.

Chapter: 16

Dante stood outside his father's door that lead to his chamber with the cloaked figure that was watching Lynn back at the inn in Draconus. They were speaking in a low volume so as to not allow Dante's father the chance to know they were outside his door.

"So, you are certain that Lynn didn't see your face as you escaped?"

The cloaked figure gave a slight nod and smirk under his cowl, "I'm sure he didn't see my face or I'm sure they would have been more adamant about chasing me down. I know Lynn and his entourage. They would have chased me down at all cost seeing as they left me in that accursed village. Verne knew I was ready to leave and find my own power."

"Well, I must say the information you have provided me with should be more than sufficient."

Dante was about to knock when Niccolo's voice somehow leaked through his mind barrier, "Dante, come in. You have been standing there too long and invite your guest in with you."

Dante growled low in his throat in frustration, pushed his father out of his mind and entered into Niccolo's chamber. Upon entering the massive room, Dante looked around until he spotted Niccolo in one of his large chairs looking out of the windows. Dante escorted his guest in front of Niccolo and was surprised to see his fathers' eyes closed and a smile playing across his lips.

"What are you smiling about father?" snarled Dante.

"Thank you grandfather," thought Niccolo before answering his son.

"You're changing, my son. Your psyche is different from what I use to sense when you were a youth," he said ignoring his son's tone.

He opened his eyes and set them upon the cloaked figure and asked, "Who are you and what do you want from me?"

"The question is what do you need from me?" said the anonymous person.

Niccolo sneered and said," You are a bold one. What is your name? Wait could you be, Macdowl? I've heard of your exploits since a one, Verne Wingo, made you leader of his clan."

Macdowl walked to the window and peered out for a few seconds. When he turned to face Niccolo once again he said, "Your son warned me of your power and I must say you are correct, yet, you don't need my name just to receive my advice."

Niccolo sat up straighter giving Macdowl his full attention, "Flattery will get you nowhere, but, advice you say?"

"Yes, advice," said Macdowl, "on a few nuisances and their weaknesses."

With Dante's help, Macdowl knew he would be able to give away just tidbits about himself to hook the big fish. He read Niccolo's face and felt the small tug at the back of his mind but brushed it away like a butterfly on a flower.

"Well, let's hear your advice," said Niccolo.

Macdowl gave Dante a look and took Niccolo by the shoulder to the ivory top table with golden intricate legs. Macdowl traced a finger across the designs of the table top. Dante knew his cue and left the room so they could be alone. Outside the chamber he formed a mist and made his way to the Caves of Moorya where he will wait with Christian for Lynn Thrax and his entourage.

They made their ascent up the side of the volcano. Some of them were being extra careful because the rocks were pulsating with heat as they went higher up. Magma filled cracks were like veins rolling down the side of the mountain side. Rocks sizzled and popped as they melted under the blazing liquid.

"Is this an active volcano?" asked Verne keeping his eyes on every spot where he stepped. He really didn't want to have his foot melted off by a mountain.

"Yes, it is. Only one problem is it has been active for centuries but never released its fury since I can recall," Maria answered while trying to navigate the path up the volcano.

As they kept going they could feel the tremors getting more and more frequent and aggressive as the summit loomed near. They would have went higher but stopped when they came to an opening in the side of the fiery behemoth. They stood there looking at the ominous opening in the mountain. It loomed like a giant mouth waiting to swallow them into its fiery belly.

"This is the entrance to the Caves of Moorya," Maria paused as a fierce tremor shook the volcano, "It has never been agitated like this before. Its almost like the mountain is alive."

The opening stood almost three times as high as Lynn stood. The surface of the ceiling in the entrance was smooth like onyx. Slippery elusive salamanders crawled here and there. The amphibious little lizards crawled easily across the stone then magma with no recourse. Lynn was amazed that the little creatures were able to skate across the molten liquid and not be consumed in its fire.

"The perfect place for those creatures," thought Lynn as he made sure not to step on any underfoot.

"Those things are amazing," Maria said barely audible enough for Lynn to hear.

"But how?" Lynn asked still confused by the unbelievable sight.

"Salamanders on this mountain, for some reason have, always been able to survive on this magma without being injured."

"Wow. Truly amazing," Lynn said as he turned back to walk into the volcano.

"I can't believe my predecessors would build something like this," thought Gaia mesmerized by the beauty and horror of this magnificent force of nature.

Nobody knew but Uri smiled behind his mask looking into the shadows of the cave. Just the allure of being in a place that housed so many shadows excited and intrigued him. Verne gripped his sword hilt over and over nervously. He didn't know what traps awaited him and his friends beyond this obstacle.

"Is there any way we can speed this trek up and get out of here?" Verne voiced his nervousness with a slight tremor to his voice.

Lilander stood there stern and ready for anything to happen. His bow was slung around his chest and his daggers slightly free of their sheath ready for any ambush. He softly caressed the hilt of one of his daggers and softly repeated an incantation under his breath.

They walked into the opening and the ground began to slope up and drift to the left. Their only source of light came from little fissures of pulsing magma. They made sure to not walk to close to these tiny fissures because some were actually miniature fissures and not just craters and would pop and hiss every now and then. They made it to a wall where the only path to take was to go left. When they took that path they came upon two more choices, straight or right.

Lynn walked up to the fork and stopped to ponder a means of operation. He turned to his fellow travelers and said, "Uri, go that way and inform me of where it leads. If there's another fork let me know as soon as you can find us. The rest of us are going this way. Do you need anyone to accompany you?"

Lynn stood looking down the right path with Uri at his side. Uri shook his head, removed his mask and changed into his werebat form. He couldn't take flight in the cave cause his lycanthrope form was too big in the narrow cave. He just lurked along in his assigned direction. Everyone else started walking straight and before long heard a slight squeak reverberate in their ears.

"Smart," said Lilander.

Verne asked still looking a bit nervous more so now that one of their party was separated, "Huh. What's smart? I don't think us hearing an unidentified noise in this cave is smart."

"No. Uri used his sonic scream to guide him through the cave."

"Yes, that is what he did. Great idea sending him Lynn," Gaia said commending the immortal.

They kept walking and the path turned sharply to the left as the ground sloped down. When the ground stopped its slope there was a long pathway with a light reflecting off the walls from the far ends. They made their way to where the light illuminated from to see a rock pillar in the middle of moving magma.

Lynn, Maria and Verne wiped the sweat from their brow. Gaia and Lilander had their own way of dealing with the heat by controlling their own body temperature. Uri suddenly dropped down from the ceiling directly in front of everybody almost startling them to yield their weapons.

"Sorry," Uri said while jumping back a bit, "but the way you sent me had a fork in it alright, one leading right and one veering left. I took the right fork and it turned sharply to the left and sloped down and lead to a large cavern with a large hole in it that lead down into another cavern that lead to nowhere."

"How did you get back up?" asked Verne.

"He's a werebat," Lilander said to Verne not showing any frustration for his question. Lilander then turned to Uri, "What about the other fork?"

"I didn't go. I came right back to tell you all what was down the other side. I smell fresh air coming from that way," Uri said and pointed to the right of where they were standing leading down a path that bent around the inner wall of the volcano.

Maria stood looking up into the night sky, "What about the opening up top?"

"I don't mean to sound rude but I said I smell fresh air coming from that way. That's what I meant," Uri said after changing back to his human form.

His mask was back on quickly since he never let anyone set eyes on his face. Uri nodded to Lynn after his mask was on.

Maria walked over to Lynn and asked, "Are you sure that we need to go this way?"

"Well, I'm not leaving until I get what I came for," Lynn said turning back the way they had come.

Halfway back down the pathway leading away from the moving magma they were ambushed by a brood of four gray short neanderthal's that resembled a ghastly looking Halfling. They were accompanied by one large troll that just about took up the path in height and width. The short abominations attacked like a pack of wild dogs hoping to overwhelm one person while their pet troll handled the rest.

Their choice wasn't a very good one because when Gaia saw them heading her way she activated her armor. She brought her palm rubies over the ruby on her chest and that immediately started the transformation. Her shoulder armor bulked up and produced an armored spine for her leading up to a helmet that covered only the top half of her face.

The shoulder armor spread its protection to harden her brassiere and drop a gold shield over her stomach to resemble a full breast plate. Her gauntlets extended to her upper arms with the golden armor bulking up a bit. Her boots produced armor also that stopped at mid thigh. The knee caps on her boots had a symbol of the world emblazoned on them.

She stood ready as they bore down on her looking like they were a group of small people plagued by some incurable disease that caused them to go mad. She didn't wield her weapons but delivered a series of punches and kicks to the little creatures. The troll attacked the others with its club held high while letting out a moaning battle cry.

Lilander nocked one arrow and shot straight for the trolls nostril. The arrow went clean in the trolls nostril and disappeared. The troll kept going not even feeling the dart pierce its brain. Before it got too close the troll stopped abruptly and fell at the warriors feet with its brains and blood oozing from its nostrils.

Seeing the troll cut down the shorter creatures stopped their assault and made a run for it back into the darkness from which they came after witnessing their key element get easily and effortlessly disposed of.

"I'm guessing it took a few good seconds for the troll to actually register in its small brain that there was an arrow in its head," Lilander said with a small smirk playing on his face.

They walked back to the fork that Lynn sent Uri to a few moments ago. They took the left path that lead straight with the walls protruding out a bit. There was a small section on the path where they had to squeeze through one at a time because the walls came together with only a few feet of walking space.

They walked a few paces to another fork so Maria asked, "Which way do we go now?"

Lilander pointed to the right, "My intuition is telling me this way."

Uri pointed to the left, "I don't doubt your intuition but I hear grunting coming from this way."

They stealthily made their way to the left which turned left sharply. Upon looking around the corner they saw a handful of thralls toying with two young women who looked to be from Draconus. Gaia's rage boiled over when she saw this happening and attacked the thralls not trying to go the stealth route anymore.

Maria went alongside her just as quickly while Lilander unsheathed his daggers and followed suit. The thralls turned to face the attackers with an evil grin showing that they were not the least bit surprised. Or frightened for that matter. More thralls dropped from the unseen ceiling of the cavern to land behind Lynn, Uri and Verne boxing them in.

Gaia, Maria and Lilander stopped in their places as they saw the trap unveil itself. The two women stepped forward with yellow feral eyes and spoke in unison, "Our masters await your arrival. If you'll follow us?"

They walked past the six warriors as comfortable as they are around each other. It almost seemed like the thralls knew that they would not be struck down by these six **guest** of theirs. The two female thralls held hands as they lead everyone back to the fork and took the path Lilander recommended before. Their hips swayed seductively with each and every step they took. Part of the vampire in them that makes them look appeasing to any unsuspecting victim.

The path started straight but then curved to the right and sloped up a little until it opened up into the center of the volcano. In the center was that same rock pillar that the six adventurers saw earlier but was now looking at the summit of that same pillar. Standing in the center of the rock pillar was . . .

Dante and Christian.

They were waiting patiently and looking at the six heroes that have wandered into their lair. The thralls all branched out to the side of the pathway to allow the soon to be dinner course to step forward.

"Welcome to the Caves of Moorya. This place is where your journey ends and mine begins," screamed Dante across the void.

Christian turned to the side to show the Staff of Locked Souls embedded in the pillar and said, "Here is your staff. You can have it only if you best me in battle and we both know since my awakening, that has been impossible for anyone. Even the likes of you."

Christian laughed and smiled his wolfish grin and stared at Lynn as if he could burn a hole through him. Lynn felt his hand slowly going for the hilt of his katana. Christian seeing Lynn's hand started laughing. Just then Dante stretched his arms out to his sides and said, "Behold, your resting place."

A mist descended upon everyone present. Thralls, Lord vampires and six heroes all together. When the mist cleared, they stood on the summit of the volcano. Dante and his thralls stood a short distance behind Christian while Lynn's friends stood a ways behind him but too close to Dante for comfort.

"There were even more thralls than the ones that escorted us," Lynn noted to himself.

Christian unsheathed his mighty sword and pointed the heavy blade one-handed at Lynn and said, "This is where we end your running around."

Lynn shook his head slowly, "The world was not destined to go the route you will lead it down. Things are destined to change, and so . . . will . . . I."

Lynn unsheathed his katana then his Blood sword from its green and pearl bottom reptile hide scabbard. A surprised look shown on Christian's face as he saw and heard the blade ring true.

"So, you found another pretty blade to replace your lost staff. Isn't that the same blade King Augustus tried to defend against me with? It won't be of any use to you. You're going to die here today and I'll have that sword also."

The wind picked up miraculously hard. Clouds began to form and rain, lightning and thunder accompanied them as if mother nature herself looked down upon this battle. The weather was almost unbearable as the wind beat the rain upon Lynn's face. Lynn looked over his shoulder and knew his friends were blind to him as he was blind to them except probably Lilander.

And that was a big probably.

Christian just stood there smiling, not moving an inch as if the rain didn't affect him until . . .

Lightning flashed across the sky.

Just as fast as it came and went, Christian was in Lynn's face swinging his blade for Lynn's head. Lynn ducked under his attack, but being a true vampire, Christian's speed was enhanced greatly. Before Lynn could launch his own attack Christian did a side kick to his face. Lynn threw his arms up over his face to defend and brace himself.

The kick sent him flying a few feet to land on his back. No sooner had Lynn stopped sliding Christian was bringing his sword down to impale him. Lynn rolled to his side to avoid the attack. Christian then tried to impale Lynn over and over. Lynn rolled to the left, right and left again with nowhere to go since he was trapped between Christian's legs.

Christian brought his sword down to try and cleave through Lynn's head. Lynn blocked the attack with both of his own swords. They stayed stalled in that position as Christian spoke, "Give it up Lynn. You're no match for me."

"Maybe," Lynn said, "but this will even the score."

Lynn kicked Christian over his head allowing himself enough time to get off his back. When Lynn turned to face Christian, he was already on guard waiting for Lynn's attack. Christian then stood straight up and did something to his sword that made a faint click sound. He smiled as he separated his sword into two single edge blades.

Lynn rushed him, attacking Christian valiantly with a lunging stab with his Blood sword in his left hand. Then he brought his katana down in an arch, then a slash with his Blood sword coming across his body and finally a running slash with his katana. Christian just dodged the first, dodged the second, parried the third and jumped over the last attack.

When Lynn turned around Christian swung both his swords at Lynn's katana knocking it from his hand to the summit lips. The katana tilted there for a brief moment then fell over the side down the slope of the volcano. Lilander seeing what happened sent Uri after the sword. Uri quickly ran and changed into his lycanthrope form while going over the side of the volcano.

"It seems you lost something and you're back to a disadvantage Lynn," Christian said with that wolfish grin he's known for.

Carried faintly on the wind Lynn could hear Dante clapping and chuckling in delight. Lynn looked left and right for any solution that could possibly show itself or come to mind. The laughter of Dante gnawed in his ear as the situation seemed dire. There was no way he could ask his friends to assist for fear that Dante was stronger than he lead on. Up until this moment he still didn't know the extent of the Prince's power.

"It's not over yet," Lynn said then turned and leaped down into the volcano.

"After him! Don't let him touch that staff," Dante screamed at his thralls.

Lynn had already put his palms together and brought his ancient power to the surface to levitate down into the volcano when the thralls leaped in after him. They were a fraction too late as Lynn relinquished his Staff of Locked Souls from the rock pillar.

The thralls fell upon him making him lose concentration over his power. Instead of biting, they held Lynn's hands away from each other as they all plunged into the magma. Lynn fell faster and faster and tried to connect his hands but the thralls that were on him held tight like some unbreakable bonds. The last thing Lynn heard over the thralls snarls was Maria and the rest of his friends screaming while Dante and Christian laughed like mad men.

In a split second Lynn thought about the events that lead up to this moment. The day he defeated Ruffio was vivid and clear in his mind. The palace of Nospherat and King Ravenholme and the beauty of the ravine. Its surrounding woods and the beauty of how nature interacted with the elves there.

He then saw himself running through Cinlae after freeing Lilander and Verne with the help of Uri at his side. The fight in the Crystal Coliseum and how the people ran for their lives while he and is friends stood and fought the onslaught of thralls and Christian. Uri laying on the brink of death in Augustus estate and Lynn using whatever control he could over his power to bring Uri back to the land of the living.

He even saw the battle aboard Admiral Jo's ship and then the battle that eradicated the thralls in the streets of Draconus. Then his final memory was of himself battling Christian then grabbing his Staff of Lock Souls only to have Dante and Christian laughing as their thralls perished with Lynn into the liquid inferno.

Lynn thought, "What will happen to Verne, Lilander, Uri and Gaia? What about Maria? They need me . . ."

Then he hit the molten liquid and everyone knew he was gone forever.

"Lynn! No!" Maria screamed from the lips of the summit down into the volcano.

Lilander, Gaia and Verne stood by Maria looking into the fiery abyss in grief. Uri landed beside them with the katana in hand and saw everything and said, "We have company."

Everyone turned and Maria peeled herself away from the sight of Lynn's final resting place. Christian and Dante stood there flanked by their thralls as the lost warriors turned to face them. Both the vampire Lord's stood there with evil grins on their faces. Dante began to walk forward slowly as Christian stood there with the grin still glued to his lips.

"You do know that no one must survive except my mother," Dante said with a smirk on his face.

"Yes," Christian finished, "she will face the wrath of Master Niccolo himself. You know what to do, now do it!"

He screamed to the thralls and they immediately jumped into action against the five remaining beaten heroes. Uri let out a sonic scream to stop a few thralls knocking them over the lip and into the volcano but it had no use against the ones behind him and the new thralls showing up from the slopes and crawling out of the lips of the volcano.

Maria, Verne, Lilander and Gaia formed a circle and laid waste to which ever thrall came into striking distance. They knew eventually that they would tire out from this onslaught and be at the mercy of Dante and Christian. The two Lord's sat back and waited. Not wanting to strike too early they wanted to avoid any altercation that could drain any of their energy. They watched as the thralls slowly began to overtake the band of heroes.

"It's not over yet," Lynn thought as he forced his eyes open to see magma flowing freely around him.

He stretched his hand out to see if it was real but the red river of fire flowed through his fingers like water. He looked around only to see the red abyss for as far as the eye could see. He didn't have any bearings of which way was up. How he was able to survive he wasn't sure.

How he was able to breathe without the air he was so accustomed to was even more bewildering to him.

"I'm alive," Lynn thought, "but how?"

He then looked down at his chest and not only saw but felt that the dragon crystal has grown in power, pulsating like it had a life of its own or like it was a heart beating in rhythm with Lynn's.

"Free."

"Something else is down here," Lynn thought as he heard the telepathic message of glee.

"Free," it whispered its telepathic voice again.

The crystal began to vibrate and pulse with power as the mysterious creature moved closer and closer to the beacon, to Lynn's dragon crystal. A monstrous crescent headed lizard revealed itself to Lynn and dwarfed him greatly. It was covered in molten lava like a protective coating from the heat.

The beast licked its massive tongue out to taste not Lynn but the energy around him. Lynn knew that at any moment it could be his last seeing as he was no bigger than the creatures tongue. Lynn floated in the liquid inferno waiting for the beast to take one big gulp and swallow him. To Lynn's surprise it didn't. It just . . .

Stared.

"You," the creature sent telepathically to Lynn, "you're the one who freed me. The one I've been waiting a lifetime for."

Giant claws came out of nowhere and wrapped gently around Lynn. Lynn felt more secure than he could ever have felt. It was almost as if he was once again a young boy wrapped in his mothers arms after a bad dream.

"What are you?" Lynn asked in amazement.

"I am a dragon of olden days. I am one of the oldest creatures that are still living. Others have come and others have gone and still we remain," said the dragon.

"We?"

"Aye," said the dragon then it thrust its hind legs and swam for the surface in one graceful movement. As they emerged from the magma, the magnificent beast flapped its great wings one time to bring its body aloft in the air. Then it spread its wings and glided there off the heated thermals and looked up. Lynn was able to peer through its claws and follow the dragons gaze just before it flapped its wings again and again to take flight up the volcano faster and faster.

As they rose into the air above the summit Lynn looked down and saw his friends tiring from the battle against so many thralls and no place to go. He saw Dante and Christian inching toward his despairing friends and knew if he didn't act soon they would be worst than dead.

They would be enthralled.

"Down there. My friends need my help," Lynn said aloud.

To Lynn's surprise, the dragon responded, "Our friends need our help."

The dragon shifted its direction and began to glide for the summit. Lynn leapt from the dragons massive claws when close enough to the summit to get his swords a little bloody. Maria and the others looked up just in time to see Lynn emerge from the dragons massive claws. Upon seeing Lynn alive, it brought new life to his friends. As for Dante and Christian, they made their escape back down into the volcano.

With both the Blood sword and Staff of Locked Souls blade in hand they began to glow fiercely red and green respectively as Lynn killed thrall after thrall. Lynn approached a thrall from behind and just as it was turning to counter Lynn's assault Lynn leapt over the thrall and took its head. Other thralls took notice of Lynn's arrival and began breaking their attack on his friends and trying to assault him. Lynn slashed and dodged his way through the wave of vampires.

Lynn finally made it through the chaos to where his friends stood and said, "Hang tight and stay close."

Lynn sent out telepathically his location to his new friend, the dragon. Within seconds, the magical beast settled on the summit behind Lynn and his party then breathed a fiery death straight into the mass of thralls, decimating them all.

The dragon made its way to the lips of the summit and released a napalm down inside the volcano. He then picked everyone up into his claws and placed them on his back as he rose into the air. The volcano shuddered just before lava erupted from the lips of the summit and began flowing down the mountain. Everything that was in its wake was laid to waste. No creatures survived on the mountain that night. All has either escaped before the doom or were consumed by the fiery rage of the mountain and dragon combined.

Chapter: 17

The volcano trembled as the dragon dealt death to the thralls above. Christian stumbled over Dante as they both tried to hold themselves up from the massive tremor. Now the heat was even more unbearable that the dragon was awake and aggravating the volcano. It was as if the volcano awoke with the dragon and was now ready to vent its frustration on those that chose to intrude upon it slumber.

"I will not accept this defeat. I will not let them take my stronghold," Christian said as Dante lead the way through the various paths of the cave.

"Oh yeah, and how do you expect to do that?" Dante asked jeering at his subordinate.

"I should go up there and destroy them-"

Dante cut Christian off by turning around and standing within inches of him with a look that could make a lion cower or a vampires blood warm up.

"You lost your stronghold for now. We will acquire you another one after we destroy Lynn. If you would've killed him instead of dallying," Dante said but knew the truth.

Christian tried hard to hide his thoughts but Dante picked them out of his mind as if he were taking fruit from the forbidden tree in the Garden of Eden. Dante knew that Lynn was too much for Christian now. They made their way to the entrance and saw that the way was clear.

They started to walk until the volcano shook again as if thunder were bottled up inside of it and it just decided to roll out. Then lava flowed over the entrance and into the cave blocking their attempt to leave that way.

"This way," screamed Dante over the noise of the rushing lava and its melted rocks sizzling and popping.

They went back to the fork and took the right path since the left caved in.

"Where are we going?" Christian asked as Dante continued to lead.

"We can't use our mist around here."

"Why not?"

"Have you not felt the power? I've tried and that dragon did something to the volcano to block our escape."

The lava seemed to come faster as if it could feel their desperation. Quickly, they took the fork and ran into the wall turning left. Dante hit the wall first and Christian tripped over him and fell to the floor of the cave.

"Damnit!" Dante exclaimed in frustration, "what is going on?"

Dante grabbed a hold of Christians ankle while trying to find a good grip on the wall. He found one and was about to tell Christian to quit struggling but couldn't get the words out because the volcano trembled again and jarred his grip loose. They both slid down the slippery slope into a cavern and into a hole.

This time it was Christian who grabbed Dante by the wrist and held onto the lip of the hole. Christian smiled and said, "Looks like our roles are reversed. Now-"

He was cut off as more large rocks and boulders fell down into the hole forcing Christian to let go and fall with Dante down the natural shaft. They hit the bottom and saw that the rocks jarred themselves just at the exit point. They settled in and covered their heads as little pebbles fell from above.

"We need to talk about your plan and the destruction of my stronghold," Christian said menacingly.

"Ahh, I'm awake," Dante heard the telepathic message.

Dante looked around and began walking towards a small hole in the wall about the size of his torso but double in width.

"Did you hear me!?" Christian screamed.

"Shhh. Can't you feel it? Can't you hear the voice?" Dante said in a hushed tone.

"Feel what?" asked Christian sounding confused while walking to where Dante now stood.

Dante reached his hand into the hole feeling for something. He didn't know what but something was telling him to. Christian peered into the hole as Dante reached in to grab hold of something smooth.

"Well, what is it?" Christian asked.

"There's two, but, only one is loose and I can't-"

Dante never finished his statement. Christian was dumfounded as he watched Dante be snatched into the hole with little resistance. Never since his awakening has Christian felt fear and now it reeked off of him so foul that it made his nose flare up. The palms of his hands became clammy with sweat as he felt the perspiration form on his forehead and down his back. This was so unfamiliar to the undead.

"Dante, come back!" Christian screamed into the hole.

Even with his excellent vision in the dark, Christian could only see a plated wall that breathed.

"Breathed," Christian thought, "what in the world?"

The wall began moving until a large slit of an eye looked out from the hole. Christian was caught in a trance until the eye blinked and drug him through also. He went in screaming but stopped when he felt a hand fall on his shoulder. He looked up to see Dante smiling and behind him was a giant black crescent headed lizard just like the first dragon but different in features in so many ways.

The dragon peered over Dante's shoulder at Christian. The beast looked almost as if it were dead from its facial features. The eyes were sunken into their sockets and its scaly skin pulled taut to its face. It's skeletal frame could be seen through the thin flat horny plates of scales covering its entire body. The dragon looked malnourished but its power and strength permeated through its body and into the air around them.

"What is this?" Christian asked.

Dante climbed into the massive claw of the beast and was placed on its back. "This, my friend, is Touruche, the black dragon."

Touruche expelled his breath which reeked of decaying flesh to Christian. To Dante it smelled like the sweet scent of his lover . . . DEATH.

Dante held his hand out to Christian, "Come, ride with me on this beautiful creature."

Christian rose to his feet and stepped into the dragon's claw. Christian settled in behind Dante when he mounted Touruche's back. Dante sent telepathically to Touruche, "Now, my friend, let's leave this place."

Touruche began shuffling towards a wall and breathed out a green flame with a black core that melted the walls all the way to the surface. The liquid residue left from the green flame dripped from the hole leading to their haven. Not knowing what the mysterious liquid was Christian reached out to touch it.

"I wouldn't do that if I were you. That stuff stings like the devil ha-ha," Dante said without looking over his shoulder.

"What is it then?"

"It is acid. It is Touruche's own unique breath weapon."

They emerged from the side of the volcano and took flight into the black soot issuing from nature's behemoth. Touruche let loose a mighty roar that could be heard for miles around and shot a black napalm, the same way Lynn's dragon did, into the mouth of the volcano.

"Why do that, Touruche?" Dante asked with his mind.

Touruche flew away from the area and replied, "Rannik, the red dragon, knew I was down there and attempted to seal me back up before I could make my escape. He took the chance of doing that and not destroy the obelisk to release his followers or mine. So I did."

"What obelisk? There was no obelisk down there."

"Oh yes there was. Melchai, the Grey Knight, trapped the dragons in an obelisk disguised as a rock pillar in the middle of the magma. Once Rannik was free to leave the volcano, he made room for me but I need a counter part. That's where you came in. Now watch."

Touruche turned in the air and floated there a moment waiting. Then out of the volcano shot a massive beam of light into the air. Miles above the ground the light separated into six separate beams and spread in different directions.

"I want those crystals," Dante said aloud to himself.

Touruche spoke in the common language letting Christian hear his voice for the first time, "You can't have them. Those dragons have already chosen their human companions and as long as my followers still exert their free will, we can have the human and the dragon on our side."

"Dante, let's get out of here and to some safe territory," Christian said but almost sounded like a plea.

Dante nodded his head and told Touruche where to go. A few miles away on a plateau stood a black stallion with a gray mane and tail. The horse reared as it felt the presence of the two dragons leaving the mountain. The horse was frantic with fear. It's rider shushed and patted the horse to calm it.

Straddled on its back, Lilandro sat there and thought as he held a silver crystal, "Now, I will destroy you and the traitor. Sharron, you're going to help me do it."

The silver dragon crystal pulsated for a moment in response. It glowed in response to Lilandro's desire Lilandro smiled and turned his black stallion towards Niccolo's aerie and started on his course to redemption.

Rannik, the red dragon settled down in a small clearing just wide enough for his colossal body a safe distance away from the volcano. Everyone dismounted from Rannik's back. Maria and Verne were the only two to show excitement from the magical creature before them.

Lilander was first to ask, "What's its name?"

"His name is-"

Lynn was saying but Rannik finished for him, "I am called Rannik."

He spoke to them in the common language. He smiled at them or what you would call a smile on that beastly visage Now Uri, Gaia and Lilander showed some shock on their faces.

"I've heard about dragons in history and tales that were told in peoples stories," Lilander said.

Maria then asked, "Why did you help us?"

Rannik put his giant eye on her. "You're Lynn's friends if I'm correct. Why wouldn't I help my friends if they needed me also?"

Uri stepped forward and said, "Let me inquire on-"

He was cut off when a roar came from the direction of the volcano like it could have won a test between itself and the likes of thunder and see which one was mightier. Rannik snapped his head up and towards the volcano as did everyone else. For a few seconds there was nothing then a beam of light shot up into the air then separated into six different lights and spread themselves out to different regions of the kingdoms.

Rannik growled low but loud enough for the others to hear. "He's loose and he's rousing his followers by releasing the other dragons," Rannik sounded a bit worried in his telepathic message to Lynn.

Lynn responded in like, "Who is **he**? How is **he** loose? And how do you know?"

"Touruche is his name. Someone has activated his crystal. I know its him from his magical essence coming through the air on the winds. The only offset is that he released the other dragons that helped put him away," Rannik answered Lynn's questions then turned to face his master. "Whoever has his crystal is in grave danger for he is master of himself and will not like the idea of being tamed."

Lynn nodded and asked, "How could I keep something as colossal as you hidden but close by? I don't want to scare any commoners."

Rannik moved one of his armored scales from over his brow to show an exact replica of Lynn's crystal. It gleamed in the light of the waxing moon in the sky. It pulsated with an inner light of its own. Its glow began to grow as Lynn brandished his crystal and creep closer to Rannik's.

"As of now my full power has not returned to me or I would change into my human form. For now, aim your crystal at mine so that they catch sight of each other. We both must concentrate on putting me in the crystal and when I'm there I will be waiting for you to ask for my help again."

Lynn nodded taking in every word while aiming his crystal at Rannik's. Rannik's body became transparent and was soon turned into little flecks of light and then sucked into Lynn's crystal like a genie being put back into its magical lamp.

"Lets move. We need to get to Niccolo and end this," Lynn said after placing the crystal around his neck.

"Why can't we just ride on Rannik up to Niccolo's front door?" Gaia asked.

Uri, knowing exactly the approach Lynn was taking explained, "If a tiger is to eat it must hunt. In the act of hunting the tiger must lie in wait for any unsuspecting prey. It stalks its prey in the bush and when its too late . . . it pounces. It ambushes and surprises its prey into drastic mistakes."

"All you had to say is we were using a stealth approach."

"Last time we tried the stealth approach, you gave us away," Uri joked.

Gaia grumbled under her breath as she distanced herself from Uri and his accusations which hit her hard. No one was surprised because they knew Uri was probably the only person she would let talk to her like that. Even with only his eyes showing from beyond his mask you can still see the smile in his eyes but it still had an adverse affect on Gaia.

"Lynn, I think it would be best if you all rested before we embark," Lilander said.

Lynn nodded and said, "Alright, but we leave tomorrow after the sun crosses the sky."

Everyone unpacked for the night ahead and got some sleep by a small fire they built in the middle of their makeshift camp. Nobody really slept that night laying under the ominous shadow of the mountain that sheltered Niccolo's aerie. The animals were quiet this night. Lilander kept watch and even with his adept senses it almost felt like he was blind in this place. It felt like there was some type of leech siphoning off his life and dulling his senses and making him drunk with stupor.

He couldn't tell but what was out there watched them with a patience but also with the sick intent of a prowler. It didn't opt to attack but watch. It maintained itself steadfast to find out any weaknesses in its prey. It was content to wait for the time they were at their weakest to then pounce. That night it did nothing. It's eyes glowed in the dark like little floating orbs as they moved from hiding spot to hiding spot.

The next afternoon they set out for Niccolo's stronghold. The sun beat on them as they walked on this side of the mountain. With the sun at high noon it really didn't matter which side they walked on the only reprieve they had was from the trees under the mountains watchful gaze. They walked under the canopy of trees not taking for granted what nature has provided for them.

By nightfall they were at the base of the mountain that housed his aerie and that was the barrier to the land of Ciena. "Here it is. The Mooray Mountains. Where Niccolo awaits," Maria said when everyone paused to look up at the dead looking mountain.

Now they stood below the mountain like a titan standing before them not even acknowledging their existence. The trees and other plant life looked almost totally dead due to its current landlord. Even with the foliage looking the way it is it was still thick enough to where they couldn't possibly cut through without alerting the residents of the forest. Maria pointed out a path on the mountain that stood wide open even amongst the trees.

"That path leads a straight climb up to his castle. We don't want to go that way."

"Why don't we want to go that way?" asked Verne.

"Because the thralls watch that path. We would be set upon by the might of the aerie in no time and even you Lynn, with all your might, power and prowess would eventually succumb. We'll take a different route."

She took everyone to another path and before going on, she warned, "Going anywhere on this mountain you must be wary of your every step. Any noise will set them off. Stay as quiet as possible."

"I think we can handle what thralls come our way, Maria," Verne said.

"Not these. The thralls that patrol the mountain are Niccolo's elite thralls. They never leave the aerie and mountain. He keeps them close at a moments call. All he has to do is think about them and they will be there before you can usher another breath."

They walked the winding path and was making good progress until . . .

SNAP!

Verne stepped on a fallen twig snapping it under his weight. He swore in a whisper and Maria quickly hushed him and everyone else. Everyone held their breath and position as if in some natural portrait that was painted not by an artist but by time and fate that brought them all to this place and at this same moment. The night noises of crickets sending their calls into the air.

Chirp-chirp-chirp.

They went on not being bothered by the strangers to their territory. The trees ruffling under the winds breath. Clouds rolled past a crescent moon hiding it then releasing the moon from their grasp once more. They started walking again but no sooner had they done that nine thralls attacked from all around them coming out of trees and bushes.

These thralls wielded weapons of their own instead of just their deadly nails and teeth. Lynn battled two thralls, one with two tomahawk axes while the other attacked with a metal quarterstaff. Uri battled two female thralls with sai who were former ninjas assassins in their mortal life. Gaia battled a giant of a thrall with gauntlets that had blades protruding from the knuckles all the way back to his elbows. Verne faced off with one thrall that resembled one of his own people.

He used two knives in his hands and knives extending from the toes of his boots. The final three thralls were slim and limber. It seemed as if they were created just to counter Lilander and Maria. They used scimitars against the elf and ex-vampire queen. Lynn fought with his Blood sword and Staff of Locked Souls glowing brighter with every swing.

The thrall with the quarterstaff was twirling the staff around his head and around his body lashing out at Lynn during his spinning spectacle. The thrall had Lynn tied up in a dead lock so to speak when—whoosh—a tomahawk came flying past his ear. The axe missed and embedded itself in a nearby tree.

The one that threw the short axe tried to retrieve his weapon but Lynn sliced through his neck just as he gripped the handle of his axe. The other thrall jumped through the air at Lynn with his staff spinning above his head. Lynn quickly advanced on him before he could land and sliced through both of the fiends legs sending him to the ground. Lynn then turned and brought his swords down through the neck of the pitiful creature crawling on the ground.

Uri used two katanas, one formerly belonging to Lynn. He held one sword upside down as the two female thralls attacked simultaneously. The thralls lunged with their sai trying to impale the ninja werebat. Uri dodged each attack so closely that he could feel the wind from the weapon being so close to his body. One thralls' thrust caught Uri's hair and spun his strands up in and around the weapon.

The thrall pulled back, yanking Uri's head to bare his neck and her teeth. Uri spun one of his katanas quickly in his hand and stabbed backwards through her chest then the other through her open mouth. The other thrall seized her moment and lunged at Uri with her sai. Uri withdrew his katana from the thralls chest and impaled the lunging thrall through the mouth also. Both thralls hung there on the blades like kabobs on a skewer. Uri withdrew both blades, spinning around and lopping off their heads.

Gaia was tiring from the blows the large thrall was dealing her as she kept blocking. Every time he threw a punch with those gauntlets and his enhanced vampiric strength it sapped even more of Gaia's strength. His attacks backed her up to a tree and he saw his opportunity as she dropped her guard. He swung with his right gauntlet and she slid easily to the left making his bladed gauntlet catch deep into the tree. He spun around with his left fist and she ducked under that causing that hand to do the same as the former.

He stood there looking as if he was stuck to a crucifix and would've freed his arms if Gaia wouldn't have launched both her swords at him cutting off his arms at the elbows and embedding her swords in the trees. Gaia used him as a springboard when he fell to his knees to grab a hold of her swords, kick off the tree, dislodging the blades and flipping back over to separate his head from his body.

The thrall fighting Verne leapt into the air kicking with his knifed up boot toes. Verne ducked under and turned around just as the thrall grabbed a hold of a tree and climbed up onto a branch. There was a vine hanging close to the thrall. He grabbed it without hesitation and swung down kicking his feet again. Verne rolled to the side but not before one blade nicked his pants slashing the side of them open.

Verne grabbed for the open cut in his leg and screamed out. The thrall swung back for another round but upside down with his knives in his hands at the ready. Verne gathered himself up and jumped above the thrall and grabbed hold of the same vine that the thrall was swinging from. The thrall was rolling itself back up the vine to reach Verne when Verne cut the vine above himself.

Both him and the thrall fell to the earth but Verne landed on the thralls chest with both boots breaking the thralls ribs. As the thrall let out a snarl, Verne cut off his head like an executioner manning a guillotine.

The thralls attacking Lilander and Maria spread out around them. They circled the two warriors like wolves would a stubborn bull moose. Lilander had his daggers out and ready for battle. The three thralls attacked in unison waving their scimitars above their heads.

At the last second, Lilander grabbed Maria and leapt straight up into the air. The thralls cut right into each others body as Lilander had planned and timed the leap just right. He released Maria in the air as they descended. When they touched ground, they ended the thralls pitiful undead lives even though they were in no shape to move. After destroying the thralls everyone checked to make sure they were alright and in one piece.

"How are we fairing?" Lynn asked his friends while still watching the trees for any more movement.

Everyone assured each other that they still had all their limbs. Verne was glad that now his body gets a chance to heal itself from the wounds he sustained.

"We need to be on the move. Niccolo knows we're here no doubt about it now," Maria said trying to hurry the friends along.

Lilander agreed and everyone resumed their walk through the hidden trail only to have Uri and Lilander stop when it seemed like they were halfway up the mountain. They both began looking around as dawn broke the horizon.

"It's just dawn, isn't it?" Maria asked.

Neither answered but Uri changed into his werebat form and took flight through the trees heading back the way they had come. His sonic scream could be heard faintly through the trees as he searched for an unknown specter.

He returned and said, "Lilander, I need your eyes to see if this is what I received back."

Lilander nodded.

Uri lifted Lilander off the ground by taking hold of his shoulders and directed his view. Lilander saw the trees falling in the forest from the way they had come, then he saw what was causing it.

They landed and Lilander quickly explained, "There's a basilisk coming our way. Maria, is there any other creatures out here like that?"

"I can't say. That basilisk has always been out here but it never messed with anyone . . . unless . . . it smells blood," she replied.

Everyone began checking over themselves again until Verne let out a gasp. Everyone looked at him to see him looking at Lynn. Lilander walked over to Lynn, reached behind his ear and pulled his hand back with dried blood from a healed cut.

"But what about your leg?" Lynn asked of Verne.

"His leg has healed back there from hence we came. He also took the time to wrap it. Your wound we knew nothing about and the dried blood remained on your ear," replied Maria.

"Run," Lilander said, "run for the castle. It's the only possible way to escape from a creature as devastating as a basilisk."

They ran as quickly as their legs could carry them up the winding path. Branches cracked under foot as they ran. Branches snagged at the adventurers as they weaved through the forest. They came up to the open castle gates from the left side. The gate stood about nine feet high with two large gargoyles seated on the post overlooking the entrance. They looked behind them to see that the basilisk was only halfway up the path.

"Let's get inside and-" Verne was saying but stopped as two looming shadows showed over them from behind.

Gaia was first to look over her shoulder then turned quickly at what her eyes had sat themselves upon.

"W-W-Watch out. They're **big**," she stuttered while taking a step or two back unsheathing her swords.

Everyone else turned to see the once two gargoyle statues alive with sulfurous eyes coming at them. They lurked closer with their big frames standing at about eight feet with grotesque animal features and wings. The grinding of their sinewy muscles were ominous to their ears. Their rock hard skin rubbing together like sandpaper.

Their bodies and joints were nothing but muscle. Tons of muscle with malicious intent in their minds portraying in their eyes. Now everyone had their weapons drawn and ready for another tough battle. The gargoyles ran at the trespassers initiating the attack. Everyone scattered as the hulking beast attacked the spot where they just were standing.

"Maria," Gaia screamed, "did you know about these two?!"

"No. I've never seen them come to life before," Maria answered back out of breath slightly.

They split up in groups of three to fight the hulking gargoyles. Verne and Gaia fought alongside Lynn while Lilander, Maria and Uri all battled together. Gaia had her golden armor spread across its respective places on her body gleaming with a celestial aura. Maria donned the Black Widow mask looking like a wingless harpy.

One of the gargoyles attacked Verne so Gaia tried her luck. She attacked from behind but the gargoyle not lacking in awareness and speed dropped to all fours and delivered a mule kick. The power of the kick sent Gaia flying into the wall of the gate, nearly crashing through the heavy thick stones.

Lynn attacked the gargoyle with both swords causing them to glow fiercely. The gargoyle threw up its arms to block Lynn's barrage of attacks. Lynn backed up to see the damage he caused while breathing heavily. The gargoyle let its guard down to show not even a slight mark or scratch. It smiled and started walking toward Lynn.

Verne jumped on the gargoyle back, between its wings and just out of reach of its prying claws, catching it by surprise. The other three were not faring any better in their attempts.

Lilander attacked with his daggers and stepped just out of reach just before it could connect on its attack. With all of its attention on

Lilander, Maria attacked using her enhanced prowess from her Black Widow mask. The onslaught kept the massive gargoyle busy with the two assailants giving Uri an opening.

Uri ran from behind with the speed of a ninja and his were animal and flipped over the gargoyle and delivered a dropkick to its face while flipping through the air. No sooner than Uri landed and seeing the gargoyle going down it would be back up on its feet resuming its attack.

Gaia was barely standing when the basilisk finally reached the gates of Niccolo's aerie. Lilander was first to see it and screamed, "Everyone! Behind the wall! You must not let it look into your eyes!"

Everyone made their way for the open gate except Uri and the still staggering Gaia. Uri ran on the side of the wall towards Gaia. He grabbed her up in his arms and leapt over the wall. Both gargoyles turned to face the large basilisk coming at them.

"Quick, inside," Maria said holding the door open to the castle.

Before going into the castle Lynn felt some immense psychic energy behind him. Lilander felt it also and turned with Lynn to see one of the gargoyles crumble to dust.

"It's fatal glare. That's why you don't look into its eyes," Lilander said while closing the door with every body standing in the foyer.

To their left was a row of panes looking out into a streaming pool and a fountain depicting a vampire holding a limp woman's body in its arms with water gushing from her throat and down his chin. No opposition seemed to be out there but a little further down to their right was a light shining through an open door.

They crept up to the door and peered in yet saw nothing in there but a few cushioned chairs. They passed up the room and walked a little further down the foyer to stop at a door on their left. Looking through that door was the outside of the castle and the streaming pool with water being fed from the grotesque statue.

A little further down the foyer to their right was a hallway leading to some stairs with a thrall pacing back and forth, blocking the way. Lynn tapped Uri on the shoulder and pointed out the vampire to get his point across. Uri nodded and bounced up and ran along the wall quickly and stealthfully as the ninja he was.

The thrall turned to look at the oncoming attack but was too late to let out an alarming cry because Uri had already beheaded the damned creature. Uri motioned for everyone to come forward now that it was safe. Instead of taking the stairs they went through a door that was in front of the stairs that they couldn't see from their previous position.

Nothing was in this room except for an expensive looking rug with a table on top in the center of the room. Adorned on the table were different tools. There were small flasks and tubes for experiments upon the table like the ornaments on a Christmas tree.

"What are these?" Verne asked picking up a small flask.

"This," Lilander began to explain, "looks like where Niccolo has performed dark magic or alchemy. It looks more like the latter."

Lilander picked up one of the cauldrons and attempted to sniff the pot to find out its contents. He pulled back unsure then took another sniff and said, "These items have never been used."

Maria asked, "What do you mean they have never been used? Niccolo used to spend days locked up in here."

"Exactly what I said, these have never been used."

Lilander began to swipe the items off the table causing everything to smash on the floor. When he was finished clearing the table only a wooden ladle remained on the corner of the table. Lilander reached over and lifted the bowl portion as far as the triggered device would allow and heard a faint click. Lilander smiled and pointed down.

Uri reached down under the table and lifted until he found out which way the hinges swung. The trapdoor opened exposing stairs that could be seen from the door. Lilander and Uri took lead as everyone else followed down the steps. The steps came down to a hall that was lit by one torch.

They walked the hall to the end to go down more stairs that curved to the left. At the bottom of those stairs was a heavy oak door. Uri pushed the door open and in the center of the room lay a still lifeless body on an altar. The body had a black cerement covering it.

Lilander pulled back the black shroud and asked, "Why would Niccolo keep a dead body around?"

Lynn saw the face of the decapitated head and knew just who this person used to be. It laid still like a cadaver waiting to be poked, prodded and explored. Lynn felt a tinge of anger welling up in him but quickly got it under control as he remembered that this person was dead by his hand.

He answered, "That dead body . . . is his grandfather . . . Ruffio."

Verne went up to the still body and peered into the face of death. The features on his face were so much like only one face that he has set eyes on . . .

Dante.

"Maria, Ruffio and Dante resemble a lot. Does Niccolo look anything like his grandfather?" Verne asked.

"Yes, they do resemble each other. You can see the same features in each sire but they all have their intricate differences."

Maria looked up from the dead body to the walls of the room. Around the room was enclosed with books on different black arts and myths along the walls on wooden shelves in the stone walls. Maria scanned the shelves for what they could possibly be about. She saw titles like *Book of the Black Earth*, *Necromancing and its Many Forms*, and *Reanimation Through Sacrifice*.

"I think he's trying to bring Ruffio back to life," Maria said after reading the titles.

Lynn pondered for a moment as everyone looked at him. He looked up into their faces and said, "Well we don't have time to figure out how he's planning on doing this but if we stop him then how can he possibly achieve this feat."

They looked at the other side of the room where there stood two more large doors. They opened them both to see where they lead and saw that they lead to separate destinations. Lynn decided to take the route on the right where the fresh air was coming from.

He thought, "How could fresh air be coming from down here?"

At the end of the hall was a hole leading outside to the mountain but on the barricaded side. There was a path grooved into the side of the mountain leading down into an unknown land. The jagged path curved in and out of the mountain side like a desert rattlesnake slithering across the desert abyss.

"That is where Niccolo was born," Maria commented when she saw what they were looking down upon.

"So that is the birthplace of this monster?" asked Lynn.

"He wasn't always a monster. Losing his grandfather was detrimental to his psyche. He couldn't handle not being without him and when Ruffio reached out to him from beyond the grave he leaped at the chance to be reunited with him."

Maria stood there looking down into the forgotten land with a sorrowful almost longing look on her face. Lynn put his arms around her and walked her away from the view of Ciena. They turned around and went back to try the other door leading off to the left. They went through the door and immediately caught scent of dead decaying flesh and heard the moans and groans of people.

There were steel bars blocking the prisoners exit but not their view of the hall. Once seeing the six travelers the prisoners that consisted of men, women, children, young and old, retreated to the far wall in fear. They looked like mice trapped between a cat and a hard place. No escape except death and they feared that. The children began to softly cry grabbing for whoever they thought could keep them safe. The adults held on tight to the children wanting to hold on to what they thought could be their only hope at life.

"Don't be afraid," Gaia spoke, "we're here to help. Uri."

Uri summoned his beast form and beat the bars back so that the people could squeeze through. They stayed back unsure until Uri changed back to his human form. They began inching forward for fear that this may be some type of ruse just to get them all out and then be fed on. Not knowing which way the slaughter would come from they kept their eyes darting back and forth but especially on Uri. The freed prisoners were lead back to the open hall leading down the mountain side.

"You must get clear of this mountain and this place as fast and as far as possible," Lynn screamed over their heads as they descended the mountain in a frenzy.

When the freed prisoners were all out and on their way down the mountain, Lynn lead his friends back to where Ruffio lay only to see Dante standing there waiting on them. He stood there smug with contempt and a smile on his face. He walked around the dead body of his great grandfather and ran his hand down the altar tracing the edge of the smooth stone slab.

"You better hurry, my father is waiting for you," he said.

Maria then spoke, "Dante, my flesh, blood, bone, why not help us stop your father? He has gone mad with what he is trying to attain. Humans and vampires can live together if—."

"Help you? Ha! I wouldn't be surprised if you even made it past father you traitorous whore. Ha! Help you. Ha! Have you forgot why father started this or has that immortal poisoned your memory as well as your thoughts?" he said as he merged with the shadows and disappeared.

Maria dropped one tear before Gaia comforted her and said, "He was never yours. Niccolo made sure of that when he plagued him, when he damned him."

They went back up to the next floor and came into one long hall that opened to the left at the end. Lilander took closer looks at the bare walls as they walked the hall. He couldn't believe what his eyes were seeing. He reached out his hand to touch and verify what his eyes were showing him.

"Are these different body parts? They look like bones, eyes and skin," Lilander asked.

Maria answered, "Niccolo is somewhat of a necromancer after all. He must've used the dead body parts of the people they ate to build golems, these walls and who knows what else."

When they rounded the corner at the end of the hall there were dead bodies hanging from the ceiling. Lynn knew he knew these people but couldn't place their identity. Verne let out a gasp when he laid eyes on the dead bodies of some of the people just hanging form their necks like a puppet with no puppeteer.

Peter Macdowl stepped from behind one of the puppet like dead bodies. To anyone who knew him, didn't know him now as he stood there smiling like a wolf with his needle point cusp and crimson pupils shining evilly.

"Finally, you made it to my masters humble, yet disturbing, abode," he said laughing afterwards.

Verne stepped forward gritting his teeth in anger asking while unsheathing his sword, "Why Macdowl? Why betray us? Why betray me?"

Macdowl continued to smile as he spoke his voice slightly more guttural than the voice that Verne remembered, "You don't realize the true power that you're missing. I wanted you to see the light but you abandoned us and went with **HIM.**"

He pointed at Lynn and brandished a look of hate on his face for the immortal. His gaze rested on Lynn as if he was trying to mentally burn a hole through Lynn's skull. He relaxed his stare for a moment to speak to his former leader.

"I'm only sorry that you have chosen to side with Lynn. These people once sided with you and your master Lynn. See what your choices have done to them? We, vampires will rule this world the way it was meant to be. Master Niccolo has the power to bring about a peace that none else could have foreseen."

"How could vampires taking over bring peace?"

"With our blessing spreading throughout every kingdom, Master Niccolo will be able to stretch out his iron grip on this world and make people bow in the name of peace. At the same time their punishments for any crimes will be dealt with accordingly . . . even if its death or this state ha-ha-ha-ha."

"That's not peace, that's suppression," Verne screamed in frustration.

Macdowl laughed as he unsheathed his scimitar readying for a fight with the six travelers. He spun the blade around in his hand and showed his new found skill with the blade. Of course his vampirism helped him become even more adept.

"No, you made your choice," Verne said before taking his stance.

Verne called over his shoulder, "I'll handle him. You guys go on ahead and deal with Niccolo."

Macdowl then said, "There's no way up but through me."

Verne and Macdowl stalked each other like lions fighting over a pride would do to size up the challenge then charged headlong at each other. They slashed and parried each others attacks constantly changing momentum. Macdowl lunged at Verne with a riposte but Verne spun around the thrust and cut Macdowl across the back of the thigh. Before Macdowl could react, Verne quickly slashed open his back with three fast strikes,

Macdowl stumbled into one of the hanging bodies. Verne charged at him but Macdowl swung the body he fell against into Verne's face. Verne, not wanting to damage the corpse of one of his people more than it already has been, caught the body instead of pushing around or cutting through it. When he moved the body, Macdowl was running up some stairs in the corner of the room.

Verne quickly pursued, everyone else followed the chase. When they made it to the next floor there were four large square pillars about four meters wide and four meters thick so it was impossible to see around even one let alone all of them. Everyone followed Verne through the pillars as he followed Macdowl going up the next flight of stairs to the next floor.

On this floor, the hall was structured exactly like the hall on the floor where Verne's dead people hang alone in death. When they made it up to the hall they found that Macdowl wasn't there nor anywhere in sight.

"Verne, are you alright?" asked Gaia.

"No," he bit back tears, "yes, it's just I want those bodies taken back to my camp for a decent burial."

Lynn put his hand on Verne's shoulder, "Verne, I'm sorry but they must stay. We don't know what Macdowl could have done to them or put in them."

Verne just nodded with a sad grimace on his face and head down. He bit back the urge to shed a tear and sniffled before regaining his composure. He didn't want to be comforted by any one. He just wanted to avenge the loss that he felt and to avenge his people for such a vile act by a traitor. Maria went on ahead and took lead.

Maria spoke up, "Up here around this corner should be-"

She looked confused and almost like she lost all hope when she saw there was nothing but a wall at the end of the hall to their left.

"Are you sure this isn't the door?" Uri asked pointing at the door straight ahead.

"I'm positive that it was down this way."

"Well, lets try this door," Lynn said opening the lone door. He stood stunned in the threshold of the door. He looked into the deep darkness that would happen if he were to fail. He couldn't bare the sight of that happening. He backed up letting the door close.

Verne thinking something was wrong with Lynn tried the door. When he stood in the threshold he saw Macdowl pillaging on their people. Then Macdowl looked at Verne and let out a laugh that echoed through to Verne's bones. He let the door shut as he was also taken aback by what he saw.

"What is wrong with you two?" Gaia asked as she opened the door and stood stunned the same way the two before her have.

She saw herself chained down back in 'The Advent' in total darkness. Yet all around her she could feel and hear the planet crying out for her help. The damage done to their home was so ravaging that the floating globe of life could no longer feel the need to go on. She was dying and there was nothing Gaia could do being chained here captive the way she was.

Then a voice reached out to her like cold fingers around her throat and sounded like an evil melody, "Mother Nature, you have failed your past. Now, your powers will be mine. They will help me rule this world and shape it to the perfect picture it was meant to be. If you refuse, this planet you so love will forever perish because you made your choice and showed everyone that you care not for this place. Now! Make your choice."

Gaia quickly shut the door with beads of sweat forming on her brow.

"It's a fear portcullis," Lilander broke the uneasiness, "Niccolo has used a great deal of psychic energy and magic to create this and hide our true path."

"What do you mean?" Maria asked.

Lilander didn't answer, he closed his eyes, lifted a splayed hand in front of himself and began to focus on more of Niccolo's energy. He turned to face the right wall and walked back the way they had come just a few steps. When he touched a spot on the wall a door suddenly revealed itself.

Lilander smiled, opened the door and stepped in followed by everyone else. This room housed various weapons along the walls and on racks. Ancient and modern swords, spears, spiked clubs, maces, bows and arrows and even throwing knives made into deadly rings. The room lead around to the left into another room where a bear skin rug laid along the floor and a chair for visitors awaiting the host. There was a door in this part of the room at the far left of the wall.

"So, you are really going to perish at the hands of my father?"

Dante appeared from behind them out of the shadows. They spun around to face the tainted offspring.

Dante spoke, "I only wish you a quick journey to hell."

Dante disappeared once again leaving the six adventurers alone in the room. They walked to the eccentric looking door and heard a voice from within, "Come, come in Lynn, and bring your friends with you. And that traitorous whore."

Macdowl stood hidden on the side of the far pillar where the ascending stairs were. He watched as his former leader and mentor came up the stairs followed by the rest of his foolish friends. They followed the thrall Macdowl sent out through the middle of the pillars obviously thinking it was him. Verne quickly followed up the stairs with the rest of his band of mild pacifist hot on his tail.

"They really think they're going to be able to defeat Master Niccolo when they can't even hope to beat me or his castle. They're going to meet their demise at the hands of Master Niccolo," he thought to himself.

He then spoke out loud to himself, "If they all die, including Niccolo, I would say this is my lucky day."

He turned around to get out of the vicinity. When he came fully around, he stood face to face with a dao-tug smiling grimacingly. His presence caught Macdowl by surprise because he didn't even sense his approach whether it was through hearing or scent it was like he just materialized out of the air.

"Traitor," Lilandro said before swinging his blade at Macdowl's head.

Macdowl dodged the oncoming attack. Lilandro threw a punch at Macdowl's face but he spun to the side dodging the attack making the punch connect with the pillar. Macdowl stood there shocked as Lilandro pulled his fist away from the pillar to show a long crack forming in the pillar. Lilandro smiled at the fear he smelt emanating from Macdowl's undead body.

"I thought you were supposed to be the pinnacle of the predators. Why is your fear permeating off you like a field of dead fruit?" Lilandro asked while smiling sadistically.

Lilandro leaned against his sword and motioned for Macdowl to attack. Macdowl charged at Lilandro, more out of fear than anger, and attacked viciously. Lilandro moved to the side away from the attack. Macdowl continued to attack and Lilandro continued to dodge.

Lilandro then swung his weapon up and caught Macdowl with an uppercut in the chin with the pommel of his sword. Macdowl fell on his back and quickly rolled to a crouching position. Lilandro scoffed at Macdowl's pitiful efforts. Macdowl growled deep in his throat and Lilandro responded with a growl of his own.

Macdowl let out an ungodly roar as he lunged at Lilandro with his blade thrusting out through the air. For all the speed his vampiric abilities gave him it wasn't faster than Lilandro's sidestepping slash that decapitated Macdowl. The head rolled from the falling body and turned to dust as it halted its rolling. Lilandro walked slowly to the ascending stairs with his blade tip dragging across the floor. As he made his way across the room he smiled a sinister smile and thought, "It's payback time."

Chapter: 18

Lynn, followed by everyone, entered into Niccolo's chamber to see him across the room looking out the window. Everyone bore their weapons upon setting eyes on him.

Niccolo turned to face them and said, "Come, feast your eyes on your new master. When you leave here, you will be like all the others who have been blessed with my gift. You see, the way I see it is that my greatest enemy will be my greatest ally and with your powers on my side it will make you a great general in my campaign for peace."

Gaia ran forward and made it halfway across the room before four thralls descended on her from the ceiling and held her there.

"You come to my castle and boast about you're going to defeat me! You release my slaves and food! You wrecked havoc upon this place and now the price must be paid," Niccolo looked at the four thralls and they turned Gaia free to face Lynn.

"You," Niccolo walked around to stop just in front of Gaia with his back to Lynn and his other followers, "you, must think that I don't know anything about you but contrary to your feeble mind I do. My grandfather has told me about you in another time. He told me about the future you come from. He has told me that it is ruled by my kind. So why would I allow you to stay and ruin what is meant to be."

Niccolo smiled and winked his eye at her. That must have been the cue because then his thralls went into action. They then proceeded to break all the rubies adorned on her garb.

While doing this Niccolo spoke, "Of course, you maybe wondering why I'm doing this. Well while watching you roam the lands and having my thralls engage you I was able to determine that your Gaia is actually the one known for aeons as Mother Earth. I was able to use my talents to determine how to send her back to hence she came. She came here to change this past from the darkness that her time is going through."

"Well, ha, her plan has failed and now she will go forward knowing that still her time will be left in darkness and shambles. The despair and hurt of everyone will still be on your hands Gaia. Good bye."

When the last ruby was broken, the thralls moved back as Gaia reached out to her friends as a void opened behind her and began sucking her in like a vacuum.

Before being sucked into the hole of nothingness, Gaia uttered one last word of encouragement to her friends, "I have and will always be with you, just look around for me and I'm always there."

She disappeared into the invisible space forming behind her never to be seen by this band of friends again.

Uri ran forward readying to attack when he saw that Gaia was actually gone. He began to change into his werebat form but those four thralls were prepared. One thrall threw some large silver chains at Uri's body while another threw some at his feet.

He fell just as his change was nearing completion.

The other two thralls quickly ran to Uri and buckled a silver mask around his mouth blocking his sonic scream. They then drug him to the window by Niccolo and hung him outside like an article of clothing being hung out to dry. They made a guttural chortle as Uri swung like a pendulum outside the window powerless to do anything through his silver bonds.

"Now, he's a dangerous foe," Niccolo started while taunting out the window at Uri, "a natural enemy to the vampire. A wereanimal. Such voracity in these abominations when it comes to hunting down my kind. I see why you enlisted his help Lynn."

Niccolo chuckled as he turned back to face the other four trespassers. Lilander released four arrows from his bow in quick succession. One for each thrall. The arrows stopped almost as soon as they left the bow and dropped to the floor.

"His psyche is stronger than I thought. Almost as if there were two of him in there. I can sense more than one persona emanating from him," Lilander said squinting at the subtle psychic waves flowing off Niccolo and around the room.

Verne ran forward and Niccolo used his telekinesis to throw him across the room to hit his temple on Niccolo's ivory top table knocking him out cold. Niccolo didn't even lift his finger or blink his eye at Verne's could be attack.

"It may be difficult to kill an immortal but it sure isn't when it comes to knocking them out," Niccolo joked to his thralls.

They chuckled accordingly.

Then Niccolo resumed his hold on Lilander by letting his mind envelope the elf's mind. Lilander tried to fight off Niccolo's attempts but succumbed to the cold darkness creeping through the crevices of his mind. Lilander was reduced to a fetal position holding himself with his eyes shut tight.

"Why do you play these games, Niccolo, when you know what we came here for?" Lynn asked.

"Oh, but this is what you came here to do. Did you not know that this would be your burial place?" Niccolo said then pulled Maria to himself using his telekinesis.

He forced her into a sleep with a quick jolt of his mind to hers.

"You see Lynn, she never knew the extent of my power because the whore left me before I had a full grasp on it. Yet, now with the help of my grandfather I am more than what I was when I started this campaign. I am so close and all there is left is you. Come, Lynn, I know the perfect place where I can lay you to rest along with your bitch," Niccolo said taking Maria and climbing up a ladder in the corner of his chamber.

Lynn followed him up the ladder and emerged on the roof. Two towers stood opposite each other in the corners of the roof with doors leading up into each. The roof was lined with rail guards that closely resembled pitch forks. Niccolo pointed up in the air directing Lynn's attention.

Above them was an open walkway connecting the two towers. When Lynn brought his attention back down he saw Niccolo disappear through one of the tower doors. Lynn strolled forward to follow only to have Christian appear out of the same door Niccolo went through with his sword drawn.

"Who ever said we would make it easy for you, Lynn Thrax?" Christian asked while easing forward more and more.

Lynn unsheathed both his Blood sword and Staff of Locked Souls blade ready for Christian to make his move.

Lilandro sheaths his sword after he sent the last of the four thralls that attacked him to the true death. They thought they could gain an upper hand while he was checking his brother, Verne and Uri. They were wrong. He made sure to pull Uri's unconscious silver poisoned body from the window. He relieved the silver chains of its prize then set his thoughts on his own prize. Without letting his presence be known he takes the ladder up to the roof. He emerged from the ladder just as Lynn was putting up his guards for Christian.

Lilandro quickly ran in between them, sword drawn, arms stretched out to his sides and said, "Lynn, this isn't your battle. Yours is up there waiting for you."

He then said to Christian, "You and me have unfinished business."

Christian hissed his loathing at Lilandro seeing that he was alive and not rotting like the corpse that he should be. Lynn ran for the opposite tower door and entered inside. Lynn took one last look over his shoulder at Lilandro and Christian. He slammed the door leaving the two crazed warriors to their own devices if that's what you would call this duel.

"Is this some joke? You're not real. I killed you back in 'The Advent,'" Christian said in disbelief.

Lilandro stood there with his sword down to his side, "Need I repeat myself? You and me have unfinished business."

Christian charged Lilandro and attacked like a rabid dog. For all Christian's efforts, Lilandro just dodged his attacks which seemed like he was exerting only a little bit of energy. After seeing that Lilandro seemed a little more powerful than before, Christian separated his double edge sword into two single blades.

That seemed to get Lilandro's attention now that he brought his sword up on guard. Christian charged again but this time around Lilander flew out of nowhere and delivered a flying dropkick to the side of Christian's face stumbling him.

Lilander stood by his brother with both daggers drawn and said to Christian, "Who ever said we would make it easy for you, Christian?"

Christian smiled showing the space where teeth used to be and more were rapidly growing in their place. He licked the newly grown dentin after they were complete. He smiled his teeth shining pearly white like they were perfectly molded and buffed for appearance.

"You should have let your brother die alone. Now, I can have twin elves as my own thralls or treat . . . whichever I feel huh," Christian said just before charging.

Lilander and Lilandro used their speed to swiftly move away. First, Lilander attacked by going head up with the true vampire. Christian swung his right sword at Lilander but Lilander ducked under and thrust his left dagger at Christian's open side. Christian brought his left sword down across his body to deflect Lilander's attack.

Lilander quickly thrust his right dagger only to have Christian bring his right sword down from his left side deflecting the attack and forcing Lilander to turn around opening himself up for an attack. Before he could attack, Lilandro leaped over Lilander's head and kicked Christian in the chest. Christian steadied himself just as Lilandro was bringing his sword down in an arc and blocked with his left sword. They held that position for a second until Christian caught sight of his opening.

When Lilander ran forward Christian raised his right sword up behind himself for a bluff then kicked Lilandro hard into Lilander. Both brothers rolled and toppled over each other a good distance from the strength in Christian's kick. Lilander and Lilandro were getting up from the ground when Christian was already on the move attacking Lilandro. His attack was stopped when Lilander used his own body to shield his brother from Christian's attack. Lilandro held Lilander as Christian gloated at his feat.

"Why place yourself in harms way for me when I haven't been much of the same brother you used to know?" Lilandro asked while feeling over his brothers wounds.

Lilander answered through short sharp breaths. "I could never stop loving you. I can sense your dormant power which is the same I felt from Lynn when he found Rannik the red dragon. It's only fitting that I should buy you some time to see what must be done. You're the only one that could hope to defeat him now. If you die here, Lynn will be next. I'm sure of it."

Lilandro pulled out some balm from his outfit. He looked down at his brothers wounds and knew that this was the only thing that could possibly save him. He knew that once he placed this on his twin that he would be in excruciating pain even worse than death. Possibly wishing for death's release rather than the healing pains of the balm.

"This will burn for a while but it will take the pain away and heal you. The dao-tug have many advance, be they cruel, ways of healing," he said as he rubbed the balm on Lilander's wounds and began mumbling an invocation under his breath afterwards. Lilander let out a bone-chilling scream and writhed around on the roof top.

When finished, Lilandro rose to his feet and shot Christian a glare that put Christian on guard. Lilandro took out his silver dragon crystal and put it around his neck. It glowed as Lilandro began to focus his intent. The crystal began to shine even brighter as the power was rising more and more to the surface.

"So, one of the dragons chose you? I'll control that flying lizard when I get through with you."

Lilandro made no attempt to answer but thought, "I need your help now."

The power within the crystal activated and washed over Lilandro. Christian stood there in shock as a silver ethereal armor with wings on the back of it washed over Lilandro. Lilandro's eyes burned a bright silver as they set upon Christian. When Lilandro spoke another voice was present also.

The voice of the silver dragon could be heard along with Lilandro as he said, "I am the silver dragon known as Sharron. You defects of nature were allowed a chance to survive with the common race and feast when necessary. Now you wish to destroy everything and we will not sit by and let that happen. You have met your destruction in me when you and your master decided to partake on this path."

Christian's lip trembled while trying to hold a snarl as the new Lilandro flapped his ethereal wings to gain flight. Lilandro charged Christian swinging his sword from right to left as Christian tried to block with his. Lilandro's blow knocked the sword out of Christian's right hand. Christian attacked with his other sword but Lilandro caught the blade in his hand.

Christian attempted to attack Lilandro with his teeth but Lilandro punched him in the torso sending him to the ground. Lilandro floated back a little as Christian rose to his feet and attacked with his claws and teeth again. Lilandro thrust both of his hands forward to bring a mighty wind that caught Christian in his charge and threw him back. Christian flew back at such a velocity that he couldn't stop himself.

He eventually stopped when his body was impaled on the pitch fork guard rail.

Lilandro landed in front of Christian's immobile body and let Sharron's power recede back into the dragon crystal. The armor slowly faded into nothing as the dragon's power receded. Lilandro's eyes changed back to the cold red orbs they were before the change. He stood there looking into Christians dying eyes thinking how much more he can make this creature suffer.

Christian spoke as he coughed up spittle laden with blood, "Well, you have me where you want me. Take my head and deal me the true death. Know then, my master will defeat Lynn then reanimate me and I will continue on my charge to destroy you and your elf race."

Lilandro turned away and took the chain from his belt. Just as Christian began rambling again, Lilandro spun quickly and threw his sword at Christian's head. The sword cut cleanly through Christian's neck as Lilandro whipped the chain back to himself with the sword connected to it.

He sheathed his sword and ran to Lilander's side and asked Sharron, "Is there any way you can help him?"

In his head she spoke, "Use my crystal."

He took the crystal from around his neck and began to use his crystal to try and heal his brother more. Now the wood elf of old showed on his face as worry crept to the surface. Not knowing what exactly would happen when he called upon Sharron's power to be used on his brother. He knew he had to do it though. He had to heal his brother but in order to do that he needed one more component that doesn't regularly come to a dao-tug.

Faith.

Lynn ran up the spiraling stairs to the top of the tower. He burst through the tower door and saw Niccolo standing in the center of the walkway and Maria unconscious by the door behind him. Lynn took slow steady steps out on to the walkway that bridged the two towers.

"Niccolo, why did you do this to yourself? You could've never aroused my attention and lived your undead life. Now, it will perish on the edge of my swords," Lynn said wielding his Blood sword from its green and pearl bottom reptile hide scabbard and unsheathing the Staff of Locked Souls blade.

Niccolo looked down over the side of the walkway nonchalantly and said, "Your elf friends fight valiantly, but, they won't beat Christian."

Lynn looked over the edge and saw Lilander and Lilandro fighting Christian. When Lynn set eyes on them it was just when Lilandro flew over Lilander's head and kicked Christian in the chest.

He brought his attention back to Niccolo when the vampire spoke, "You made my life a living hell. You took my grandfather from me and forced him into my mind. Now, I'll take your life and resurrect my ancestor and it will be how it was meant to be."

"You think your grandfather was righteous? He took my whole family. He deserved what he got. It was way too good for him," Lynn retorted.

Niccolo unsheathed his sword from his hip to show one side of the blade was smooth and looked like it never tasted blood while the other side was a jagged edge like a row of sharp teeth from a saw. It was a beautifully grotesque blade with its two-faced sides. The blade was made with the purpose of going in smoothly and ripping as it exits.

"Let this battle decide who will go on to reign," Niccolo said going on guard.

"I'm not fighting to rule but to rid the world of your parasite."

Niccolo became enraged and his face took on that metamorphic change anytime a vampire was readying to feed showing his beastly features before both combatants charged each other. Lynn brought both his blades down in an arc only to have Niccolo parry and counter by rolling back using Lynn's weight to launch him over his head. Lynn flipped through the air and landed on his feet coming to a sliding halt.

They faced each other again and stared at each other intently in a face off admiring each others power. Lynn charged Niccolo again swinging both of his swords one after the other trying to draw Niccolo out. Niccolo dodged Lynn's attacks with his vampiric enhanced speed and threw the hilt of his sword into Lynn's stomach and then into his face.

Lynn fell back about ten feet from the power and force in Niccolo's blows. Lynn leapt up quickly to his feet and paused for a moment. Lynn wiped away the blood from his lips and looked at Niccolo smiling with delight. Lynn's smile confused Niccolo making him even more angrier.

"Why you-" Niccolo growled at Lynn.

Lynn finally realized why his swords have been glowing that eerie red and green glow. This must be the staff that was meant for Dania. Just at the thought of his sister both blades shined even brighter. Lynn brought both blades together and witnessed them fuse together in his hands.

When the light died down Lynn held one combined sword in his hands. The hilt was long with the soul orb at the pommel and His blood orb sat in the hand guard. The blade was double edged and as tall as

Lynn's shoulder with his birthmark surrounding the blood orb as the hand guard. Niccolo charged at that moment with his blade held high.

Lynn placed his hands together to bring about his ancient latent power to help him one more time. Slowing time down now would do no good seeing as Niccolo's psyche is powerful enough to not be effected. Lynn dodged to the left then as Niccolo swung his sword at Lynn, Lynn flipped over Niccolo and landed on Niccolo's blade when he came about face.

As quickly as Lynn landed on the blade he took a stab at Niccolo's head. Niccolo caught Lynn's blade in his free left hand and used his strength to toss Lynn over himself. Lynn landed on his feet and used his telekinesis to throw Niccolo back, forcing him to release Lynn's blade. When he flew back, Niccolo used his own powers to stop his momentum and land back upright.

Lynn put both hands on his hilt and stood on guard waiting for Niccolo to make another charge. Just then Lynn felt a dangerous presence coming in from the air as the hairs on the back of his neck prickled. Niccolo felt it also because he laid flat on the ground just as Touruche tried to take his head off. Lynn kept his eyes on the beast and knew it was Touruche then recognized Dante straddled on his back. Dante aimed Touruche at Lynn this time around.

Lynn readied himself for the full force of Touruche until Ursula appeared from the tower door where Lynn entered from and leapt onto Dante. Her surprise attack threw Touruche off course. Touruche flew past and almost collided with one of the towers as Dante was wrestling with Ursula.

Lynn heard an evil voice in his head that sounded even more menacing than Dante or Niccolo, "Dante, what is this fly doing on me?"

Dante sent back, "She is after her maker, Touruche. She's a raving lunatic and I think we should teach her how to fly."

Lynn reached for his dragon crystal and let loose Rannik. The red dragon came flying out of the crystal almost like it was going through a forced exorcism and it was emerging through Lynn's chest. Rannik wrapped himself around the tower right above where Maria was laying unconscious. He looked down on Lynn waiting to hear why he was summoned.

"Rannik, there he his. There's Touruche. Keep them away from here while I finish this," Lynn sent telepathically to the red dragon.

Rannik nodded his giant crested head and flew after Touruche, Dante and Ursula. His giant wings beat up a fury of a wind draft causing Lynn to cover his eyes and keep Niccolo pinned down for just a few more seconds. Rannik's body rose slowly into the air and began gaining speed as his body moved higher and further away from the walkway. He angled his body for the other dragon and sped off with even greater speed than Lynn has seen before then.

"So that's what I felt developing in my son. I will control this world with those lizards as long as my son has one under his control and I will gain yours once I drink of your life and take your essence. I must have that power," Niccolo said watching Rannik depart.

The two combatants brought their attention back to the battle at hand and took slow steady steps towards each other. When in range, Niccolo swung for Lynn's head with his sword. Lynn leaned back to avoid the attack so Niccolo attempted a punch at his body. Lynn caught the fist and twisted Niccolo into the air then delivered a leaping kick to his chest.

Niccolo flew across the walkway and stopped when he hit the tower. He rose slowly to his feet and seemed a bit exhausted. Lynn walked forward as Niccolo charged him. Lynn ducked under his slash then spun around and parried Niccolo's turning slash. Niccolo tried to sweep Lynn's feet out from under him but Lynn stepped back each time he tried. When Niccolo saw his efforts were getting no where, he brought his sword up in an upward slash.

Lynn dodged to the right and stepped past him, cutting through Niccolo's stomach as he did so. When behind him Lynn brought his sword around and down, slicing Niccolo's back open. Niccolo came upright due to the pain of the attack. Lynn seeing his best opening yet, stabbed his fused sword through Niccolo's back.

Niccolo dropped his blade as all his energy drained from his body from the stab delivered through his back. Lynn pulled the blade out of Niccolo's back and spun with both hands on the hilt to gain momentum for the final blow. Before he could finish his spin, both dragons fell through the walkway sending Lynn, Maria and Niccolo plunging to the roof below. Lynn grabbed Maria in the air as they fell past the roof where Lilandro knelt over Lilander's immobile body. Niccolo bounced of the side of the roof and continued to fall.

"Rannik, I lost my concentration on my powers. Help!"

Lynn sent out to the red dragon his desperate message. Suddenly his descent slowed and he was lifted back upwards with Maria in his arms. Lynn looked up over his shoulder and saw Lilandro with an ethereal armor covering his body shining like an angel and some ethereal wings flapping. Lilandro put Lynn and Maria safely on the roof then let Sharron's power subside once more. Lynn put Maria softly down and ran to the rail to look over and see if he could catch sight of Niccolo.

Niccolo lay strained and broken boned across pieces of the broken walkway and ground just outside the gates. Niccolo laid there slowly catching his breath as his lungs began to refill with air. His body started to heal but due to the loss of so much blood it wasn't as fast as usual.

He thought, "Just a little longer and I will be healed. Let them think I'm dead and when I am back to my old self they will beg me to change them."

Niccolo heard the rustling of bushes and trees coming from the forest beyond his head. He couldn't turn his neck around to see what it was but something told him there was something out there with ill intent and not caring whether he was a vampire or not. The gargoyles were now gone but the basilisk slithered out of hiding beyond the trees and fell upon the vampire Lord. The basilisk constricted Niccolo and Lynn caught a hint of a smirk on Niccolo's face before the basilisk took his head with one mighty snap of its jaws.

Rannik landed partially on the roof and said, "Lynn, they flee. Should I pursue?"

Lynn shook his head of sweat and drenched locks, "Let's finish off here and go home."

Verne emerged from the ladder with Uri in tow. Verne looked around in a bit of confusion and said, "Oh great, I finally get to be knocked out in the battle of my life."

Lilandro grabbed his dragon crystal and let Sharron out onto the other side of the roof opposite Rannik. Once the silver dragon was summoned and settled in Lilandro turned to Lynn. His dao-tug features still kept the seriousness of a true killer but his voice belied them.

"Tell my father and brother let things be. Tell them I am content with where I am now. This is why I was born. I feel it. I just can. There is work to be done and I will see them again . . . one day," Lilandro said while hopping on Sharron's back.

She flapped her wings and caught a draft of wind and rose quickly since she was much smaller than Rannik and lighter. Once air born she settled in on an air current and rode it only flapping her wings periodically. Lynn didn't utter one word to try and change his mind because he knew Lilandro's was made up.

"Now what?" Verne asked.

Lynn still looking at Lilandro's silhouette answered, "Get everyone on Rannik's back. Rannik, set this place ablaze and destroy all life on this mountain."

Lynn pulled Maria's unconscious body onto Rannik's back and Verne held Lilander while Uri sat behind him. Rannik took flight and circled the mountain. Rannik began to set the mountain on fire from the bottom and circled up to the castle. Anyone within a ten mile radius could see the beacon of fire in the night. Probably in a five mile radius or more they could feel the intense heat. Seeing that everything was done here, Lynn sent Rannik the direction to Kamma. The red dragon turned in the air and made his way for the Grand Straight.

Chapter: 19

Rannik flew over the Grand Straight using the winds off the waters to glide to save his energy from flapping. Maria awakened and felt a warm kiss on her brow and a warm embrace around her. She looked up to see Lynn smiling down at her. She fell back into her slumber happy that her love was alive. She couldn't think of a better or safer place to be in than his arms wrapped around her like when she was relaxing in the sauna in the elves home of Nospherat.

When they finally entered Kamma, the citizens were a little frightened at the sight of the dragon. Most ran for their lives but the few that were stunned and shocked were rooted to their spots as if their feet dug into the ground like a trees tough roots. Once they set eyes on Lynn though, the fright turned into excitement from the sight of the heroes returning. Rannik's enormous bulk was so large that if he tried to land in the streets of the city he would cause more damage than a war could.

Rannik was barely able to land in King Augustus' estate. The back pathway leading to the horse stables and the Dining Hall was just big enough for his body but he made the ground shake and caused a lot of noise when he landed since he couldn't fly in low and had to land from higher than suitable. By the time Lynn and everyone else were off Rannik's back, Augustus, Le'Anne, Loraine and most of the servants were out back staring in awe at the giant mystical beast.

"King Augustus," Lynn said with a bow, "Niccolo is no more. He may be gone but Dante, his son, is still on the loose with a very powerful ally."

Augustus was still transfixed on Rannik but the red dragon said, "The ally is my brother Touruche. He is the most vile dragon amongst our kind. We must find them and put him back in his cage."

Augustus never taking his eyes off Rannik said, "I see Gaia is missing. Where is she? And what's this one's name?"

The last question was for Rannik but directed at Lynn. Before getting started on all the events that happened since they left, Lynn called Rannik back into his crystal. A dinner was arranged that would take place that night. There Lynn told Augustus everything while he sat and listened intently without interruption.

Lynn told Augustus about the attack in the Isle of Lost Songs. Also he made sure not to omit their stay in Draconus and how they rid the port city of the vampires that preyed on the patrons there. He then told him of their travels through the Caves of Moorya. Lynn gave every detail about the fight with Christian and his fall into the volcano only to be saved by Rannik.

Finally Lynn told him about their journey up the mountain to Niccolo's aerie and their many battles that happened traveling up the mountain. He told Augustus about the gargoyles and the basilisk. He described the final duel between him and Niccolo and his fall from the walkway above the two towers. He told of how the basilisk fell upon the vampire Lord and consumed the undead fiend. Then finally he told him about the words Gaia left with him to spread to everyone.

When Lynn finished, Augustus spoke, "Wow, so all that happened in almost a weeks time. And in this same crystal is what saved you in the volcano?"

Augustus held Rannik's crystal in his hands, turning it over and over to look at it from all angles. Lynn looked around the Dining Hall to see Lilander and Le'Anne's heads close together talking, smiling and looking lovingly deep into each others eyes. Loraine had Uri on the floor teaching him ballroom dancing. His movements were almost assassination to the eyes they were so brutally bad. Even though he wasn't very much a dancer, he seemed relaxed with his hair down and mask off and different attire and a large smile across his face.

Lynn knew Uri still had his uniform on under his outfit just in case he was needed. Lynn smiled at the thought. Lynn looked around for a double take and found his target. He dismissed himself from Augustus' side to begin his pursuit. Maria was so caught up in her own world that she didn't even notice Lynn until he put his hand out to take hers.

She took his hand and followed him to the dance floor. Lynn held her close as they danced and just felt the soft and tenderness of her touch. Maria felt as if her feet were not even on the floor as they glided effortlessly across the floor. Their bodies moved with the music and it seemed as if they were the only two dancing in the room.

Lynn leaned a little closer and whispered, "Where do we go from here?"

She put her head on his chest and said, "Anywhere with you. I'll go to the ends of the earth for you."

Lynn quickly took her hand and secretly informed Augustus that Maria and himself were making their exit.

"My king we must depart from your company now. We have a flight to make and get back to our kingdom," Lynn told Augustus.

"What of your friends Lilander, Uri and Verne?" Augustus asked.

"Tell them I said to stay here, and enjoy the leisure of a free life. When I'm needed again I will know. I will come."

Lynn turned to leave but stopped with one more message, "Oh, there's another message for Lilander from his brother, Lilandro. He said to tell both his father and brother that he feels this is what he was born to do and that when its time he will be there. Don't go looking for him because he will always be near."

Lynn left quickly with Maria in tow.

When they made it to the edge of Kamma, Lynn summoned Rannik, "Are you up for another trip my friend?"

Rannik happily accepted and took the twosome onto his back. Rannik felt some one was watching them so he snarled at the shadow that was making its way toward them. Lynn leaped from the dragons back with his Blood sword at the ready.

"Show yourself or me and my friend here will make you rue the day you decided to cross paths with us," Lynn bellowed.

"Of course I would like to accompany you too seeing as I have taken an oath."

Lynn let a sigh of relief wash over his body as he housed his sword back in its sheath after seeing that it was Verne there with tears forming in his eyes but refusing to let the damn holding them back loose.

Lynn chuckled, "How could I forget and leave you my dear friend. Get on."

Rannik placed Verne on to his back seated behind Lynn and Maria and took the three passengers up into the clouds. He caught one of the many wind currents and rode it to the city of Fawn and flew low over the castle Maru startling everyone inside the city. Rannik landed on the roof of the castle and was formerly introduced to Lynn's god son, King Aurelius.

Aurelius spoke to Rannik, "If you so please master Rannik you may take your rest and slumber up here on my roof."

Rannik refused with, "Forgive me your highness but I would feel more comfortable for now in my crystal by my masters side."

"Farewell, as you please then master Rannik."

Lynn, Aurelius, Maria and Verne all went to Aurelius' chambers. They told Aurelius the story leading up to this moment. Aurelius sat listening with intent as they relived the stories. Each friend taking turns to tell the story how they saw it and filling in the blanks where one of the others may have erred. He laughed when they laughed and inquired when something didn't quite add up.

When they finished with the feats of bravery and epic battles, Aurelius said, "Seeing as Niccolo is gone, will you stay and be my counselor as you were for my father? You and Maria are more than welcome to stay. Verne also. He is family if you say he is indeed like a brother to you."

Lynn gladly accepted his offer this time around. The next day, Aurelius announced Lynn's return and his decision to stay. Maria and Lynn were greatly cheered and accepted by the people of Fawn. Verne enjoyed his fame from the background. Aurelius then announced that Lynn and his lady Maria would be formally wed in front of the people of Fawn with the king's blessing. Lynn blushed as the people cheered and approved of the pair for they were loved amongst the people for restoring this peace that they now have the opportunity to enjoy and bask in.

Before the ceremonies Verne chose to be kept a low profile for the safety of Lynn and Maria and that he may perform his duties more efficiently. He figured if no one knew he was the personal guard of Lynn then he wouldn't be suspected to be a threat to a potential threat, if there were any. When Lynn found some time to himself that day he made sure to send a message to his family, whom he left years ago for their safety, to inform them of his safe return and where he could be found should they need him.

That night they celebrated in the throne room. Lynn danced with Maria and looked into her eyes and knew this is where he is supposed to be. They kissed long, deep and passionately into the night. Aurelius made a toast to the newly weds and bid that the party go on for the remainder of the night. The celebration did in fact go on as the king bid and it was lively all the way through.

Epilogue

Dante stood in the rubble that used to be his home, his fathers' castle. The whole mountain was burnt, dark and reeking of death. He looked around at the destruction that Lynn and Rannik caused. On Dante's face it wasn't remorse for his father or anger at the ruin of his home it was the look of serenity. He smiled knowing that now he can come and go as he please and put his plan into full effect. His great grandfathers plan.

"Just the way I like it," Dante thought.

Touruche landed from his flight from surveying the rubble from the air and settled in behind Dante just as Dante asked, "Did you find her?"

"No. She has some how evaded us and went into hiding."

Dante lifted a skull and looked it square in the face. He looked over his shoulder and said, "She felt my power. She's not stupid. So why did she attack?"

Touruche made what looked like a shrug of his gigantic shoulders. Dante walked to the peek of the mountain and looked down. He knelt down at the lip of the summit still holding the skull in his hand. With the flex of his hand he crumbled the skull and let the dust fall down the mountain side.

"No matter. We will rebuild this place to our liking. This will be our home, our stronghold, our seat of power. This will have no rival and make the one my father built look like some child's play in a mud pit," Dante laughed after saying that.

Touruche interrupted his laugh with, "And what about Lynn Thrax?"

Dante held Touruche's crystal at a distance looking into it. Looking at the many colors that passed through the jewel as he turned it in his hand. Dante let out a deep and hearty laugh as if he had not a care in the world and the person who destroyed his home was not a threat. He looked at his dragon Touruche and placed his hand on Touruche's brow.

"We will deal with him when the time comes. Unlike my father I will be prepared for Lynn and **I WILL KILL HIM**. For now, we have work to do."

Dante went to Touruche's shoulder, climbed onto his back and took flight. As they left the mountain a piece of the fallen decrepit castle moved and out came a slender figure. Dust and dirt fell from the figure as if it were sand falling through an hour glass. Red eyes focusing on the fading black dragon Ursula emerged from the rubble and smiled.

"So it worked," she thought, "I have finally mastered hiding my psyche from his probes."

"It won't be long before you will be mine," she said in a low hiss.

THE END